MW01517225

COLD BETRAYAL

A.J. MCCARTHY

Black Rose Writing | Texas

The author grants the final approval for this literary material.

First printing

This is a work of fiction. Names, characters, businesses, places, events, and incidents are either the products of the author's imagination or used in a fictitious manner. Any resemblance to actual persons, living or dead, or actual events is purely coincidental.

ISBN: 978-1-68433-196-3
PUBLISHED BY BLACK ROSE WRITING
www.blackrosewriting.com

Printed in the United States of America
Suggested Retail Price (SRP) $19.95

Cold Betrayal is printed in Chaparral Pro

This novel is dedicated to my husband and my two beautiful daughters.

COLD BETRAYAL

To Sharon,

Never stop reading!

JMcCarthy

27/4/2020

Chapter 1

Without having to touch it, she felt the lump swell on her forehead. She'd hit the steering wheel with such force the vibrations resonated down her spine. For a full minute, she stared dazedly at her hands gripping the wheel, until she lifted her gaze to see the hood of the car crumpled in front of her. She swore loudly.

Tori couldn't believe it. Snowbanks looked so innocent from a distance. Now, she discovered the kind of havoc they could wreak on a vehicle. She thought she'd been careful, but careful or not, her lack of experience had been her undoing.

The realization sank in that she had to get moving. Tori optimistically put the car in reverse and tried to back out of her predicament, but it was soon obvious it wouldn't happen. Her tires spun uselessly on the snow and ice, the car held firmly in the grip of the great white monster in front of her.

Tori mentally berated herself for naively travelling to Quebec in wintertime, unprepared for the climate. And she hadn't even had the common sense to stay in the city where the road conditions were better. No, she'd ventured out into the countryside, onto a little-used crossroad that was hardly more than a wide path. Tiny patches of black asphalt peeked through the snow, and the snowbanks on each side of her towered several feet high, making the road resemble a long, white tunnel.

She couldn't even call for help. Her mobile phone had suffered its demise this morning, crushed under the heel of a heavy boot. The boot in question belonged to a person with whom she had more important things to worry about besides the fact he had destroyed her phone.

There was nothing else to do. Tori had to continue her journey by foot. It was a matter of time before they found her, their knowledge of the area so much greater than hers.

Fumbling for the latch of her seat belt with shaking fingers, she noticed the blood on her jacket. Touching her forehead, she felt the warm stickiness.

"Great. Just what I need."

Knowing it could be worse, she found a box of tissues in the console beside her and pressed several to the wound. She couldn't allow a bump to the head to slow her down.

Tori glanced at her attire. It had been suitable for driving in a car with the heater set at its maximum, but it was sorely lacking for traipsing around in the great outdoors, particularly in this great outdoors. Her jacket was warm enough for a cool Florida evening in December, but it hadn't taken her long to discover it wouldn't withstand a frigid January day in Quebec. It fell as far as the top of her jeans-clad hips. Her footwear consisted of a pair of sneakers, and a thin pair of leather gloves provided the only protection she had for her hands.

On top of it all, she didn't have a hat to cover her head and ears. She'd have to make do with what she found in the car and hope she soon came across some sort of shelter where she could be safe and warm. Her immediate concern was to get as far from this car as possible. When they found it – and they would – they'd scour the area in search of her, and she couldn't afford to let them find her.

Tori had a light silk scarf that had been designed for use as a fashion accessory. She wrapped it around her head, covering her ears, and shoved more tissues between the cut on her forehead and the now multi-purpose scarf. Zipping her coat up to her neck, she flipped up her collar, grabbed her keys and gloves, and stepped from the car. A blast of cold air slapped her face.

Recovering, Tori realized she had another dilemma. She didn't know in which direction she should walk. She couldn't go back. That would be the direction from which her pursuers would come. If she continued along this deserted stretch of road, her blue jacket and jeans would stand out against the pure white background like a beacon. She'd have to scramble up onto the snowbank to escape them. But, would she be able to move quickly enough?

No, she had to venture into the forest while she had the opportunity. But which way? Both sides of the road were identical. There was so much sameness, so much whiteness, eased slightly by the grey of the leafless maple and poplar trees. A few evergreens, heavily laden with snow, offered some color relief.

She shrugged and chose a direction at random, hoping for the best, and climbed up the bank. This was no small feat. The top of the hard-packed snow bank loomed at least a foot higher than the top of her head. She jabbed holes into it with the tips of her sneakers and made footholds for herself. After much grunting and a healthy dose of swearing, she hauled herself to the top.

Tori fell to her knees, gasping for breath. A wave of dizziness washed over her, no doubt from the combination of exertion and the bump to her head. She couldn't rest long. Not only did she have to move to outrun her pursuers, but she had to avoid freezing to death. Lounging in the snow was not the ideal way to do either.

Tori stood, waited a moment for her legs to get over their shakiness, and struck off toward the trees. Since the weather had cooperated lately, she wasn't bogged down by soft snow, but it was cold, which made it miserable to be outside. She sought comfort in the fact the trees would protect her from the wind. By continually moving, she'd keep herself warm. She knew she wouldn't survive long in these conditions. She'd have to find shelter soon, or she'd die in this beautiful, cold, white landscape.

Tori concentrated on putting one foot in front of the other until she noticed the sun high in the sky. Glancing at her watch, she saw it was midday. It had been two hours since the car had crashed. During that time, she hadn't seen a sign of another human being. Of course, she realized she may not have covered much territory either. It was hard to judge how far she'd progressed with so much sameness surrounding her, so much snow and forest.

Walking was more difficult than she'd expected. Sometimes she'd take several steps on top of the hard crust, until one leg would break through, and she'd find herself in the awkward position of having a limb swallowed by the snow. She'd struggle to extricate her leg, just to have it happen again a few steps later.

Tori came to a full stop. She'd heard of people having mirages in the heat of the desert when they were exhausted and parched with thirst, imagining a cool pool of water. Did people also have mirages when they were exhausted and frozen?

Up ahead, a cabin was nestled in the forest, like a picture on a postcard. Using a tree to support her tired body, she squinted, straining her eyes to see the small plume of smoke curling from the chimney.

Her knees shook, both from weariness and relief. There was hope she would escape this penetrating cold. Her fingers and toes were numb, and her ears had long ago decided the pretty silk scarf was useless. Her eyelashes were heavy and white with frost.

She approached the cabin from the back. Tori didn't know who she'd find in residence. It could be a kind, gentle person just as easily as it could be a dangerous brute. Then again, she was in immediate danger of hypothermia, not to mention the fact that proven dangerous brutes were already on her trail. The choice was obvious, but she didn't intend to waltz into another treacherous situation without checking it out first.

Piles of snow surrounded the cabin, high enough for her to easily peer into the windows. At the back, she saw a small bedroom with a dresser and two beds, a double and a twin. Through another window on the side, she had a view of a larger room furnished with a sofa and armchair at one end. At the other, a table, three chairs, a kitchen counter, and cupboards completed the furnishings.

What caught Tori's attention, apart from the fact the building appeared to be empty of human life, was the wood stove that sat in a corner with a pile of split logs stacked neatly beside it. She had to get inside and warm herself. She'd deal with the inhabitants of the cabin if and when she encountered them.

Tori approached the front door and knocked noisily, despite her suspicion the structure was empty. No sounds of movement emanated from inside the cabin. Tori reached for the knob, hoping to find the door unlocked. She didn't have to worry. It swung open easily. She hesitated for a moment before calling out.

"Hello. Is anyone here?"

No response. She ventured over the threshold.

Tori scanned the contents of the cabin. It had a lived-in look, but it was tidy, everything seemingly in its place. She eagerly crossed the room to the wood stove.

With difficulty, she tugged off her flimsy gloves and fanned her fingers out as close as possible to the heat. She huddled beside it for several minutes before a small amount of warmth crept into her extremities, but the cold had burrowed deep into her bones. She questioned whether she'd ever enjoy warmth again.

Tori considered her next step. Should she seek help from the occupant of the cabin or should she strike out on her own again? It didn't take a genius to realize the person who stayed here was not a quiet, genteel woman. It would be an outdoorsman.

Would she be safe, one woman alone? She wasn't stupid. She knew the dangers. She'd experienced many of them over the past few days. She'd survived, but that didn't mean she'd throw herself on the mercy of the first person she met and damn the consequences. Unfortunately, she didn't have a lot of options.

Reluctantly, she left the warmth of the wood stove to explore the small cabin. The kitchen and living area seemed innocuous. A quick peek into the tiny bathroom didn't reveal anything dangerous. Venturing into the bedroom, on the wall she hadn't seen through the window, there was a well-stocked gun cabinet that rivaled anything she'd ever seen before. Not only did it contain rifles, but it was equipped with large, dangerous-looking knives. It also had an empty spot where a rifle should have been.

Tori's stomach clenched. The owner of the cabin, while temporarily absent, could be armed. She became less enamored with the idea of hanging around to see who lived here and if he could help her. She'd already relied on her wits to get out of a bad situation; she'd continue to do so.

Tori searched the cabin for some items she'd need to survive until she reached civilisation and could find someone she trusted, if indeed such a person existed. In the bedroom, she came across a dresser that had warm, wool socks in one of the drawers. She gratefully pulled them over her still-cold feet. In the closet were men's boots that were many sizes too big for her and too heavy to make walking easy. She'd have to depend on her own shoes, even though she had to untie the laces to squeeze her wool-clad feet into them.

Tori smiled when she found a warm sweater so large she could pull it on over her jacket. The sleeves needed to be rolled up to accommodate her much shorter arms. She topped off her outfit with a fleece-lined man's jacket that she put on over all her other clothes. It fell almost to her knees. She wondered if it was over-kill to wear so many layers, until she remembered the temperature outside and the fact she might spend the night in the woods. She decided it could never be too much. She knew she resembled the Goodyear blimp on a bad day, but her biggest concern was survival, not her appearance.

Tori thought about the size of the man who wore these clothes. She realized she'd made the right decision to escape the warmth and relative safety of the cabin, but she'd have to hurry. She didn't know when he'd come back. Rifling through the kitchen cupboards, hunting for something to eat, she shoved bags of dried fruit and nuts into her pockets, along with a few apples. A wave of guilt flowed over her at the idea of stealing from someone, but her life depended on it. She vowed she'd return the clothes and replace the food as soon as she could. She didn't have time to worry about it now.

Having donned an enormous pair of fleece-lined gloves and tucked her long brown hair under a woollen cap, Tori took a last glance around the cabin. She gazed wistfully at the stove, and hastened out into the winter frontier. In front of her was a large, almost perfectly circular clearing. She headed toward it, wondering if it would be easier to hike across such an expanse since it was so flat and clear of trees. On the other hand, it would make her more visible. Tori decided to be cautious and skirt the clearing, hiding in the shelter of the woods.

Loud barking exploded behind her. Looking over her shoulder, her eyes widened, and her heart thumped. A man stood beside the cabin, and even from this distance, she saw he was big. She had no doubt he was the owner of the clothing she'd borrowed. But, her attention was drawn from the man to the great beast that lunged toward her, growling furiously.

Without a second thought, Tori swiveled and ran, heading for the clearing. The bulk of the clothing she wore impeded her progress, her knees hampered by the weight of the heavy coat. The collar she'd turned up to shield her from the wind bobbed up and down in front of her face as she ran. She had difficulty seeing the ground in front of her. The surefooted animal could outrun her, but she wouldn't give up without a fight.

When it hit, it hit hard. A great weight landed on Tori's back, and she found herself lying face-down in the snow. The pressure of the dog's paws penetrated the heavy layers of clothing, two on her shoulders and two on her buttocks. Her arms came up to defend her face from the teeth that were inches away, his loud barks ringing in her ears.

Unexpectedly, his barking stopped, and the animal's weight left her. Squinting from behind her collar, she saw the dog, a German Shepherd, standing to one side, panting without taking his eyes from her face. His tongue lolled out of the side of his mouth, and his breath created great clouds of frosty air.

Tori dared to glance back toward the cabin and spotted the man striding in her direction. He had a thick black beard, shaggy hair sticking out from under his wool cap, and a distinct scowl on his face. What caused her the most distress was not his size, or even his scowl, but the rifle he carried under his arm. Again, without a second thought for the consequences, she jumped to her feet and leapt forward. The man bellowed, but she couldn't make out the words and didn't know if he shouted at her, or if he ordered the dog to attack. Tori didn't stop to find out.

Without warning, her right foot didn't connect with the hard snow beneath her anymore, and she pitched headlong. As her body was engulfed by freezing water, she realized she'd run onto a frozen lake, or at least a partially frozen lake. She grabbed ineffectually at the edge of the ice, but the water swallowed her up, her body weighed down by heavy clothing. Panicking, she flapped her arms and kicked her feet, trying to dislodge the boots. Surfacing briefly, she opened her mouth to scream and inhaled icy water as she dipped below the surface again.

Tori's wrist was painfully clasped in a sharp grip. She saw the watery image of the huge dog crouched on the ice with her arm clenched between his massive teeth. She didn't know if he wanted to make a meal of her arm, or if he intended to save her, but she didn't care. His efforts dragged her head above the surface, and that's all that mattered. She'd gladly sacrifice an arm for her life.

A low growl came from behind her, and Tori worried there was another dog joining in the attack. Someone or something grabbed the back of the heavy winter coat and pulled upward with a quick jerk. She was lifted up and out of the hole in the ice. But, when the dog released her arm from his iron grip, she slid out of the overlarge coat, and with a muffled scream, slipped back into the water and felt it close over her head once more.

•   •   •

The man couldn't believe his eyes as he stood on the ice holding an empty coat – his own coat – in his hand. The person had disappeared from inside the garment.

Riley had been the first to spot the stranger, and his bark had alerted both humans. The man was surprised to see the small figure ambling awkwardly toward the lake. The cabin was private, as it was meant to be. He couldn't remember the last time he'd seen anyone in the area.

The man's surprise turned to alarm when he saw the person run toward the lake and the ice-fishing opening directly in his path. His shouted warning made the person run faster. He swore soundly and took off at a run, hoping to intercept the kid before he reached the hole.

The man was convinced the person was a teenage boy, intent on causing mischief. He wasn't big enough to be an adult man, and he'd have no other reason to run if he hadn't done something wrong. As the man grabbed onto the coat and lifted the boy out of the water, he was relieved he wouldn't have to dive into the bone-chilling depths to rescue the troublemaker. His relief was short-lived when he was left holding an empty coat. He tossed it aside, tore off his own coat and boots, and dived in to find the rapidly-sinking body.

•   •   •

Tori fought against the invisible force that dragged her toward the bottom of the lake, kicking with her legs and pushing upward with her arms, but her clothes were too heavy, and her limbs were too numb with the cold. When the strong arm circled her waist, she stopped fighting and let it haul her to safety. A shaft of light filtered through the dirty lake water as her savior towed her toward the opening in the ice, her lungs straining against the pressure. They broke through the surface of the water, and she was pushed up and out of the lake. She gasped for air, spit out dirty water, and silently blessed the solid feel of the ice underneath her.

A grunt and a splash sounded to her right, and she turned her head to see her rescuer pull himself out of the hole onto the ice, where he knelt with his hands on his knees, and his head bowed, panting heavily. The dog barked and raced energetically between the two people, enjoying this new and strange game.

Tori dazedly pulled herself up onto her hands and knees. She had to get her wet body off the ice, but she trembled violently, both from shock and cold. She didn't think her legs would support her.

It turned out her legs weren't needed. To her amazement, the man had already recovered from the unexpected swim and tugged on his coat and boots. He threw the coat she had worn over his arm, scooped her up, flung her over his shoulder, and carried her in the direction of the cabin. It didn't even occur to her to protest. She was wet and frozen, and in no condition to go anywhere on her own.

"*Es-tu fou? Tu ne m'as pas entendu? Je t'ai dit d'arrêter.*"

Tori had no idea what he said, but she knew by his tone of voice he wasn't happy. She couldn't blame him. If he felt half as miserable as she did, his anger was justified.

Arriving at the cabin, he shoved open the door, and unceremoniously deposited Tori on a hard kitchen chair. She folded her arms around herself and curled into a ball, seeking warmth. She wasn't given the chance. The heavy wool sweater, soaking wet, was grasped, and the man tried to yank it over her head. The combination of wet, stretching wool and tightly-clasped arms worked against him.

"*Aide-moi. Lève tes bras.*"

In apparent frustration, he grabbed her arms and jerked them upward. The sweater followed, sliding over her head in a cold, sopping mess. In the process, the borrowed wool cap came off, and her wet hair tumbled down over her shoulders.

"*Christ. Une femme.*"

A combination of astonishment and anger distorted his face.

"*Qui es-tu? Qu'est-ce que tu fais ici?*"

Tori shook her head and answered through chattering teeth.

"I don't understand. I don't speak French."

"Who the hell are you? What are you doing here?" he said in perfect English.

He was an imposing person, quite tall, with broad shoulders and what might be a muscular physique, although it was well-hidden by his layers of wet clothing. His long, bushy hair was in dire need of a trim, and he had a thick, dark beard covering most of his face.

From behind the cloak of hair, his eyes were dark brown, almost black, and they blazed with anger. His heavy brows were lowered, and she was reminded of a large brown bear she had seen in the zoo, snarling with irritation. Oddly, despite all these less-than-reassuring traits, Tori didn't feel afraid of him. She mentally reminded herself not to trust a total stranger.

"I'm cold. Could I please have a blanket?"

"I'll be right back," he said, shaking his head, seeming to realize she sat before him, totally drenched, as was he.

He trudged toward the room at the back of the cabin, to reappear with a large blanket. He tossed it onto her lap.

"Here, get undressed and wrap yourself in this. I'm going to get changed."

When he disappeared through the bedroom doorway, Tori set about getting undressed. She unzipped and removed her jacket with little effort. She even removed her sweater without too much trouble, but undoing her jeans was a difficult challenge. Her fingers, numb with cold, couldn't handle the button, and the heavy material was pasted to her body in such a way she knew she wouldn't get out of it unaided. But she'd do her best rather than face the unappealing prospect of asking the stranger for help.

"Can I come out?"

His voice carried clearly from behind the closed door of the bedroom.

"No!"

After a few moments of silence, "Do you need help?"

"No."

Frustrated with her attempts to remove her jeans, Tori discovered the harder she tried, the worse it became. She stood in the middle of the room, clad only in her bra and the recalcitrant jeans, when the man entered, dressed in dry, warm clothing. She grabbed the blanket off the chair and clutched it firmly in front of her.

"No. I'm not ready."

"You need help."

"I can do it."

"No, you can't. You're too cold, and your clothes are too wet."

He spoke in a matter-of-fact voice as if it was an ordinary occurrence to have a distressed, half-naked, soaking-wet, frozen woman standing in the middle of his cabin.

"You don't have to worry. The last thing I'm interested in is your body, and I doubt you have anything I haven't seen before."

Tori didn't know how to respond. Aware she'd never get undressed on her own, she was mortified at the idea of this strange man helping her get out of her jeans. However, she noticed an impassive look now replaced his scowl.

He took over and applied himself to the task at hand. He moved closer, reached behind the blanket, and unbuttoned the waistband of her jeans. As he slid down the zipper, she noticed him glance up at her face. Tori swiveled her head toward the wood stove, willing it to swallow her up, her cheeks red with embarrassment.

•   •   •

The man took advantage of the moment to get a good look at her. She appeared to be in her late twenties or early thirties, with long, brown hair and brown eyes, pretty despite her recent mishaps. She was also very tense, which was perhaps understandable under the circumstances.

As he tugged the wet fabric down her legs, he did his best to divert his line of vision, but at one point, he had no choice except to look at her and was rewarded with a view of an excellent set of legs. They were hidden from his sight when she secured the blanket around her body, stepped out of her jeans, and pulled off her socks. He occupied himself with picking up the sodden clothing while she made a cocoon of the blanket. Without so much as a glance in her direction, he dragged a chair to the stove and draped the jeans and sweater over the back of it. A second chair followed, and he wordlessly indicated she should be seated.

•   •   •

Tori didn't hesitate. She hobbled to the chair, holding onto the blanket tightly. After several minutes of absorbing the warmth, she looked over her shoulder to see her rescuer standing mutely behind her. Feeling uneasy under his scrutiny, she redirected her attention to the stove in front of her.

"What's your name?" he asked.

After a moment's hesitation, she said, "Tori. What's yours?"

"Benoit. Ben, for short," he said. "Tori. I've never heard that name before."

"It's short for Victoria."

"What are you doing here?"

Again, she hesitated. So far, she'd worked under the premise that absolute secrecy was necessary. She resolved to stick with that plan.

"I had a car accident. I was looking for help."

It was weak as far as explanations went, but it was the best she could do on short notice, and it was close to the truth. She didn't dare look at him, knowing her expression would betray her. Ben placed another chair at a right angle to her and sat. He stretched his long legs out in front of him and crossed his arms over his chest, as if he was settling in for a long inquisition.

"You're a few kilometres from the nearest road. You're telling me you walked all this way searching for help instead of just going back the way you came?"

Tori fought to keep her face blank, suppressing a wince when she heard how stupid her explanation sounded coming from his lips.

"I walked a short distance into the bush, but I got lost and couldn't find my way back. Luckily, I came across your cabin."

"And you were so desperate for help you started to run as soon as you saw me."

"You scared me. You're so big...and...your dog, he frightened me."

They both stared at the accused. He lay peacefully in front of the stove at their feet, and seeming to sense they talked about him, he lifted his head and wagged his tail happily. Tori shifted in her chair.

"What kind of car were you driving?"

She wondered at the relevance of the question but chose to answer it anyway.

"A Ford Tempo. Why?"

"Just curious. Did you have an airbag?"

"No. It's an older model. That's why I have this bump on my head," she said, lifting her bangs.

"Yeah, I noticed that."

His dark eyes were firmly fixed on hers, holding her attention.

"But I have to question what kind of car could make such a mark on your cheek and around your throat."

Tori lifted a trembling hand to her neck and turned her face from his scrutiny. Her breath quickened as the memory of how those marks had been sustained came rushing back to her, the feel of large hands squeezing the life from her body.

Her thoughts were interrupted by the big dog as he came over to place his chin on her knee, his tail wagging and eyes pleading. She wondered if the animal sensed her fear and wanted to offer her comfort. She returned the favor by petting his head and scratching him behind his ears.

"What's his name?"

Tori forced the words past the constriction in her throat, hoping to display a casualness she was far from feeling. She needed to change the subject.

"Riley."

"Riley? That doesn't sound like a French-Canadian name."

"It's not. I grew up in the West End of Montreal."

Ben spoke as if this explained everything, but for her, it explained very little. He must have noticed the puzzled expression on her face.

"My mother was an Anglophone; my father French-Canadian. I grew up with both languages in the house."

"You appear to be the exception," she said wryly.

Since coming to Quebec City a few days ago, Tori had struggled to communicate with the people. Many were understanding and tried their best, but she came to realize there weren't many people who spoke English fluently. All the signs were solely in French, and only the large chains of fast-food restaurants and department stores were familiar to her. She was unprepared for the culture shock.

"Where are you from?"

His question evoked a sharp glance from her, which in turn elicited a raised eyebrow from him.

"Florida," she said.

"Florida? This time of year? Are you running away from all the Canadians headed in that direction?"

Tori squared her shoulders.

"I wanted to experience winter, and was told there'd be no better place to do it."

"Well, you're correct there. So, I suppose you've visited *le Vieux Québec* and been skiing at Mont Sainte-Anne, perhaps had a tour of the Ice Hotel."

Tori knew he was suspicious, wanting to uncover her real intentions, but she wouldn't give him any more information other than misinformation.

"No, I haven't had time yet. I just arrived yesterday," she lied.

"Really? So, the first item on your itinerary was a trek through the bush forty kilometres north of Quebec City."

His voice was laced with sarcasm.

"No. I went for a drive. The trek through the bush was a bonus."

Tori heard the foolishness of her own words, but she didn't care. Let him believe what he wanted. She'd be away from here as soon as possible.

Chapter 2

As Tori shivered by the stove, Ben puttered in the kitchen, heating a can of soup. He'd obviously recovered from his impromptu swim in the frigid lake much more quickly than she had. But, to her relief, his questioning had stopped, and he seemed disinterested in her and her reasons for being there.

Curiosity ate at Tori. Who was this strange man who had saved her life? What was he doing in this cabin deep in the woods? Did he live here year-round? How did he survive? She wanted to ask all these questions and more, but his remote behavior wasn't encouraging. She might not be afraid of him, but she didn't feel she could demand answers just to appease her curiosity. He might feel she should return the favor.

"Soup's ready. You can come to the table."

Tori gazed longingly at her clothes draped over the chair, but it was obvious they were still dripping wet. She felt uncomfortable eating while swaddled in a blanket. She'd have to hold onto it with one hand. Apparently, Ben understood her dilemma.

"Hang on," he said.

He handed her another one of his heavy wool sweaters and a warm pair of socks, before discreetly turning his back to her.

Tori let the blanket fall to the floor and pulled the cozy sweater over her head. It fell to mid-thigh level, and the sleeves swallowed up her hands. She didn't care. Sitting at the table, with the blanket covering her bare legs, she was grateful for the borrowed clothes. She rolled up the sleeves while sniffing appreciatively at the steaming bowl of soup Ben had set in front of her.

Tori hadn't realized how famished she was. She flashed Ben a quick smile of thanks, grabbed her spoon, and ate ravenously. It was late afternoon and she'd worked up a ferocious appetite since breakfast.

The meal was conducted in silence, a silence Tori found to be surprisingly companionable, considering the circumstances in which the two of them had been thrown together.

Ben cleared his throat, and Tori anticipated another string of probing questions she wasn't prepared to answer.

"Is your car severely damaged?"

"I'm not sure," she said, relieved to discuss a relatively safe topic. "I hit the snowbank. I tried to back out, but the car was stuck, so I had to leave it. The front was crumpled up a bit, but maybe it can be fixed."

"It's going to be dark soon. It'll be more difficult to find someone to pull you out at this hour. I suggest we wait until morning. It won't snow tonight. Your car will be all right there until tomorrow."

Tori had misgivings about staying overnight in the cabin, but they had nothing to do with fear of this stranger. Rather, she sensed he cherished his privacy, and she'd intruded upon it.

"It's all right," he said. "The couch is comfortable and close to the stove. You'll sleep well and so will I."

Her feelings must have been obvious, but his tone led her to believe he wished she'd never come upon his cabin or fallen into his lake. The latter she would also have happily avoided.

Tori stood, laid her blanket across the back of the chair, and picked up some dirty dishes. The least she could do was help, she thought. When she stood on her tiptoes and stretched to put an unused glass in a cupboard, he intervened.

"I'll do that. You go sit in front of the stove."

"I'd like to help."

"Thank you, but I want you to sit in front of the stove. And, take the blanket with you."

His voice was firm and allowed no room for disagreement. Tori picked up the discarded blanket and curled up on the couch near the wood stove. Despite her good intentions, it was wonderful to take advantage of the warmth and comfort of the well-worn piece of furniture. She snuggled lower into its soft depths.

Drowsiness overcame her, and her eyelids grew heavy. A buzzing noise broke through her stupor, getting louder and closer. Strangely, it sounded similar to a lawnmower, but Tori knew it wasn't possible. She roused herself and glanced at Ben. His body was stiff, his head cocked slightly to one side.

Fear crept under her skin. She didn't know the source of the sound, but Ben's reaction to the buzzing noise wasn't reassuring.

"Get up and come with me," he said. "Bring the blanket."

He strode over to the chair by the stove, grabbed her clothes from the back of it, and led her by the elbow into the bedroom at the back of the cabin. It didn't occur to her to protest or ask questions. She instinctively placed her trust in him, sensing this wasn't the time for lengthy explanations.

Inside the bedroom, he opened a closet and shoved her in amongst a motley collection of clothing, a broom, and various other household supplies.

"Stay there," he said unnecessarily, shutting the door.

The buzzing noise reached the cabin and stopped with a smothery gasp. She heard Ben crossing the cabin to the front door. She held her breath and tried not to fidget. The inner walls were thin and far from soundproof.

Knuckles rapped on the door, and a draft of cold air swept across her feet as the wind invaded the small cabin and snuck through the cracks in the walls. Her shivers transformed into tremors when she recognized the voices of the new arrivals. The conversation was conducted in brisk French, and she couldn't understand a word of it, but panic welled up inside of her.

She searched her mind for a way to escape the cabin without attracting notice. The bedroom window was high on the wall. To get it open and climb through it soundlessly would be impossible. They'd hear her and be upon her immediately. Besides that, she wore nothing more than a sweater and a pair of socks. She'd freeze as soon as she landed in the snow piled outside the cabin.

Tori closed her eyes and took several deep breaths. The men continued their questioning of Ben, and she suspected she was the main topic of their interrogation. The fact Ben hadn't yet led them to her was a good sign. Maybe he didn't intend to cooperate with them, although she couldn't fathom why. She thought he'd be glad to see the last of her.

Tori hated her feeling of helplessness, hoping they'd soon leave empty-handed. She cautiously moved her right arm, searching for a makeshift weapon with which she could defend herself. She connected with a broom handle and grasped it with a death grip. It'd be useless against a gun, but it could be used to knock a knife out of someone's hands, or to hit them in the throat. She decided it was better than nothing.

The door thumped closed, and the cold draft swept through the cabin again. She held her breath until the buzzing noise started once more. She realized it was a snowmobile that had brought the men through the bush to this remote location. She closed her eyes with relief when she heard the vehicle moving away, but she knew Ben would soon come to confront her. She didn't know how she'd explain this one.

Chapter 3

Ben stared blankly at the closed door, assimilating everything that had happened. The arrival of the girl had been a surprise, and he'd suspected from the beginning that she hid something. Now, he knew it was something dangerous. Tori had an excellent reason for not following the road back into town. She was running from someone and that someone had just come knocking on his door.

The two strangers had followed her footprints through the snow. Even in the dark, the headlight of the snowmobile clearly exposed them. It had taken a lot of explaining on his part to convince them it was his footprints leading to the cabin. He wasn't sure he'd succeeded.

There'd been no question of handing Tori over to them. True, he valued his time alone in his cabin, and he would've preferred she'd chosen someone else's lake in which to fall, but he wasn't cold-blooded enough to hand her over to a couple of goons. She was in trouble, and he wasn't going to make it worse for her.

Ben pivoted and stared speculatively toward the bedroom where she hid. He knew she'd heard everything, but she wouldn't have understood them. He also suspected she'd recognized the voices at the door. He was convinced those men were responsible for her injuries, and several pieces of the puzzle now fit together. There were still some gaping holes but, if he handled this wisely, he might fill them. The question was whether he wanted to do so or not. After all, this cabin was meant to be his refuge, not a hotbed of intrigue.

When he pulled open the closet door there was no sign of his visitor. Pushing aside the clothes on hangers, he saw her pale face with wide, frightened eyes peering at him from behind a mop.

"You can come out now," he said.

Tori kept her gaze locked on his, seemingly trying to decipher his thoughts, but Ben carefully kept his expression impassive. The daylight dwindled, the interior of the cabin darkening, and the shadows would make his face even more difficult to read. She stepped out of the closet, clinging to the broom, and visibly fought to master her fear and appear casual. She opened her mouth to speak but slammed it shut. Ben felt certain she couldn't decide what to say without further incriminating herself.

He left the bedroom without another word. In the main room, he dropped the blinds on each window, blocking the shimmer of the sunset on snow. Tori waited on the threshold, watching him. He hoped she got the message that he was willing to protect her from the people who meant her harm. Despite the fact she'd intruded on his life, stolen his clothing, and forced him to dive into the frozen lake, he'd offered her shelter and safety.

Ben rummaged inside a cupboard, found some matches, and lit two lanterns fixed to opposite walls in the main room. He didn't look in Tori's direction as he added two pieces of wood to the fire and poked at the coals. He sensed her glare on his back, and he knew she waited with impatience for what was to come.

He glanced her way.

"Are you planning to use that or are you going to put it away?" he said, nodding at the broom.

Chapter 4

Tori's cheeks reddened as she realized she'd forgotten to leave the broom where it belonged. She rushed to put it away.

"Do you want a coffee, or something?" Ben asked when she returned.

"No thanks."

With an economy of movement, he made a pot of coffee. While waiting for it to brew, he steadily worked in the kitchen, tidying up, and digging through the cupboard for a box of cookies.

Tori ran a jerky hand through her hair and hoped the tension didn't show on her face. She wondered if Ben purposely drew out the moment, knowing how the wait affected her.

Setting a plate of cookies in the center of the table, he sat with his cup of coffee. Blowing softly on the steaming brew, he fixed her with a penetrating gaze.

"So, Tori, what *exactly* are you doing here in Quebec?"

Tori was tempted to lie again and repeat the story she'd told him, but she sensed he was past believing it. She didn't think he deserved any more lies. He'd done more than enough for her already. But, she couldn't tell him the truth. She decided to be honest with him in another way.

"I'm sorry. I can't tell you that."

One of Ben's eyebrows lifted in surprise.

"Why not?"

She hesitated for a moment, unsure how she should answer.

"It's something I have to take care of myself. I don't want to involve you or anyone else."

He gave a humourless snort.

"I think it's a little late for that. I think I'm already involved."

She nodded.

"Yes, to a certain extent. But at least I can limit your involvement."

"What if I told you I want to get involved?"

"I wouldn't believe you. I'd assume you were just being kind."

She paused, considering her words.

"Ben, I may not know you very well, but you strike me as the kind of guy who likes to keep to himself," she said, waving a hand around the cabin. "I appreciate what you've done; fishing me out of the lake, and letting me dry out. I especially appreciate that you didn't hand me over to those men, but I refuse to drag you into this any further. If you don't mind me staying here tonight, I'll be out of your hair by tomorrow morning, and you can pretend you never saw me."

His expression was doubtful.

"I've told you there's no problem with you staying here tonight. Don't worry about it," he said.

To her surprise, he abruptly changed the subject.

"So, what part of Florida are you from?"

"Tallahassee. Have you ever been there?" she said, relieved to have a break from their uncomfortable conversation.

"No, but I've been to Fort Lauderdale a couple of times; the standard March break trip for a lot of college students. Of course, most of it's a drunken blur."

Ben's reference to college surprised her. He struck her as the type of guy who'd lived most of his life in the bush. She had trouble imagining him poring over books and taking part in student parties.

"Where did you go to college?" she asked.

"John Abbot, in Montreal."

"What did you study?"

"This and that."

His tone was brusque, and his expression was stiff. An awkward silence followed, but his obvious reticence intrigued Tori. Her natural curiosity urged her to question him further, but her conscience advised her it wouldn't be welcomed, and she'd abuse his grudging hospitality.

Chapter 5

Riley, who lay on the floor between them, perked up, and growled low in his throat, his attention drawn to the door. Tori stiffened and pivoted to face Ben, her eyes wide with fear.

"It's probably nothing," he said. "But, maybe you should go back into the bedroom. I'll check it out."

Tori scrambled off her chair and into the other room, taking up residence in the closet again.

Ben listened for noises. It wasn't unusual for the dog to catch the scent of a rabbit, even from inside the cabin, but so close on the heels of the other visit, he wasn't taking any chances. From the cupboard positioned high above the sink he removed a handgun from the top shelf. It was the second time he'd taken it from its hiding place in the past hour, which was unusual. But, this had turned out to be an unusual day. He pulled on his heavy jacket and boots and stepped outside the door with Riley bounding ahead of him.

The sun had set, but the sky was clear of clouds, and the moon was almost full, reflecting off the snow and creating an eerie brightness. The large dog hesitated for a second on the porch before racing through the trees to the right of the cabin. Ben took that as a good sign. The dog wasn't headed in the same direction the snowmobile had taken. It went a long way to convincing him that Riley chased the scent of a small animal.

The night was quiet, and Ben stood still, listening for any noise that didn't sound natural. He whistled and was rewarded by the sound of Riley crashing through the trees toward him. The branches on each side of the dog were whipped by his tail, and he appeared unconcerned. Ben relaxed, but he was aware he couldn't give up his vigilance.

After filling his lungs with the crisp winter air, he returned to the interior of the cabin and called out to Tori as he pulled off his boots and coat.

"All clear. You can come out now."

Brooms and containers rattled before he saw her peek around the doorway leading into the main room.

"It was nothing. Just a false alarm," he said.

"But why would Riley react like that? He must have heard something."

"He smelled something. It was probably just a rabbit or a fox. Most of the larger animals are hibernating." Her expression was far from confident. "Don't worry. Nothing will happen to you here."

Ben slid his hand to his back and touched the gun tucked into his waistband, hidden by his sweater. He'd keep it on him rather than hide it in the cupboard, but that information wouldn't be shared with her.

"Are you hungry? Thirsty?" he said, forcing a casualness into his voice.

"No, thanks. I'm fine."

Ben didn't think she looked fine. She stood in the middle of the room wearing his oversize sweater and rubbing her arms as if she was cold. He suspected it was fear and not the temperature that gave her the chills. Riley, as if sensing her discomfort and thinking she needed a distraction, went up behind her and pressed his nose, which had recently been in a snowbank, upon her bare thigh. Tori's reaction was instantaneous. She squealed and jumped several feet away from the offending nose, twisting in midair. They both chuckled at the sight of the German Shepherd wagging his tail, immensely proud of himself.

"Riley, you scared me," Tori said.

At the sound of his name, the dog raced over to stand in front of her, surely expecting a reward. Tori scratched him behind his ears, and Riley's tongue lolled out of his mouth with utter contentment. Ben observed the exchange with amusement. At least his guest had momentarily forgotten the unwanted visitors.

As Tori and the dog bonded, Ben moved around the room, preparing a meal for supper. He felt Tori's gaze on him, until she seemed to take note of the equipment in the cabin. She peered at the gas stove and the lanterns on the wall, and studied the narrow metal piping running up the wall to the lights. She stared at the refrigerator with a furrowed brow.

"Do you have electricity here?"

"No."

"How does the fridge work?"

"With propane gas, same as everything else."

"Where does the gas come from?"

"I have two tanks outside."

"How do you get them filled?"

"I take them out and get them filled."

"Do you live here year-round?" Her voice rang with disbelief.

"Not really."

"What do you mean by 'not really'?"

"I mean I don't really live here year-round."

"Where do you live when you're not living here?"

"Somewhere else."

Her head tilted to the side, and she pursed her lips. He was purposely vague. He didn't want to talk about himself, and he knew she couldn't insist, since she'd soon find the tables turned on her.

After their dinner, Tori helped clean up. When she asked how he managed to get running water in the cabin, he gave her a short lesson in physics involving underground streams and gravity.

By this time, it was late, and the combination of a full stomach, a warm wood stove, and the exhausting events of the day had clearly caught up with Tori. Her eyelids were heavy.

"Um...if you don't mind lending me a pillow I think I'd like to go to sleep now," she said, giving in to her fatigue.

"Just go into the bedroom and take a bed."

"Oh, no. I couldn't do that. That'd be an imposition. I'll sleep on the couch."

"I'd rather you sleep in the bedroom. There're two beds in there. We won't have to share."

"No, Ben. I'll sleep here. The couch is very comfortable."

He spoke purposely, looking her in the eye.

"Tori, I think it'd be better if you slept in the same room as me. Just in case those guys decide to come back."

Her eyes widened. She obviously hadn't considered that possibility, and she now appeared to agree with him wholeheartedly.

Ben followed her into the room and watched her crawl into the single bed, leaving the double for him. She curled onto her side and hauled the covers up to her chin. An hour earlier, he'd lit the stove to warm the room. He now adjusted the thermostat on the small propane stove to prevent the room from getting too warm while they slept.

About to extinguish the lights, Ben saw Riley pad into the room. Instead of taking his usual place on the double bed, the dog crossed over to Tori and climbed up beside her. She looked momentarily surprised, but smiled and wrapped her arm around him as he burrowed himself in, nestling his head against her chest.

Shaking his head in disgust, Ben shut off the lights and removed his sweater, sliding the gun under his pillow. As he slid under the covers, he considered how German Shepherds were supposed to be the most loyal dogs a person could own. But, all it took was a pretty face and a nice set of legs, and they'd abandon you without a second thought.

Chapter 6

Tori slept like a log.

The sound of heavy footsteps and the smell of coffee awoke her. For a moment, she was disoriented, until she remembered where she was and how she'd come to be there. Her furry source of warmth was missing, making her pull the covers closer. She glanced over at Ben's bed and saw it was neatly-made without so much as a wrinkle in the blanket. She was curious if he was extra tidy because she was here, or if he was always so meticulous with his belongings.

She lay in the bed for a few more minutes and thought about her unwilling host. She wondered what kind of person preferred to live in complete isolation rather than among other people. While his cabin was well-equipped as far as the necessities of life were concerned, it'd be considered rudimentary by most people's standards. She found it comfortable, even charming, but she didn't think she could live in such isolated conditions year-round, not in this climate.

Then again, she thought, as she dragged herself out of bed, it wasn't something she'd ever have to do. This morning, she'd get her car out of the snowbank, go back to her motel, and figure out what her next move should be. With those thoughts in mind, she was surprised to be hit with a pang of regret when she entered the main room and saw Ben efficiently preparing breakfast.

He'd made her feel safe and protected. He'd given her food and shelter. It'd be easy to give in to the temptation to hide here for a few days, just to relish that perception of security and well-being. But that wasn't an option for Tori. She'd never been a person to run from her responsibilities. She knew she'd bitten off quite a bit when she made the decision to come to Quebec, but she'd chew it anyway.

"How do you like your eggs? Scrambled or fried?" Ben asked, interrupting her pensive mood.

"Either one will be fine, thanks."

He shrugged and deftly cracked four eggs into a large cast-iron frying pan.

"Don't tell me you have chickens here somewhere."

"No, why would I?"

"Where did you get the eggs?"

"At the store, like everyone else."

"There's a store near here?"

Again, he shrugged. "Not close, but not too far either. I make a trip every once in a while."

"I guess you have to. There's only so much you can fit in that freezer," she said, nodding toward the refrigerator.

He glanced at her with a hint of amusement on his face and gestured toward the window.

"I've got a pretty big freezer out there."

"You mean you put food outside? What about animals? What do you do in the summertime? You do have summer, don't you?"

He laughed out loud. Tori couldn't help but smile. She'd never heard him laugh.

"Do you see that small building over there?"

Tori joined him at the window and craned her neck to see over the pile of snow that mounted halfway up the panes of glass. She saw a structure measuring about a hundred square feet. Strangely, the door stood open.

"Yes."

"That's an insulated building, and it holds six forty-five-gallon drums filled with water. They freeze solid in the winter. In the spring, I shut the door to keep them insulated and use that as my cold room for the summer."

"That's ingenious."

"It's no big deal. A lot of people do it. It's not as if I invented the idea."

"It's still ingenious."

Ben shrugged his large shoulders and went back to his cooking.

"If you want some coffee, there's a fresh pot on the stove."

Tori's mouth watered at the offer of a cup of hot coffee. She wasn't disappointed. Ben seemed to be good at everything he did.

Riley padded over and rested his head on her lap as she sat at the kitchen table. She smiled and scratched him behind the ears.

"So where did you disappear to this morning? I woke up to an empty bed."

The dog studied her dazedly as her fingers evidently found his favorite spot.

"Riley's a bit of an early riser. I had to let him out for a run."

"So, that makes you an early riser too, doesn't it?"

"I don't mind," he said, shrugging.

Ben set a plate filled with bacon, eggs, and toast in front of her. Her eyes widened.

"I won't be able to eat all this."

"Give it a try. What you don't eat Riley will be very happy to finish."

If it hadn't been for a smattering of sympathy for Riley, she may have polished off the whole plate, but his big, pleading eyes reminded her she should save a bit for him.

After breakfast, in preparation for the retrieval of her car from its chilly parking spot, Tori changed into her own clothing. Standing with his hands on his hips, Ben scanned her up and down. He went over to a large chest and rooted through it before giving a positive-sounding grunt. When he straightened, his arms were filled with items Tori had difficulty deciphering.

Without preamble, he yanked a woollen cap over her head and handed her a large pair of mittens and woollen socks. An oversize bush jacket was thrust at her. She wrinkled her nose at the musty smell that battered her nostrils.

"Pull those socks over your shoes. It's not much, but it's better than nothing. It won't take us very long to get back to your car."

Tori's brows drew together. It had taken her several hours to reach this cabin, even though she might not have taken the most direct route.

When they were bundled up, they stepped into the frigid air, Ben leading the way. Tori was again struck by how penetratingly cold it could be in this area of the world. Evidently, global warming had avoided the province of Quebec. She tucked her head as deeply as possible into the jacket, leaving just her eyes visible between the collar and the edge of her cap. Ben turned when he heard her groan.

"It's not that bad. It's only minus ten degrees," he said, seemingly amused.

"Minus ten! Good God!"

"Celsius, of course."

"What's that in Fahrenheit?"

"Oh, about fifteen degrees or so."

"That's still cold – way too cold."

"To tell you the truth, minus thirty is cold. Once you experience that, you'll think the temperature today is balmy. Trust me."

Tori followed him as he trudged through the snow, not wanting to imagine what it would be like at minus thirty degrees Celsius. She hoped she never had the opportunity to become familiar with it. She hesitated when she saw him head to the other side of the cabin, toward the building he'd described as the cold room. She thought they should go in the opposite direction.

Ben circled to the far side of the structure, and she lumbered gracelessly through the snow, struggling to catch up to him. Riley ran back and forth between them, understanding better than Tori what was happening. The animal trembled with anticipation.

Tori came up behind Ben and peeked around him.

"What's under there?" she said, pointing at the large, odd-shaped object covered by a green canvas tarp.

Ben picked up a corner of the tarp and removed it from its resting place. She frowned at what was underneath.

It was a snowmobile; what seemed to be a large one even to her inexperienced eye. It was a flashy red model with the words 'Arctic Cat' displayed across the cab. She squinted at Ben to see him watching her expectantly. He obviously waited for some sort of reaction, but the one thought that bounced through her head was the fact he expected her to get on that thing with him. She managed a weak smile.

"It's...uh... nice."

"Nice? Is that all you have to say?"

What surprised her most was that her normally calm and aloof host, a man who lived a simple life in a basic and rustic cabin, cared so much about a showy machine.

"Ben, you have to remember I've lived all my life in Florida, and not even on the coast. I've never been on a Sea-Doo, much less a snowmobile. I don't get very excited about this type of thing."

"Hmmph," he said with a shrug. "Let's get going."

Ben shoved a large, red helmet into her hands, which she stared at for a moment before looking at Ben with raised brows.

"I have to wear this? It's huge."

"Don't be a baby," he said, taking the helmet from her and dropping it onto her head. He hooked it under her chin before she had another chance to protest. He climbed onto the snowmobile, twisted a switch, and the machine roared to life.

Tori opened her mouth to suggest they walk to her car instead, but anything she had to say was drowned out by the sound of the large red 'cat'. Ben motioned with his head toward the back of the machine. She took a few tentative steps and stopped. There wasn't much room on the seat of the snowmobile; Ben's bulk took up most of the space. When she was within reach, he grasped her arm and pulled her closer, shouting into her ear.

"This seat is made for one person, but you'll be all right. You can hang on to me."

"Maybe I should walk. I mean, if it's not big enough to carry both of us..."

Tori didn't finish her sentence. Ben yanked her arm until her rear-end made contact with the cold vinyl behind him. Resignedly, she adjusted her legs until she straddled the seat. She tentatively gripped the sides of Ben's jacket, knowing her cheeks were pink, and not only because of the cold. She hardly knew this man against whom she was forced to huddle.

The machine whined loudly and took off with a burst of speed. Flung backward with the force of the launch, Tori wrapped her arms around Ben's middle and clenched her thighs against his hips. Her heart leapt into her throat as she questioned whether she'd survive this excursion.

The snowmobile bounded through the trees, and Tori witnessed the immense power of Ben's pride and joy. She clung to him like a baby monkey clinging to its mother's back. To handle corners, Ben would shift his body weight to one side or the other, tugging Tori sideways with his movements.

With each bump in the trail, her head, heavy with the weight of the helmet, banged against his back between his shoulder blades. She lost control of her limbs as they were jolted and tossed on the back of the machine.

Amongst the trees, the branches whipped by Tori's face and stung her cheeks, until she buried her face in the back of Ben's coat. Curiosity eventually got the better of her, and she strained to peer over his shoulder to see where they were headed. She glimpsed a trail leading through the forest, but her eyes watered and her face stung from the freezing air. She sought the shelter of Ben's back once again.

Behind her, Riley barked. She peeked over her shoulder and saw him keeping pace, his tongue lolling out of the side of his mouth, and his breath producing great clouds of steam.

She didn't comprehend Ben's obvious attraction to this strange sport, but she assumed it was a guy thing – and a dog thing. As far as she saw, it was a noisy, possibly dangerous, and definitely smelly activity. The exhaust fumes emitted by the vehicle were different from any other she'd ever smelled. She'd forever think of it as 'Eau de Arctic Cat'.

After ten minutes of bouncing along the rough trail, the snowmobile slowed and descended a snow bank until they arrived on hard, level ground. Assuming they'd reached their destination, she relaxed her grip on Ben and peeked over his shoulder, hoping to see her car.

The road in front of them was deserted. Ben spun the machine around until it faced down the snow-covered lane, and he hit the accelerator. They surged ahead, unhampered by trees and ruts in a trail. Tori's heart pounded in her chest as she encircled Ben's waist with her arms. The powerful engine whined like a jet plane at takeoff. Within a few minutes, he slowed until they came to a complete stop, and he shut off the motor.

Ben pried Tori's fingers from his waist, got off the machine, and looked down at his passenger.

"That was fun, wasn't it?"

Tori nodded faintly. His hand snaked out toward her head. She flinched and blinked in surprise when he snapped the helmet's visor down in front of her face.

"Next time, you should keep that down," he said before pivoting and strolling away from her. Feeling foolish for not having noticed the visor, she scrambled off the snowmobile to follow him to her car, yanking off the offending helmet along the way. Riley came skidding to a stop beside her, his tongue dangling, and his great chest heaving.

Ben stood with his hands on his hips and stared at the front of the crumpled vehicle. He shook his head.

"Well, you earned that bump on your head. You got yourself in good and deep. It's going to take a tow truck to pull it out of here."

Tori's mind jumped ahead to everything she had to do to become mobile again and back to civilisation.

Ben opened the driver-side door, and his body stiffened as he peered inside the car. Curious about the cause of his glower, Tori took a step toward him. Ben swung around, blocking her view.

"What is it? What's the matter?" Distress rang in her voice.

Ben fixed her with a hard look and said, "Tori, someone left you a message. I'm not going to hide it from you, but I want you to be prepared."

Tori stared into his eyes and nodded, bracing herself for what was to come. Ben moved aside. She felt his scrutiny as she looked through the open driver-side door. A spasm of shock passed through her, and she fought to clear her face of all expression.

Tori sensed Ben's presence close behind her as she witnessed the damage that had been wrought upon her car. The seats of the small sedan were cut to shreds, her clothing was ripped and strewn around the car, and the dashboard was smashed. Her gaze was drawn to the object that lay on the front seat. It was her beige duffel bag, and someone had used a black marker to scrawl a short message across the side – YOU WILL DIE.

Tori tried to appear devoid of emotion. She grabbed her bag and stuffed the ruined clothing inside. Her efforts were stopped when a large hand gripped her arm. Ben spoke brusquely, clearly hoping to break through the wall she'd erected.

"Leave it, Tori. There isn't anything worth keeping. Besides, we have to leave everything the way it is for the police."

She dropped her bag on the seat and turned wide eyes on him.

"No. There will be no police."

Anger and fear battled for control of Tori's emotions. Her voice trembled, and tears burned her eyes. She blinked them back, and knew the best way to forestall them was to push those emotions aside. It was another blow to her spirit, but she wouldn't allow it to drag her down.

Ben sucked in a quick breath and stared at her.

"How can you say that? You've been threatened. These guys are serious. You have to talk to the police."

Tori didn't respond. She grabbed her bag, leaving most of her clothing lying where it was, in shreds. She stalked away from the car, but swung around when Ben grasped her arm again. He didn't attempt to hide his anger.

"I didn't say very much about those marks on your neck, and I didn't say a word about those two goons showing up at my front door, but I'm not as stupid as you think I am. You're in trouble, and if I wasn't convinced before, I'm very convinced now. This is no time for fooling around. You need help, and that means calling the police."

She was taken aback by his tone, but she soon recovered.

"I appreciate your concern, but I can take care of myself, thank you very much," she said stiffly.

"Yeah, I can see that."

His glaring sarcasm made her angrier and more stubborn. She spun on her heel and marched down the road in the direction from which she'd arrived the previous day, knowing she'd ultimately reach civilisation.

"Hey. Get back here."

Tori didn't stop. She knew she owed Ben her life and she should express a proper goodbye to him, but she was hurt, scared, and angry. She had to get away to sort out her thoughts and decide where she'd go from here.

Seeing the desecration of her car and the threatening note had hit her hard, even as she went to great pains to hide her reactions. Strangely, the overriding emotion was hurt, with confusion running a close second. She couldn't fathom why she'd be threatened with death. Tori's intentions were, and always would be, noble.

Behind her, the silence was deafening. Relief and disappointment fought for a higher ranking in her emotions.

"Okay, you win," he said, his voice monotone, "no police. But, you're coming back to the cabin with me until we figure out what to do."

Tori slowed. She couldn't decide whether to ignore him and forge ahead on her own, or accept his help. She'd have to reclaim her independence at some point, but she was still shaken by the sight of her car, and baffled by the turn of events. The prospect of leaning on Ben's strength and kindness, at least for the time being, appealed to her. She walked toward him, her eyes trained thoughtfully on the imprint of her footprints in the snow. When she saw the tips of his winter boots in front of her, she stopped and raised her head to peer at him.

"All right. I'll go back with you now, but tomorrow I'm going to have to go to my motel."

He eyed her intensely for a moment but remained silent.

Together, they walked to the snowmobile. With her helmet firmly settled on her head and the visor in place, Ben drove back to the cabin. He travelled at a more leisurely pace than the last time. Whether it was because he mulled over what had just transpired, or because Tori had only one arm available with which to hang on – the other one clutching her duffel bag – she was thankful for the respite from the hair-raising speed of their previous ride.

CHAPTER 7

Tori was deep in thought, contemplating what had happened over the course of the past week, and how she should move onward. She knew she was in a lot of trouble, more than she had ever thought possible. She was at a point where she needed to decide if she should go back home without having accomplished what she had set out to do, or if she should keep on with her original plans. She sat in front of the wood stove, gazing at the burning logs without seeing them or appreciating their warmth.

She thought about her mother, sick and alone in Florida. She thought about Danny, who was desperately in need of her help, even though he refused to admit it. She thought about the terrible misunderstanding between them that had led to those two thugs trying to kill her. It was such a comedy of errors she would've laughed if the terror she'd felt when she was at their mercy didn't still lurk in the forefront of her mind.

In her twenty-nine years, she'd never experienced violence of any kind, and like most people, had believed it could only happen to someone else. She'd naively thrown herself into an unfamiliar world, and she now had the choice of forging onward or backing away. Fear prompted her to back away, but loyalty compelled her to endeavor, once again, to talk to Danny. Her fierce devotion and natural optimism won out, and she decided there'd be no turning back, not until she had at least one more chance.

Having made that decision, she glanced over at Ben, who moved restlessly around the cabin. His brows were lowered, and his expression didn't invite conversation. He'd remained silent since they'd returned from the site of the damaged car.

"I'll be back," Ben said, pulling on his coat.

Tori's eyes widened when he went into the bedroom and reappeared with a rifle under his arm.

"Where are you going?" she said, alarmed.

"Hunting. Keep the doors locked. C'mon, Riley."

Man and dog left, and Tori slid the lock closed behind them.

"I feel sorry for any animal that crosses his path today," she said.

She paced the floor until they returned shortly before five o'clock. The darkness had crept into the room, and Tori had worried about what she'd do if he didn't come back. She hated to admit she was so dependent on this stranger.

Despite his rough appearance and his unconventional way of life, Tori knew Ben to be dependable and trustworthy, and he was the type of person she desperately needed at this time. But, during her hours alone, she'd concluded she must stick to her plan, complete her mission, and do so with the least amount of involvement from anyone else, Ben included.

After a quiet meal of steak and eggs – Tori couldn't eat the poor little rabbit – she broached the subject of her plans for the following day.

"I need to get back to my motel. If you could show me the shortcut you took today, I'll be able to walk to the nearest town, have my car towed, and get back into the city."

"I'll drive you to your motel."

His voice was matter-of-fact and devoid of emotion.

"That won't be necessary. I've imposed on you enough as it is. From here on in, I can take care of myself."

"It's no problem. I have to go into the city anyway."

Tori didn't understand why this surprised her. He had every right to go into the city. He might do it regularly, but she found it difficult to picture him lumbering along the streets. With his hairy, unkempt appearance he could be mistaken for a homeless person. Where was his home when he wasn't here? And how did he earn a living? These were questions she wanted to ask, but it was a territory into which she couldn't venture.

"Maybe if you could get me to the nearest telephone, I could call a taxi," she offered, not wanting to involve him in any more of her problems.

"I'll take you to your motel, Tori."

His voice was firm, warning her not to disagree with him again.

Tori sighed and acquiesced. After all, it wouldn't do any harm for him to drop her off. She didn't want to start an argument, not after everything he'd done for her. But, she was curious about one thing.

"Um…we won't be going by snowmobile, will we?"

The question evoked a small smile from the usually serious man.

"No. Believe it or not, snowmobiles aren't licensed for the streets."

"We were on a street today."

"Most people would call it a country road, not a street, and it's one that's rarely used. Driving on it may not have been legal, but the possibility of having a police car in the area was unlikely."

"So, how will we travel tomorrow?"

"We'll go as far as a friend's house by snowmobile. I have a truck parked there."

"Is it far?"

"Far enough, but you'll make it. Don't worry."

"I'm not worried," she said.

The next day, she recalled her foolish words. Again, he jammed the helmet on her head, fastened it, and nudged her toward the snowmobile. Again, she climbed onto the back of the machine and thought with dread of the journey ahead of them.

She was dressed like the abominable snowman, wearing even more layers of clothing than the day before, since the trip would be longer. A smile tugged at Ben's lips when she emerged from the bedroom resembling the Pillsbury dough boy and moving with much less agility. He wisely kept his comments to himself, hurrying her out the door before she collapsed under the weight and heat of her clothing.

Riley trembled with anticipation, having understood they were about to have another adventure.

They took the same trail as they had the previous morning, but branched off onto another, leading them in the general direction of the city. Ben travelled at a reasonable speed, and Tori relaxed when she realised she didn't need to keep a death grip on his waist.

Most of the time, they were on a large flat trail reserved for snowmobiles. On one occasion, they crossed an ice-covered body of water. Tori held her breath, her body stiff with bad memories, despite Ben's reassurances that it was hard-packed, and there was no danger.

After an hour of driving, with a few rest stops for Riley's benefit, Tori saw they approached a more highly-populated area. She caught glimpses of houses and farms, and she was hopeful they'd almost reached their destination.

Ten minutes later, Ben pulled the snowmobile to a stop outside a two-storey, white clapboard house with dark green trim and an attached one-car garage. Obviously built in the 50s, it seemed well-maintained, and it was surrounded by large maple trees, their branches bare. Tori could imagine how beautiful they'd be in the summertime. The area was rural, and a few neighboring farms were visible in the distance.

She turned to Ben inquiringly. "Where are we?"

"At my friend's house."

"I mean, what's the name of the town?"

"It's a small town, Saint-Gabriel-de-Valcartier."

It sounded like a mouthful to her.

"Okay, and how far from the city are we?"

Ben shrugged his large shoulders. "About half an hour."

He threw a tarp over the snowmobile and secured it in place. She followed behind as he strode over to the garage and entered a security code into a panel. The garage door rumbled open to reveal a shiny black pickup truck parked inside.

"Your friend is home?"

"No, the truck's mine. I leave it here while I'm up at the cabin."

"He must be a good friend to give you full use of his house and property like this."

"Yeah."

"Where is he?" she asked.

"Who?"

Tori gritted her teeth, mustering as much patience as possible.

"Your friend."

"He's not here," he said, frustratingly stating the obvious.

Tori sighed, putting any other questions aside.

By now, they were inside the house, and she scanned her surroundings approvingly as Riley bounded past her, scampering about the tidy, modern kitchen. Ben filled a large bowl with water and, while Riley quenched his thirst, a bag of dog food was retrieved from a cupboard.

While her companion prepared a pot of coffee, Tori covertly tried to get a better look at the ground floor of the house. Since Ben didn't welcome her curious questions, she needed to discover as much as she could on her own.

The living room was also tidy, and though she wouldn't go so far as to describe it as stark, it didn't have a lot of extras, leading her to believe the house was inhabited by a bachelor. When she asked if she could use the washroom, her theory was confirmed. The room was relatively large and clean but devoid of any signs of a feminine presence.

Returning to the kitchen, she glimpsed a small pile of unopened mail sitting on the counter and saw several envelopes addressed to 'Jean-François Lafond'.

"Is that the name of your friend? Jean-François?" Tori stumbled over the name, not sure how to pronounce it. The smile on Ben's face told her she'd mangled it badly.

"Jean-François," he said, with his perfect French accent. "Yes, it is. Here's your coffee."

She would've liked to learn more about this friend and why Ben was so comfortable here in someone else's house, but she knew where any questioning on her part would lead.

Instead, they enjoyed a hot cup of coffee together, and she listened as he made a couple of phone calls to plan for the towing and repair of her car. He gave her the information for the garage on a piece of notepaper, which she considered dubiously. She had no idea how she'd communicate with these people, or how she'd find the money to repair her car, but that was a concern to be put aside for now.

"You should take off some layers," Ben said.

Tori wrapped her arms around her waist.

"I still haven't warmed up."

"You won't need it in the pickup, and if you get too warm in here, you'll feel the cold even more when you step outside."

He removed his leather snowmobile suit and replaced it with a sheepskin coat as Tori stripped off most of her layers and folded them tidily on the couch.

They climbed into the truck, leaving a disappointed but tired Riley behind. As Ben drove along the winding road, Tori took the opportunity to study the scenery surrounding them. The countryside in winter was beautiful, she thought, particularly when seen from the inside of a warm vehicle.

Reaching the end of the road, they turned left at a flashing red light and drove through a small village.

"This seems like a nice place to live," Tori said.

"Yeah, it's close to the city, but you're still able to enjoy the country life."

"Have you ever considered living here?"

"At times."

"Do you live far from here?"

"No."

"Would you care to elaborate?" she said.

"No. Would you?" he said, his brows raised.

Tori pressed her lips together and willed herself to be silent. Before she knew it, they were on a highway, speeding toward the city, which was visible in the distance.

"What's the name of your motel?" Ben said.

"The Flamingo Rose."

Ben glowered at her with raised eyebrows. "The Pink Flamingo?"

"No, The Flamingo Rose."

"That's what I said. 'Rose' is 'Pink' in French. And what kind of a place is that to stay in?"

His voice was harsh.

"The cheapest one I could find, that's what it is," she said. "Do you know it?"

"I know *of* it. Cheap is definitely the best way to describe it."

She knew he didn't refer to the cost of the rooms. Tori's cheeks warmed, and she straightened her shoulders.

"Well, that's my problem. I'll take care of it."

"How?"

"My own way."

She could be evasive too. He'd discover he didn't own exclusive rights to that quality, she thought.

They lapsed into silence for the rest of the drive and soon pulled into the parking lot of the motel. It had been two days since Tori had last been here and, she admitted to herself, it was a depressing sight. The garish neon flamingo had seen better days, and the row of motel rooms were nothing short of decrepit. She knew from first-hand experience the interiors of the rooms were even worse.

"Which one is yours?" Ben said gruffly.

"Number eight."

Thankfully, the key to the room had been zipped into her coat pocket and had survived the trek through the woods and the unforeseen dunk in the lake.

Before she could protest, Ben got out of the truck and strode toward the door of her room. She had no choice but to follow. As he watched, she unlocked the door and pushed it open. The inside of the room was as she had left it. It was still ugly and smelly, but at least it hadn't been destroyed, and there were no death threats written on the walls.

A small smile of satisfaction played over her face, but it disappeared when she saw Ben's reaction. His eyebrows were lowered over narrowed eyes, reminding her of the first time she'd seen him.

She knew, despite his appearance, he was a kind, helpful, gentle man. She was struck by a deep sadness as she realized she'd never see him again. She felt as if she was saying goodbye to a friend she'd known for years.

"Ben, I want to th..."

"Don't mention it, Tori."

"But, I have to. You saved my li..."

"I haven't saved anything."

His face was turned from her, and his voice was deep and low. Tori thought she detected a trace of emotion in it. Deciding to cut it short for both of their sakes, she stood on her tiptoes and planted a kiss on the tiny portion of his cheek that wasn't covered by his beard.

Ben swiveled away and left the room, mumbling a quiet 'Goodbye, Tori' as he strode out the door.

Chapter 8

The first thing Tori did was indulge in what she'd missed the most at the cabin, a long, hot shower. To stand under a steaming spray was a luxury she'd never expected to relish to such an extent.

Dressed in dry, warm clothing, she sat on the edge of the bed and studied her surroundings. She chuckled wryly when she realized the cabin appeared lavish compared to this dreary motel room. She was struck with a new determination to finish what she'd come here to do. She wanted to go back to her home and the life that had been put on hold.

During the long snowmobile ride to Ben's friend's house, through the constant bumping and jostling, she'd reflected upon her predicament. Despite everything that had happened, she'd come too far to turn back. She'd find Danny and make him realize what she wanted from him.

Tori blamed herself for the results of their previous meeting. She'd been wrong to threaten him, no matter how empty her threats had been. She should've known he'd misunderstand. He'd always been paranoid, but she'd been desperate to get through to him, and her desperation had led to stupidity. And that stupidity had led to the second misunderstanding when the two goons had mistakenly assumed Danny wanted them to kill her. If she hadn't delivered a well-placed kick to the crotch of her attacker, she wouldn't have escaped.

Tori spent a long, solitary evening in the motel room after picking up a tasteless submarine sandwich at a nearby convenience store. Her thoughts drifted to the cabin and Ben. She wondered if he'd gone back to his isolated home after doing his errands, or if he'd gone to his other home, the one he wanted to remain a secret. Perhaps, he visited a woman while in the city.

Maybe he was unwilling to talk about her. Was she married? Was he caught up in an illicit affair?

Tori smiled at the direction her thoughts had taken. She was creating an imaginary life around Ben that, for some reason, didn't seem to fit. Perhaps it was because she envied his simple life, free of stress, and not having to worry about anything more important than whether he'd fish for his supper or hunt for a stray rabbit. Did she need to wrap him up in intrigue simply because her own life teetered on the edge of danger?

Tori wished she'd learned more about him. She was curious about his odd situation. He lived in what she considered the most basic of comforts, yet he owned a recent-model snowmobile and pickup truck. He had to have some sort of income to afford such luxuries. Did he have a job? Had he inherited money to let him live his life in whatever way he pleased?

Ben had the qualities of a loner, used to being on his own, yet he had friends or at least one close friend by the name of Jean-François Lafond. His appearance was rough, dishevelled, hermit-like, yet she knew him to be kind, and capable of dealing with a distressed female.

He was worldly enough to recognize those horrible men for what they were and to choose to protect her from them. Yes, he was an oddity, and maybe that was the source of her sense of affinity with him. She had never felt more like an oddity in her life as she had since she became Alice and fell into this wintry Wonderland. She was still contemplating the puzzle that was Ben when she drifted to sleep in her lumpy, lonely bed.

The next morning, she was pleased to find she still possessed the same determination to get to Danny, her courage unfaltering. It was a sunny day, although certainly just as frigid, and she wouldn't see it wasted.

Grimacing, she remembered she'd have to contact that distasteful little man by the name of Yvon who'd led her to Danny the last time. She knew, after all that had happened, Danny would've relocated and disappeared, once again, into the woodwork. As loathsome as the task would be, the slimy dope pusher was the best and quickest means of finding out where Danny was holed up. She'd pretend interest and avoid his lascivious advances by promising him an encounter at some future date – a promise she had no intention of keeping.

Fortunately, just a few of her possessions had been in the abused duffel bag, so she changed her clothes and ran a brush through her hair before calling a taxi. She struggled to tell the driver she needed to go to 'De la Couronne Street', but he seemed to understand. He made his way to the area of Quebec City that was known to the locals as 'Lower Town'. Tori had heard it was a section of the city that, historically, was known for being rundown, housing bars and establishments with a bad reputation. Many of them were covers for drug operations or prostitution.

The city had taken control and changed the image of the sector. Businesses had built modern office buildings in the area, and new housing projects were constructed. The graffiti was covered up with beautiful and original murals on the buildings and on the concrete pillars supporting the overpasses that gave access to 'Upper Town'. Although a shady area still existed, it was much smaller and less visible.

The driver dropped her off at her destination and, as she stood on the cold sidewalk, she took a deep, strengthening breath. She wanted to get this over with as soon as possible. She headed into the bar where she'd found Yvon the last time. Entering the dimly-lit establishment, she paused in the doorway to let her eyes adjust to the light, or lack of it. There weren't many people in the room; a couple of men leaning on the bar, and another man and woman sitting at one of the booths. They all looked as if they'd never seen the light of day, with their pale skin, bloodshot eyes, and the lethargy common among people who spend their days with no useful purpose in life.

Tori approached the bartender, a different one from the previous time, ignoring the interested stares of the other occupants of the bar. The large man working behind the counter stopped wiping beer glasses, plainly curious about this strange woman who looked so out of place. He didn't return her smile.

"Uh, hi. I was wondering if you could help me."

Tori spoke slowly, thinking he'd have trouble understanding her English. When all she received in reply was a blank stare, she rephrased the question.

"Could you help me please?"

"You from where?" His accent was heavy, and she knew she was in for a linguistic struggle.

"Florida."

His face brightened. A foreigner was more interesting than a local Anglo who wouldn't speak French.

"What you want?"

"I'm looking for Yvon."

The man's eyes narrowed. "Why?"

Tori shrugged noncommittally. "I need to see him."

She wanted to give the impression of a woman in need of drugs, but she wasn't sure she pulled it off.

"He's in the back."

He nodded his head in the direction of the door to the right of the bar, the same one as last time. Obviously, Yvon had permanent lodgings in the establishment. Trying to be positive, Tori told herself she was fortunate to have found Yvon in the first place. Arriving in Quebec, she hadn't known where to start her search. She'd never been in need of a drug dealer before, in any country. The fact that she'd hit the jackpot on her first attempt had to be worth something.

Bracing herself for the encounter, she knocked on the door hesitantly, part of her hoping he wasn't there. When she didn't receive a response, she peered over her shoulder at the bartender. He indicated with a nod of his head and a wave of his hand that she should open the door and enter the room.

Again, Tori found herself inside the relatively spacious but dreary office. Yvon reclined in his chair with his feet on the desk, talking in French on a cell phone. Spotting her, he stopped speaking long enough to give her a yellow-toothed smile and to lower his feet to the floor. He ended his conversation and stood up to circle the desk. She stiffened but didn't back away.

"Ah, *chérie*, I hoped you would come back to see me. I was beginning to think you might not keep your promise, but I should never have doubted you."

Yvon's English was quite good, with a slight trace of a French accent.

"I don't have much time now. I came to ask another favor of you."

Tori spoke in the most pleasant voice she could muster, hiding her distaste at the sight of him. If the man made an effort to clean up his act he might be considered attractive by some women, but his hair was long and greasy, streaked with premature grey. He was tall but overly thin, with sallow cheeks and bloodshot eyes. He needed to put some meat on his bones and inject a dose of health into his body.

Presently, those glassy eyes stared at her in surprise.

"Another favor, Tori?"

She forged on, despite the look on his face.

"Yes. I need to talk to Danny again."

He laughed. He howled until he had to sit on the edge of the desk for balance.

"Are you crazy? I heard what happened, and I'm lucky Danny never found out it was me who sent you to him. I'm not going to make the same mistake again."

His laughter was her undoing. She had to get the information she needed, and she couldn't keep the desperation from her voice, forgetting her resolution to be cool and reasonable.

"He won't know, Yvon. I won't tell him. It'll be different. He'll be happy to see me. I know he will. You see, the last time was a big misunderstanding. I made a mistake, but we're going to work everything out now."

He laughed again, with a harsher edge.

"Work everything out? Danny doesn't work things out, he just eliminates them, and that's what he'll do with you. As much as I'd like to help you, *chérie*, I don't plan on being eliminated along with you."

"Yvon, please," she said, hating to hear the pleading tone of her voice.

His expression turned serious, and he took another step toward her, his hand coming up to stroke her cheek.

"Tori, you still haven't kept that date you promised me last week. I've been waiting for you, and now you say you have no time, but you expect another favor. Tsk, tsk."

She gave him what she hoped was her most charming smile.

"It's true, I don't have time now. I have to be getting back, but I swear I'll come to see you next week and we'll have that date."

She wondered if he noticed her skin crawled at his touch.

"Why don't you tell me where you're staying, and I'll meet you there?"

"I'm leaving there tonight, and I don't know where I'll be staying."

She was impressed with her new proficiency at lying.

He stared at her until she felt even more uncomfortable. A smile played across his lips.

"Ah, my sweet, I've always been so easily influenced by a pretty face. It's something that will be my downfall. Now I will again put myself on the line, and I'll find out for you, but you better not forget what you owe me."

Tori breathed a sigh of relief.

"I won't. Don't worry. Where is he, and how do I get there?"

"Hold on. You weren't listening. I said I'd find out for you. I don't know where he is."

"You don't?" she said, her shoulders slumping.

"No, I haven't had word from him yet, but I should be able to let you know in a couple of days."

"A couple of days? I need to know sooner than that."

He brought his hand up to her cheek once more.

"Patience, *ma chérie*. You see, I have to be patient waiting for you. Now, you have to be patient to get what you want from me."

Any further arguments would fall on deaf ears, Tori realized. She'd have to give in and wait to get news from Yvon.

"All right, I'll be back here in two days at the same time. Are you sure you'll be able to tell me then?"

"I will try, *ma belle*. I will try."

Tori left the bar feeling frustrated. She hated the idea of being delayed by two more days. She'd expected to be well on her way back to Florida by now, but ever since she'd arrived in this Godforsaken place everything had gone wrong.

She roamed the streets, hardly noticing the people hurrying along the sidewalks or shivering in the doorways. After a few blocks, she stopped to get her bearings. She was across from an area lined with stores and shops, nudged in between a Holiday Inn and an office building. She searched for a place to collect her thoughts.

Tori found a coffee shop and ordered a large cappuccino, hoping it'd take the chill from her bones. After paying the cashier, she spotted a solitary table for two left unoccupied in the corner of the crowded shop. She wasn't the only person seeking some warmth from a cup of coffee.

When she was seated, she took off her meagre pair of leather gloves and wrapped her bare hands around the hot cup, watching the steam rise from the dark liquid. She stared at it as if hypnotised, thinking about her conversation with Yvon, and pondering what she'd do to pass the time in this strange, cold city for the next two days.

The coffee shop buzzed with dozens of voices chattering in a language she couldn't grasp. She tuned it all out. Because of this, and the fact that her face was turned downward, she didn't see the man who stood beside her table, nor did she hear his voice. When he bent to place his face in her line of vision, she was startled and almost spilled her coffee. He smiled at her apologetically and nodded toward the empty seat facing her.

"*Désolé, mademoiselle. Est-ce que je peux m'asseoir ici?*"

Tori may not have understood the words, but she discerned from his gestures that he wanted to share her table. She didn't feel like company but, glancing around the shop, she saw he had nowhere else to sit. She nodded her agreement and hoped he didn't expect conversation along with the chair. Thinking he'd take the hint, she grasped her cup with both hands and turned her attention to the scenery outside the window. She was rewarded when she saw from the corner of her eye he'd settled down with his coffee and a newspaper.

Tori glanced at the front of the paper and realized it was the same one she'd seen on other occasions in coffee shops and restaurants throughout the city. *Le Journal de Québec* evidently had a large readership. She noted almost half the patrons pored over a copy.

As her gaze returned to the man in front of her, she saw he also observed her. He smiled genially.

Fearing he'd strike up a conversation she wouldn't be able to sustain, Tori swiveled her head and pointedly stared out the window. She wasn't a shy person, although she'd never been described as gregarious, but today she had too many troubled thoughts running through her head. The idea of struggling to communicate with a stranger added to her stress.

Tori noticed the man had returned to his perusal of the newspaper, and she took the opportunity to study him.

Tori guessed he was in his mid-thirties, a few inches over six-feet tall, with what appeared to be a muscular build, even though it was hidden under his overcoat. He was clean-shaven, with dark brown hair and eyes of the same color. He wore rimless glasses and, at the moment, a serious expression, giving him the air of an intellectual. His dark suit made her think he was a businessman, perhaps someone in banking.

He was quite good-looking, with a nice square jaw and clean-cut features. There was something about him that was vaguely familiar, something she couldn't quite put her finger on, until she realized he had a Clark Kent look about him, apart from the color of his eyes. She wondered wryly if he was Superman coming to save her from the big bad men.

Still smiling at her whimsical wish, she peeked at the newspaper open in front of him and froze. It didn't matter that the large black and white picture was upside down. She'd recognize that face anywhere, from any angle. It also didn't matter that she couldn't understand the headline accompanying the picture. She knew it wouldn't be good news.

"Qu'est-ce qu'il y a? Est-ce que je peux vous aider?"

The voice jolted Tori out of her daze. Unintentionally, she had leaned ahead to get a closer look at the picture, and she felt certain the blood had probably drained from her face. The man's expression of concern and his outstretched hand was the confirmation she needed. She straightened and shook her head wordlessly at him, hoping it was the appropriate answer to his question. His brows lowered in a puzzled frown.

"Do you speak French?"

His English was heavily accented, but she understood him. Tori didn't want to have a discussion with this man. She needed to get her thoughts and emotions under control. But, she had to give some sort of response.

"No, I don't," she said, forcing a smile. She clutched her coffee cup again and gazed around the coffee shop, hoping to relay the message that she didn't want to be disturbed. 'Clark' either didn't take the hint, or he was determined to ignore it. He closed the paper, pushed it aside, and leaned his elbows on the table.

"Are you not feeling well?" he said, his tone soothing.

"I'm fine," she said.

Tori resolved to push the subject of the picture from her mind. The newspaper article wouldn't reveal Danny's present location to her, and the fact he was featured in the tabloid shouldn't surprise her. Danny had always managed to attract attention to himself, no matter where he was, or whether the attention was positive or negative.

"Where are you from?"

Tori heaved an inward sigh and realized the only way to put an end to this stranger's questions was to leave the coffee shop. She swallowed the last of her coffee and zipped up her jacket. As a concession to the fact that he struck her as a nice guy, she chose to generously answer one question.

"Florida."

"*Eh, tu n'es pas sérieuse.* Did you take a wrong turn somewhere?"

She grimaced.

"Yes, I think I did."

"I'm joking. Lots of tourists come to Québec to enjoy the beauty of the city. You must be looking forward to the carnival."

Tori gaped at him with raised eyebrows. Was this guy pulling her leg? The beauty of the city? What carnival? Most of what she'd seen so far was violence, a filthy barroom, and a sleazy motel. With the exception of her stay in the rustic peace of the cabin in the woods, there wasn't much about Quebec City for her to recommend to her friends. In light of this man's enthusiasm, she decided it'd be more polite not to let him know her true opinion on the subject.

Too late, he'd correctly interpreted her expression, and in true Gallic fashion, waved his arms to emphasize his next words.

"What? Have you not seen the city yet? How long have you been here? You must have just arrived. Where are you staying?"

Since he didn't give her a chance to answer his first questions, Tori hoped she wouldn't have to answer the last one, but he continued to look expectantly at her. She had no intention of revealing the whereabouts of her motel. She shrugged and smiled dimly. Undaunted by her lack of communication, the man held out his hand, and Tori had no choice but to offer hers in return.

"My name is Mario Leclerc, and I'd like to welcome you to Québec."

He grinned disarmingly at her and, against her will, her smile blossomed. She retrieved her hand from his warm grasp and answered genially, "I'm Tori Anderson."

"Ah, Tori, that's a nice name. Are you staying with friends, or relatives, perhaps?"

"No, I'm here on my own."

He frowned, and she wondered if she'd given him too much information. Maybe she shouldn't be so forthcoming with this man, but despite the fact she knew nothing about him, he didn't appear threatening to her.

Shifting in his seat, she had the impression he considered whether he should speak or not. He smiled shyly at her.

"Tori, I know we don't know each other, but I wondered if I could have the pleasure of showing you the city of Québec. It's much better to see it with the help of someone who knows it, and there's nothing I love more than to be a tour guide."

Tori hesitated, not out of fear, but out of guilt. She hadn't come here to play tourist. She hadn't come here to have a good time. She'd come here for a purpose, and she wouldn't go home until she'd achieved her goal.

However, her plans were stalled for two full days, and she didn't look forward to sitting inside that dreary motel room for the duration of that time.

Her decision made, she smiled brightly at Mario.

"Why not?"

CHAPTER 9

Tori paced her motel room, alternating between flipping channels on the television and staring out the window. The image of the photo in the newspaper haunted her. It had been a shock to see Danny smiling arrogantly from the pages of the daily paper. She didn't know where or when the picture had been taken, but he'd seemed quite relaxed. He hadn't been in handcuffs or sandwiched between armed guards. Perhaps that was good news.

Tori's thoughts strayed from one dismal subject to another. She reflected on her mother at home in Florida and wondered how she was. Tori had never revealed the real reason for her trip to Canada. She used the same excuse she'd given Ben; she wanted to have a winter experience, and Quebec had been recommended as the perfect place to do so.

She'd called her mother once since leaving home, before her cell phone had been destroyed. She'd been given the classic response when Tori had inquired about her parent's health. She was fine, and there was nothing to be concerned about. Tori was instructed to enjoy her vacation and return rested.

They both knew Clarissa Anderson was lying. She wasn't fine and hadn't been for a long while. Her heart condition had become progressively worse, and it took more effort to do the small things everyone else took for granted.

Tori spent more and more time helping her mother with her daily needs. Clarissa had relinquished her driver's license a year ago, so Tori took care of picking up groceries and other necessities. She prepared meals for her mother ahead of time, so they could be reheated in the microwave. She made arrangements for a woman to come in a few times a week to take care of the laundry and the general household work.

Before leaving, Tori had set up a schedule with a neighbor who would take over those tasks. Knowing her mother was well cared for while she was gone lifted a considerable burden from Tori's shoulders.

The doctors hadn't given Tori any hope for Clarissa's recovery, stating it was just a matter of time. Most days, she refused to believe her strong-willed, determined mother would give truth to their predictions.

With an effort, Tori shook off her moroseness and went to take a shower and get dressed for the evening.

After having agreed to meet Mario at a restaurant for dinner, she'd taken a taxi back to her motel while he went back to work. She'd discovered during their conversation in the coffee shop that he was a mid-level executive for a high-tech corporation and not a superhero in disguise.

Tori looked forward to her unexpected date with a stranger. Although she doubted she'd be enthralled with Quebec City, she was confident Mario's company would be a much-needed distraction.

He'd told her to meet him at the D'Orsay restaurant. He also informed her she should dress casually and warmly because they'd tour the area on foot after eating. Dressing casually wasn't a problem, but Tori didn't have proper footwear for cold weather conditions. She settled for a pair of unlined low-heeled boots. The rest of her attire consisted of black jeans, a periwinkle blue turtleneck sweater, and her short jacket. As she thrust her hands into her thin leather gloves, she vowed she'd find a discount store and spend a few dollars on a scarf and a pair of woolen mittens.

Seated in the back of the taxi, she let her mind drift to her ultimate mission of getting to Danny. Her first attempt had been disastrous, the memory of those cruel hands fastened around her throat sending a shiver up her spine. Of course, she'd been misunderstood. Danny would never have ordered anyone to kill her. He'd taken her foolish threats seriously and, in a panic, had said something that was misinterpreted by one of his goons.

She was lucky to have escaped, her self-defense lessons remembered at the last possible moment, and she had ultimately ended up at Ben's cabin. She'd been fortunate in her misfortune. She couldn't have asked for a better protector. Even with his unpolished appearance, after her initial fear, Tori had believed herself to be in good hands. Stepping away from those trustworthy hands had been difficult, but necessary. She wouldn't want to be responsible for harm coming to anyone else, especially Ben.

The next time she saw Danny she'd make him understand she hadn't meant her words. She wanted him to know she'd never hand him over to the authorities, and he had nothing to fear from her.

Tori's attention was pulled back to the here and now as the taxi turned and climbed a large curving hill. The landscape changed, with modern hotels and conference centers on each side of the street. At the top of the hill, they drove onto a cobblestone street that curved around a beautiful circular fountain. Her head swung to her right to see a majestic, old building, sitting behind an expanse of snow-covered lawn. She must have gasped because the driver glanced over his shoulder and answered her unspoken question in halting English.

"That is *la Colline parlementaire*, the Parliament buildings."

"Oh..."

To her left was a large structure that appeared to be made of snow. The driver chuckled as he anticipated her question.

"*Le Palais de Glace*. Uh... the Ice Palace... for the Carnival."

Mario had mentioned a carnival, she thought, taking a mental note to ask him about it. She gazed in awe from one side to the other as the taxi turned to the left and drove under a stone archway. The driver continued along a narrow street lined with old stone buildings that housed modern boutiques and restaurants. In another life, hundreds of years ago, they could have been home to some of the first settlers in North America.

The streets were crowded with people, bundled up against the cold, as they strolled along the picturesque lanes.

Tori was captivated. The streets were beautiful; tastefully decorated without being garish or gaudy; retaining the splendor of the old buildings while offering the modern attractions of shopping, restaurants, and pubs. She looked forward to seeing Mario and having the opportunity to explore this unexpected delight.

Despite the heavy traffic, they arrived at the restaurant within minutes, and Tori entered the establishment to find Mario waiting for her at a table along the outside wall. She slid onto the upholstered bench across from him and was thrilled to see the long wood-framed windows running the length of the wall from the seat of the bench to the ceiling, allowing an unhampered view of the city streets and the tourists. Staring around her, Tori was impressed by the rich mahogany furnishings and the warm, cozy atmosphere.

Her cheeks reddened when she shifted her attention back to her companion. She'd barely acknowledged his presence. He chuckled when he saw her expression, guessing her thoughts.

"That's okay. I don't blame you for ignoring me. It's a beautiful night."

"I'm sorry. I never expected this. I haven't been to this part of the city yet."

"This is the part everyone must see."

"I regret waiting so long," Tori said truthfully.

The waitress approached and took their drink orders, speaking in perfect English. When she strode away, Tori looked at Mario with raised brows.

"This area is full of tourists," he said, understanding her surprise. "Most of the people working here have to be bilingual, or at least able to get by in English."

"I can't wait to see more of the city."

"In that case, we'll order our food as soon as possible, so I can show you as much as I can tonight."

The next hour and a half was pleasantly spent, eating delicious food and drinking excellent wine. Mario proved to be an engaging dinner companion, patiently answering Tori's ceaseless questions about his native city and the Quebec Winter Carnival, an event that had existed for over fifty years. They shared a laugh when he reminded her of her earlier skepticism about the beauty of the city.

"But why did you come here if you didn't expect to find beauty and enjoy the activities? Surely, you didn't drive so far all alone in the middle of winter to visit a place you didn't think was worth seeing?"

Tori diverted her gaze to the crowds of people out on the sidewalk and shrugged nonchalantly.

"I had some free time, and a friend had recommended it to me, so I came."

"Free time from what? What do you do for a living?"

"I work as a clerk for an insurance company. Nothing very exciting, I'm afraid."

"So, for excitement, you get in your car and drive a few thousand miles to visit strange places by yourself?" he said, smiling.

He didn't seem to expect a response, so Tori didn't offer one. Instead, she took the last sip of her wine.

"Where is your car? Did you leave it at the motel? You arrived by taxi."

"My car is out of commission. I had an accident, and it's being repaired."

"An accident? You weren't hurt in any way?" he said with concern.

"No, just this," she said, lifting her bangs to show him the remnants of the bump on her head. It had diminished to a large yellow bruise.

"When will your car be ready?"

"I don't know. They haven't called to give me an estimate of the repairs yet."

Tori didn't add that she couldn't afford the repairs even if they did call. She'd have to find an alternate means of transportation back to Florida. As she considered the direness of her predicament, her good mood slipped away. Mario, with his infallible timing, pulled her back.

"It's time, my friend, to explore. There's much to see and do before the end of the evening."

Explore, they did. Mario guided her along many of the streets of the old city of Quebec. She was enchanted by the loveliness of the buildings and the cobblestone streets. When they approached the famous Château Frontenac, majestically overlooking the St. Lawrence River, Tori audibly gasped. It was postcard perfect. Light snow fell, and the effect was magical.

Spontaneously, Mario grabbed her hand and tucked it into the curve of his arm. When his hand closed over hers, he drew in a sharp breath.

"Your hands are freezing," he said.

"Yours are so warm. How is that possible in this temperature? And, how can you traipse around without even zipping up your jacket or wearing a scarf?"

"It's only minus seven Celsius. Last week, it was minus thirty, forty-two with the wind chill factor. This is like being in Florida for me."

"Hardly," she said wryly.

They wandered along Dufferin Terrace, commonly called "the boardwalk". It lay beside the Château Frontenac, atop the cliffs bordering the St. Lawrence River. The ice chunks flowed down the river, and the lights of the city of Lévis twinkled at them from the opposite shoreline.

Arm in arm, they strolled along the cobblestone streets and browsed through boutiques and souvenir shops. When Tori laughingly admired a pair of woolen mittens emblazoned with comical moose heads, Mario insisted on buying them for her.

"They are...how do you say...tacky?...but they'll remind you of your little visit of Quebec, and they'll keep your fingers much warmer than those leather gloves."

Tori thanked him for his gift and wiggled her fingers inside the garish red mittens, grinning appreciatively.

When the evening came to an end, Mario insisted on driving her home, despite her protests.

"It's too late for you to be taking a taxi. I want to make sure you arrive safely."

"I'll be totally safe. There's no need for you to drive me," she said. After Ben's reaction to her motel, she didn't want to have a repeat performance with Mario.

"Where are you staying?"

Tori studied her hands twisted together in her lap.

"Tori?"

"The Pink Flamingo," she said in a low voice.

"Really? I can't believe you're staying in a place like that."

"Well, it's...uh...affordable," she said, uncomfortable, knowing she should've insisted on taking a taxi.

As they entered the motel room, she saw it through his eyes and knew how bad it appeared.

"It's too affordable, maybe. There's a certain class of people who stay in a place like this," he said.

He seemed to realize how his words must have sounded, and he was instantly contrite.

"Not that you're like that. I meant that it isn't safe for a woman to stay here alone. Why couldn't you have found something better?"

Tori smiled at him in what she hoped was a reassuring manner.

"It's all right. You don't have to worry about me."

To put an end to his questions, she raised herself up on her tiptoes and brushed a kiss across his lips. Before she had time to land back on her heels, he grasped her by the shoulders and tugged her closer for a not-so-light kiss.

Setting her down, he lowered his head to stare into her eyes, his face no more than two inches from hers.

"Tori, I don't like it."

She was momentarily confused, her mind still focused on the kiss.

"I mean this place. I know we've just met, and it wouldn't be right for me to invite you to stay at my place, but I have a sister. You could stay with her."

Tori was horrified at the idea of imposing on someone she hadn't even met.

"No, Mario. I mean it. I'm perfectly all right here."

"A dog wouldn't be perfectly all right here. Most of these rooms are rented by the hour. You don't know what kind of people are here."

"I'm being very careful, and I've hardly seen anyone, so you have nothing to worry about."

A deep frown creased his forehead. She knew he was building up for another lecture, and she wanted to head him off at the pass.

"I can't accept your generosity, Mario, but thanks anyway. And thank you for the wonderful evening. I can't remember the last time I enjoyed myself so much," she said truthfully. He was a nice guy, and she wondered why she'd never met anyone as nice in Florida.

With that, she turned him around and gently shoved him out the door.

CHAPTER 10

The next morning, Tori woke early. Her sleep had been disturbed by images of Danny, and all that had happened. Often, she wondered if she'd wasted her time, coming to Quebec. Then, she'd think about all that would be gained if she was successful and her determination would return.

She had just fallen asleep again when a heavy object thumped against the wall next door. This was followed by raised voices and more items banging on the wall. Apparently, the couple in the next room disagreed about something and didn't have any respect for people who might want to sleep.

Staring at the chipped stucco ceiling, Tori thought about the previous evening. She'd agreed to meet Mario because she had time to kill and hadn't wanted to sit in the motel room for two days while waiting to see Yvon. She'd never expected to have so much fun.

Mario had introduced her to the beauty of Quebec City, and he'd been an entertaining and charming companion for the evening. She admitted she was attracted to him, and she smiled when she remembered the first time she'd seen him. Perhaps it was his appearance, with his glasses and conservative style of dress, along with his easy-going personality, that made him blend in with the crowd.

But, Tori had discovered another side to him. He had a dry sense of humor and a certain way about him that let a person relax and forget their problems. She should know. For the entire evening she'd put her concerns aside and enjoyed herself.

Of course, their relationship – if she could call it that – didn't have a future.

Tomorrow, she'd meet Yvon, find Danny, and get back to Florida as soon as possible. But, there was still today. Mario had invited her to spend the day with him, taking in more of the Quebec Carnival sights. With that pleasant thought in mind, she jumped out of bed, took a quick shower, and got dressed.

As Tori mulled over where she would have breakfast, there was a sharp rap at the door. Her heart raced. She couldn't imagine who'd want to see her at this hour.

She stood frozen to the spot, her eyes wide with fear, and tried to think of a means of escape. Another knock sounded at the door, followed by a voice.

"Tori, are you there?"

Her knees almost gave way with relief. She hurried to the door and flung it open, unprepared for the rush of frigid air. Mario stood on the doorstep, warmly dressed, his smile fading to an expression of concern.

"What's wrong? You're white as a ghost."

Tori tugged him into the room, slamming the door on the cold outdoors.

"Nothing's wrong. I'm just surprised to see you."

In reality, she was thrilled to see him. He was a welcome sight compared to what she'd expected to see on the other side of the door. She smiled at him brightly, happy when her smile was reciprocated, and no further explanation was requested.

"I'm sorry to show up so early, but I thought maybe I could take you to breakfast."

"Oh, I was just thinking of that."

"Great, because I remembered this morning is the Calgary pancake breakfast."

"What is that?" she asked.

"Every year, a group of people from Calgary, Alberta come to Quebec for the carnival, and they host a pancake breakfast outside the ice palace. I thought you might enjoy it."

"Sounds good. I'll get my coat, and we can go."

It was one of the strangest things Tori had ever heard of, but she'd eat anything anywhere if it meant leaving the motel room.

"Um… before we go, Tori, I wanted to talk to you about something."

His tone was unusually serious. Tori dropped her coat on the bed and waited expectantly.

"I spoke to my sister last night after I got home, and she'd love for you to stay with her."

Tori was horrified.

"Mario, I can't do that. She doesn't even know me, and now you've tried to saddle her with me."

"Saddle? What is that?" he asked. Tori had forgotten that Mario mightn't catch the usual English expressions.

"It means...it means...I'll be imposing on her... I'll be in her way."

"No. She's happy. She used to have a friend living with her, but now she's alone, and she doesn't like it. When I told her about you, she insisted you go to stay there."

"I'm fine here. Really, I am."

He scanned the room, and she followed his gaze, taking in the decrepit furnishings. His nose wrinkled against the smell of stale cigarette smoke and mustiness. He turned back to her, one eyebrow lifted in disbelief.

"It's not that bad," she said.

Tori flinched when the argument broke out again in the room next door. The walls were so thin, and the screaming so clearly heard, it was as if the people stood next to them. Mario didn't say a word. He stared at her, obviously waiting for her to come up with a better reason for staying in this motel.

"Okay, so it's not that great, but you and your sister shouldn't feel you have to take me in. Not that I don't appreciate the offer, but I'd feel bad about it."

"If you say no, it's Chantal who'll feel bad. I don't look forward to telling her you won't come."

He had such a downcast expression on his face Tori experienced a little twist in her heart, as if she'd grabbed a piece of candy out of the hands of a young child.

"Oh...Mario...okay, I'll go."

His face broke out in a grin. She couldn't help but smile, but she shook her head at him nevertheless.

"She's a very easy woman," he said, as they drove to his sister's apartment, leaving the motel far behind.

"I think you mean easy-going. The term 'easy' in English can sometimes be taken the wrong way," she said with a giggle.

"Oh, I'll be careful then, because, even though she is 'easy', she has a temper when she feels insulted."

Tori smiled. Ever since making the decision to take Mario up on his offer, she'd relaxed. She detested the motel room and had never felt safe there, but it was the most she could afford. She'd find a way to make it up to Mario and his sister.

Tori saw they drove through a densely populated area of the city, with stores and restaurants interspersed among the small apartment dwellings.

"Chantal lives not far from Cartier Avenue. It's a busy part of Upper Town, and you'll be closer to all the Carnival activities."

"Perfect."

Tori reminded herself to play the part of a tourist in Quebec City during Carnival time. After all, it was her excuse for being here.

Mario turned onto Cartier Avenue, and Tori understood what he meant by it being a busy part of town. The street was lined with stores, boutiques, restaurants, and bars. People were everywhere, and the traffic crawled along the street. Mario turned off onto a quieter side street and pulled up to a small, brick, apartment building.

"*Bon*, we're here. I'll get your bag."

He led her to the top floor of the three-storey structure and down a short hallway to an apartment at the back. After one knock, the door was thrown open by a tall, willowy, strawberry blond. The woman gave Mario a quick hug and a kiss on each cheek before she enthusiastically grabbed Tori's arm and drew her into the apartment.

"*Bonjour*, Tori. I am so happy you will stay with me."

Before Tori could respond, she was also pulled into a hug and had a kiss planted on each of her cheeks.

"Th...thank you."

Tori was taken aback by the unexpectedly warm welcome, but she didn't have time to dwell on it. Chantal grabbed her bag, spun around, and marched down the hallway to disappear into a room. Within seconds, she reappeared. Tori glanced at Mario and smiled, covering up her astonishment. His sister had such an abundance of energy she created a whirlwind doing the most basic of tasks.

"Mario, *va chercher les tasses.* Would you like a coffee?" Chantal said, with a heavy French accent, much heavier than her brother's.

While Mario set about following his sister's orders, hunting in the kitchen cupboards for coffee cups, Chantal got the cream out of the refrigerator and prepared the brew. She didn't wait for an answer from Tori, but poured three cups and gestured for her to add cream and sugar if she liked.

Tori felt certain she'd get along fine with Chantal.

She observed the siblings as they bantered back and forth in French. She thought she couldn't have found two people more different. Chantal's light coloring and blue eyes were in stark contrast to Mario's dark hair and brown eyes. Whereas Chantal had a high energy level, Mario was much more relaxed and laid-back, willing to be an easy observer.

He was also perceptive. He appeared to know what questions ran through her head.

"I take after my father, and Chantal is just like my mother."

"Do you have any other brothers or sisters?"

"No, there is just us," Chantal answered. "But that's enough. I wouldn't want to have another brother to take care of," she said, looking at Mario with affection. He, in turn, smiled at her benignly.

Wistfulness drifted over Tori. She longed to be with her own family in this way, relaxed and happy, not worrying about her responsibilities, or looking over her shoulder to avoid danger.

Mario interrupted her musings as he set down his empty cup of coffee and addressed his sister.

"Chantal, we're going to the Calgary breakfast this morning, and I wondered if you could lend Tori a pair of boots. She doesn't have anything warm, and we'll be outside most of the day."

His words threw his sister into a flurry of activity. Before she knew it, Tori wore a warm pair of fur-lined boots, a sheepskin coat that fell almost to her knees, and a fluffy scarf with matching hat and mittens.

"But you may need these," Tori protested.

"Not at all. Do you think those are the only warm clothes I have to wear? When you live in Quebec, you have clothes for every occasion. Besides, I don't expect to be taking in any outdoor activities today."

With that, she wished them a good day and ushered them out the door.

Chapter 11

They left Mario's car outside Chantal's apartment and walked along a street named Grande Allée to reach the Ice Palace, an open-air structure made entirely of ice. It was swarming with people, and they lined up to receive their share of pancakes, sausages, and hot coffee. It was a novel experience for Tori to eat breakfast while standing ankle-deep in snow inside a frozen castle. She'd never have guessed such a thing existed.

From there, they roamed the streets within the walled section of the old city until they reached the Dufferin Terrace, where they'd been the previous evening.

As they walked, Mario filled her in on the history of Quebec, pointing out that the Château Frontenac was built at the end of the nineteenth century as a luxury hotel to accommodate travelers on the Canadian Pacific Railway, and had been host to many famous and distinguished guests. It had even been used as a strategic meeting place by Winston Churchill, Franklin D. Roosevelt, and William Lyon Mackenzie King during World War II.

The hotel itself had been built not far from the Plains of Abraham where the famous battle between the British General Wolfe and the French General Montcalm in 1759 led to the defeat of the French and was a decisive moment in Canadian history.

The area was crowded with people, enjoying the ice sculptures, visiting the various kiosks, and sliding on large round tubes down a snow-covered slope. At one point, Mario grabbed her hand and towed her toward a kiosk in front of which a small crowd was gathered. She saw a sign marked *La Tire* on top of the wooden shack, and as she opened her mouth to inquire what it meant, a delicious smell wafted past her nostrils.

"What is that?"

"*La tire.*"

"Oh, I thought it was pronounced 'tire', like on a car."

He laughed. "No, I don't think car tires would taste quite so good. It's pronounced 'tire'; it rhymes with 'ear.'"

"What is it?"

"It's made from maple syrup. It's like a toffee. Come, it's our turn."

A man poured a hot, golden brown liquid onto a layer of fresh snow packed into a wooden trough. Everyone was handed a wooden Popsicle stick. She copied Mario as she saw him twist the stick in the hardening sweetness until he formed a thick ball of taffy on the end.

"Mmmm.... Thith ith delithuth."

She held her hand over her mouth as she tried not to giggle. It took a moment before the candy melted, instead of sticking to the roof of her mouth.

"It's a ritual in Quebec in the springtime to have parties where people eat '*la tire*' and other traditional French-Canadian food, most of it cooked in maple syrup," Mario explained.

"It sounds very fattening."

"It is, but like everything else, it must be taken in moderation."

Later in the afternoon, back at Chantal's apartment, they had time to warm up and have a short rest. Ensconced in a cozy armchair, Tori was in danger of drifting off to sleep. The many hours of walking in the fresh, cool air had left her tired and relaxed, but Mario wouldn't let her give in. He grabbed her hand and dragged her from the chair.

"No, you mustn't get too comfortable. We still have a lot to do. And, I have a surprise for you."

With a groan, Tori pulled on the heavy winter clothing.

Twenty minutes later, they parked the car outside a section of roped-off streets. He guided her into a restaurant called 'Ashton's', and instructed her to save them a seat. It was a fast-food establishment, serving the usual hot dogs and hamburgers, so she assumed he had something up his sleeve for later as a surprise. When he reappeared, he placed a container in front of her filled with French fries that were drowned in gravy and cheese curds.

"What is this?" she asked, staring at the strange concoction.

"*Poutine.*"

"What?"

"*Poutine.* It's a Quebec invention."

She snickered.

"*This* is my surprise?"

"Don't laugh. Try it."

She did.

"This is amazing. It could even be addictive."

"It's been known to be *very* addictive."

"Why are you not fat if you eat like this all the time?"

"Moderation, remember?"

Next on their list of activities was a nighttime parade, complete with floats, marching bands, and clowns. Perhaps the most enjoyable part was when she stood with her back to Mario's chest while he folded his arms around her for warmth. It gave her a sense of peace and comfort, along with a healthy dose of physical attraction.

The parade's finale was the float transporting *le Bonhomme Carnival,* an energetic man in a large snowman costume with a multi-colored scarf tied around his waist. Tori was disappointed that the evening was over, but her feet were numb with cold, despite Chantal's warm boots.

Mario opened the door to his sister's apartment to reveal a darkened room lit by the flickering of the television. Chantal lounged in an armchair, the remote control in her hand. It was the first time in their brief acquaintance that Tori had seen the other woman indulge in any form of relaxation.

Tori flopped onto the couch.

"I'm exhausted, but I had so much fun."

"I knew you would. My brother is an excellent tour guide," she said, smiling at Mario.

"I'm afraid I can't stay," Mario said. "But I'll call you tomorrow, Tori."

Tori rose to escort him to the door and thank him for the evening, Chantal following a few paces behind. Mario wrapped his hand around Tori's arm and moved her to stand in front of him, blocking her from Chantal's view. His lips came down on hers in a warm, deep kiss. He broke it off, grinning at her stunned expression.

"Sleep well," he said, before throwing a glance over his shoulder at his sister and leaving the apartment.

When the door closed behind him, Tori glimpsed the look on Chantal's face and interpreted it as disapproval. She hesitated for a moment, wondering how to phrase the question she wanted to ask, but Chantal broached the subject first.

"My brother moves fast."

She sounded angry, and Tori's mind raced, searching for a reason.

"Is he already seeing someone?"

"Seeing someone? You mean does he have a girlfriend? No."

"Why are you upset? Is it me you disapprove of?"

Chantal's expression was remorseful.

"No, absolutely not. I think you're very nice. It's that you're not from around here. You'll be going home soon, and someone will be hurt."

Tori smiled reassuringly.

"I don't think either of us is that serious about the other. We're having fun, and I enjoy Mario's company, but as you said, I'll be going home soon, maybe in the next few days. I appreciate your concern, but there's nothing to worry about."

CHAPTER 12

The next morning, as she drank her coffee with Chantal, Tori was tense and anxious while attempting to appear calm. There was no lack of conversation as her companion took it upon herself to do all the talking, although Tori had trouble paying attention. Their discussion from the end of the previous evening had been set aside and all but forgotten.

Tori was eager to meet Danny again, and the two-day delay had frustrated her, but now that the time had come to contact Yvon, she was nervous. What if something went wrong? No, she couldn't think like that. It would get her nowhere. She had to be optimistic and confident. She knew Danny, and he knew her. One would never willfully harm the other. They'd find a way to deal with their problems.

The ringing of the telephone jolted her from her thoughts. Chantal answered it and berated the person on the other end of the line in rapid-fire French. Tori couldn't hide her surprise when Chantal calmly passed her the handset.

"It's for you. It's Mario."

Tori hesitantly took the phone, wondering what the argument had been about.

"How did you sleep?"

His voice sounded even deeper over the phone, and if he was bothered by whatever Chantal had said to him, he kept it well-hidden.

"Fine, thank you. And you?" she said politely.

"Great. I wanted to know if I could take you out today. We could go to Mont Sainte-Anne."

"Mario, that would've been lovely, but I've other plans for today."

There was silence on the other end of the line, and Tori noticed Chantal had shifted to study her with a curious gleam in her eye.

"Okay, that's fine."

The disappointment was clear in his voice, and Tori felt a wave of guilt. She had no choice. She had an appointment with Yvon today, no matter how much she dreaded meeting the revolting little man.

"Maybe tomorrow we could go," she said, hoping to make it up to him.

"I have to work tomorrow, but I'll call you in the evening."

Tori hung up the phone in frustration. She would've enjoyed another day with Mario, and she hated to lie to him and his sister, but there was no question of involving them in what she had to do. She hadn't come here as a tourist. She'd come here with a purpose, and it must remain in the forefront of her mind.

"So where are you going today?" Chantal asked as she refilled Tori's coffee cup.

"There's a friend of the family, actually a friend of my mother's, an old woman that I promised to visit today."

"Where does she live? I could take you there."

"Thank you, but I'll take a taxi. It's not far from here. Really, there's no problem. I don't mind. I can do it"

Tori realized she babbled nervously, so she made a quick retreat to the spare room to change her clothes and prepare for her meeting.

Ten minutes later, she was dressed, wearing her own outerwear rather than Chantal's. She didn't think she'd spend much time outdoors. Chantal had called a taxi for her, and Tori was relieved to hear the beeping of the horn before she was faced with having to answer any more uncomfortable questions.

Inside the vehicle, a sigh of relief escaped her lips. This type of deception was difficult for her, especially when it involved people she liked so much. She focused on the upcoming encounter with Yvon and hoped he'd tell her where to find Danny.

The downtown bar was quiet, understandable for a Sunday morning, but Tori was nevertheless surprised to see five or six people sitting at tables in the gloomy establishment. It was sad to think this was the best place people could find to spend their Sunday mornings.

She found Yvon in the back room where he always seemed to be, and mentally braced herself for one of his slimy overtures. As expected, he leered at her, looking her up and down. She shivered with revulsion.

"What do you have to tell me?" she said, wanting to get to the point as promptly as possible.

"Ah, I have good news for you."

She brightened. "You do?"

"Yes, I've convinced Danny to see you."

"Great. When?"

"Now."

"Now? He's here?"

"No, he's not here. I'll bring you to him."

A knot instantly formed in her stomach. She wasn't comfortable going anywhere with Yvon. It must've been obvious by the look on her face. Yvon lifted his shoulders and turned his hands out, palms up.

"You have to trust me, *chérie*. I'm the only connection you have with your Danny."

Knowing he was right didn't make her feel better. There was no guarantee he'd take her to Danny.

"Let's go," she said brusquely, wanting to get it over with.

Tori followed him out the back door of the bar to a small parking lot. He led her toward a black, late-model, BMW sedan and solicitously opened the back door for her. She stared at him with narrowed eyes.

"Why do I have to get in the back?"

"Because, *ma belle*, I'm afraid our Danny doesn't have faith in you."

As he spoke he removed a long, narrow, black cloth from his back pocket. She took a step back.

"You don't mean..."

"Yes, I do mean. Turn around," he said, advancing on her.

"No, I won't."

She grabbed the blindfold and tried to jerk it out of his hand, but he had a firm grip on it. Tugging back and forth, Tori lost her balance and landed against his chest. He gave her a yellow-toothed grin, and the smell of stale tobacco and alcohol wafted toward her. She righted herself and shoved away from him.

"Do what I say and you won't be hurt," he said. "Otherwise, I'll have to knock you out and put you in the trunk. I don't think you'd like that, eh?"

Tori didn't respond, frantically considering her options. She didn't trust Yvon farther than she could throw him. She'd already had a narrow escape at the hands of Danny's friends. She didn't want to go through it again.

Her decision made, she swivelled and sprinted toward the closest alleyway. It ran alongside the bar, and she hoped it led to a side street in the back.

Luck was with her. Without the sound of footsteps behind her, she knew she'd taken Yvon by surprise, and her getaway was imminent. Rounding the corner of the building, she wanted to scream. The reason why Yvon hadn't hurried to catch her was obvious. There was a ten-foot-high fence blocking her way.

Tori searched for something to climb onto to get her over the obstacle. Her heart sank. There was nothing. She was trapped. She swung around to see Yvon standing at the end of the alley, blocking her way. He smiled, but it wasn't a pleasant smile.

"I told you to do what I say, and you wouldn't get hurt. Do you not understand English?" he said, laughing at what he thought to be a joke.

Tori's back was against the fence. She had no doubt Yvon would hurt her if she didn't cooperate. The best she could hope for was that he'd bring her to Danny unharmed, and this whole episode would be behind her. But, something told her the best wasn't on the agenda today.

Yvon grabbed her arm in a painful grip and twisted her around to face the fence. He shoved her up against the rusty metal, pressing his body close.

"Maybe you like to play rough. Is that it, *chérie*?" he said, as he tied the coarse fabric across her eyes.

Tori clenched her teeth and struggled when he yanked her arms together behind her back, but he twisted her right arm until she was paralysed with pain.

"I wouldn't complain too much," he said when she whimpered. "I'm a pussycat compared to some of Danny's friends. You don't know how lucky you are."

Yvon hauled her to the car, paying no attention to her stumbling and moans of pain. She was thrust onto the floor of the back seat area. Seconds later, the engine started, and she felt its movement as it left the parking lot.

Unable to see for the duration of the trip, Tori analysed the sounds she heard, with limited success. They'd travelled with many stops and starts in heavy traffic for the first part of the journey, but had eventually moved onto a highway. At one point, there'd been strange bumps on the road, all evenly spaced.

When they came to a stop and the engine was extinguished, her heart pounded in her chest. The door would soon open and presumably Yvon would help her out of the back. If, as a result of this excursion, she saw Danny, it'd all be worth it, she thought. However, if Yvon had lied to her and brought her here for some other odious reason, she couldn't bring herself to think of the consequences.

The voices outside the vehicle were muffled, and she couldn't make out what they said, or what language they spoke. A draft of frigid air entered the car as hands grabbed her by the arms, yanking her out of the car.

"Come on, *ma petite*, we're here. You can see your precious Danny now."

Tori hoped what Yvon said was true.

The ground under her feet was rough and uneven, and she stumbled often, but was dragged upright by the hand that gripped her upper arm. A door creaked, and she was shoved from behind before warmth surrounded her.

Her blindfold wasn't removed until she was led through a maze of twists and turns to what she expected was her destination. With relief, Tori felt fingers untie the knots at her wrists and the back of her head. She blinked several times while her eyes adjusted to the light.

Scanning the sparsely furnished room, she took in the dust and grime that coated most of the surfaces. The one item that looked reasonably clean was a large metal desk. It held a laptop computer and a few scattered papers. The room had one window, grey with dirt, and partly hidden by a dark brown curtain, allowing a trickle of light to fall across the desk.

Yvon stood in front of her and smirked. No one else was in the room. She couldn't hide her disappointment. All she could think was that it had all been for nothing, and she'd now have to deal with him.

"Don't worry, *chérie*, he'll be here."

At that moment, a man stepped into the room and nodded at Yvon, who left through the same doorway. Danny didn't speak. He stared at Tori with a blank look.

For a few moments, Tori was unable to speak either. She wanted to study him, to reassure herself that he was in good health. She took note of his wavy, blond hair and sky-blue eyes. With his six-foot-two height and his muscular build, he'd been blessed with movie-star good looks. She thought ruefully that he could've been anything in life. His looks, in combination with his charm and intelligence, would've opened up a world of possibilities for him.

Instead, Danny Wilcox had chosen a career in crime, and it was something Tori couldn't comprehend. Instead of doing something useful and fulfilling with his life, he'd decided to devote it to the world of drugs. Instead of wanting to settle down and have a family, he wanted to tear families apart by introducing them to addiction. It broke her heart to see the wasted potential, but it filled her with a deep resolve to get him away from here. She loved him too much to give up.

"Do we have to go through this again?"

His voice was deep and resonant, and it held a grim note of warning.

"Danny, I said some things I didn't mean when I last saw you. You have to know I'd never hand you over to the police. Never."

"Really? I wish I could be so sure."

"How can you say that? You know me. You know I'd never betray you," she said.

"How can I say that?" he repeated. "You're the one who said it, remember? I distinctly remember you saying if I didn't come back to Florida with you, you'd have no choice but to tell the police where to find me."

Tori took two steps and closed the gap between them. She laid her hands on his forearms and stared up into his hard, cold eyes, the same eyes she knew were capable of warmth and laughter. She longed to see the smile she appreciated so much, the smile that could light up a room and had been known to cause many a female heart to flip crazily.

"I didn't mean it. I was angry and frustrated. I want you to leave here so much I lost control. I'm sorry."

"Well, you're wasting your breath. I'm not leaving here, Tori. Not until I'm ready."

"Why not? What kind of life is this?" She gestured with her arm around the room. "You're constantly on the run, moving from one dirty place to another. The police are snapping at your heels day in and day out. Why would you want to live like that?"

"There are lots of reasons, but you wouldn't understand any of them."

Her temper rose again.

"You're right. I don't understand them. I could never understand why you'd prefer to be a criminal instead of living a decent life back home in..."

"Oh, come off it, Tori. You're living in a fantasy world. Do you really think I could go back there with you and pick up where I left off? Do you think I'd want to?"

His words pierced her heart, and she lashed out in response.

"It's better than this. This is all about power and money. What kind of power is it? Power to control slime balls like Yvon? And what can you do with all your dirty money? Nothing. You spend your life hiding in old houses and barns."

"Don't worry. I have a lot of fun with my dirty money, as you like to call it. More fun than you're having in your little house in Florida with its white picket fence," he said, a sneer marring his handsomeness. "Besides, I have a job coming down soon that'll make me richer than you could ever imagine. Then I'll leave here and head south, but it won't be to Florida. It'll be much farther south than that."

Her heart brightened with hope. "You're going to give it up?"

"Of course not," he said with a derisive snort. "But there'll be a change of venue. I have a new partner in South America with very powerful connections. In a few weeks, the Quebec police will have me out of their hair for a while."

"Danny, please, we were so happy before..."

"No, Tori. You were happy. I was miserable. I was meant for much bigger things than what you cooked up in that little mind of yours while sitting behind your little desk in your little cubicle. You may get a kick out of that type of life, but I certainly don't."

"Do you think I didn't get that? Of course, I knew you could do much better, but for God's sake, Danny, is this it?" Again, she swept her arm around the dingy room, her expression disbelieving. "Surely, you could've done better than this."

"You have no idea what you're talking about," he said, his face reddening. Tori had pushed him too far. She saw it in his eyes.

The door burst open, and a large, burly man rushed into the room.

"Jean-Marc just called. He saw someone coming through the back way. It looks like the cops."

"Jesus Christ." Danny shouted. He whirled on Tori. "You. You did this."

"No, I..."

Danny struck her across the face with a backhand slap so strong she landed against the wall and slid to the floor, half dazed. He advanced on her, jerked her up by one arm, and threw her at his bulky assistant.

"Get rid of her," he growled.

Tori stretched her arm out toward him.

"Danny, I didn't do it. I swear."

He turned his back to her, grabbed his cell phone from the desk, and got on with the business of disappearing.

Cʜᴀᴘᴛᴇʀ 13

Tori fought desperately as the man dragged her roughly through the dense growth of trees, to no avail. Her captor was much larger and stronger than she was. Her struggling had little to no effect on him. But, she wouldn't give up without a fight.

The words 'get rid of her' echoed in her head. What had Danny meant? How did he want her gotten rid of? She pushed the thought from her mind and concentrated on making the brute release his iron grip on her arm.

Unaffected by her kicking and hitting, as if Tori was a tiny mosquito slamming against a hot lightbulb, he never slowed his gait. He hauled her through the trees, uncaring of the bare branches scratching her face and the fact that her boots repeatedly slipped on the icy path. She tried to scream, but she was breathless from fighting both the man and for control of her limbs. Her voice came out in little more than a squeak.

A noise intruded on Tori's frantic mind. She assumed it was the roaring of blood in her ears until she understood it came from a source somewhere in front of them.

She saw it. It was a white-water river. It had huge chunks of ice along each bank. A rapidly-tumbling tunnel of water coursed down the middle. Tori's struggles increased with the force of her desperation, but she had no effect on the man.

"Let me go," she yelled. "He doesn't want you to kill me, you idiot."

The man ignored her, but he slowed his pace as he negotiated his way down the slippery slope toward the icy bank. Losing control, Tori's feet slipped out from under her, and she slid past him. As he tightened his hold to stop her descent, her arm felt like it would leave its socket. But, fear for her arm was overridden by knowing the only thing between her and the pounding water below was the man's hand.

The man bent over her, grinning malevolently. He knew he didn't have to drag her any farther. All he had to do was release his grip.

Making a quick decision, Tori twisted her arm and grasped the sleeve of his coat in her hand. The move caught the man off-guard, and his own precarious hold on the steep, slippery hill was lost. Falling headlong into the snow, he futilely tried to grab hold of something solid to stop his fall. Screams of terror echoed through the woods as he began an uncontrollable tumble end-over-end.

Tori had no more control than her aggressor. She followed him down the hill with a horrible sense of helplessness, knowing there was no way to stop her plunge toward the icy killer below. The farther she went, the faster her momentum became. All she saw were alternate images of white snow and blue sky rolling by faster and faster like a videotape on fast forward.

Tori came to a sudden jolting stop, with the wind knocked from her lungs, and her body bent into a 'V' as her stomach met a tree. Fighting to catch her breath, she had a clear view of Danny's friend bouncing off the ice and plummeting into the rapids. She watched in horror as he was swept downstream, arms and legs flailing.

It was several minutes before Tori could move, as much because of the effort it took to breathe as because of the image of the certain death she had witnessed. She pulled herself out of her uncomfortable position and sat with her back against the tree, her arms wrapped around her knees. She shook uncontrollably, partly from the cold and partly from the terror she'd just lived through.

Tori lifted her head and looked up the hill, assessing her chances of climbing it without falling back down to join her erstwhile companion somewhere in the icy depths of the river. She spotted an area with a denser population of trees that she could use as support to tug herself upward, and she decided it would be the wisest direction to take.

Still, Tori hesitated. When she reached the top, what would she do? She could go back to the house that, by now, had surely been abandoned by Danny and his cohorts, and would presumably be safe. On the other hand, it'd be flooded with police officers and, because of that, wholly unsafe. How would she make it back to Chantal's place? She didn't have any idea where she was, and she had no means of transportation. She had a limited amount of money in her pocket. Knowing they had travelled quite a distance to get here, she might not have enough cash to pay for a taxi.

Tori didn't see that she had much choice. She'd find her way back by foot, asking for directions when she could. In the meantime, she needed to avoid running into any of Danny's men. Seeking help from the police wasn't an option either. They'd be sure to question her about Danny's whereabouts. Despite everything that had happened, it wasn't something she'd consider.

As Tori pulled herself upright, pain echoed throughout her body. Her right arm and shoulder ached, and her ribs were sore. It hurt to breathe, but she didn't think anything was broken. At least, she hoped not.

Using her left arm to grab onto the trees, Tori finally reached the crest of the hill, and with one last backward glance at the raging water below, she made her way through the trees, avoiding the obvious pathways.

Tori had no idea in which direction she went, but she stayed positive and had faith that, sooner or later, she'd come to a road leading her to help of some kind.

After thirty minutes of beating a path through the trees, not knowing if she'd gone in circles or not, Tori heard the rumble of a heavy vehicle. It told her there was some sort of roadway up ahead. When she emerged from the trees, she found herself on a road without any sign of cars or houses. She stood for a moment, pondering which direction she should take. With a shrug, she turned to her right.

Outside the shelter of the woods, the wind battered her and the cold bit into her flesh. Again, Tori was inadequately dressed, and she wistfully thought about Chantal's clothing she'd worn the previous day. She raised the collar of her jacket and checked to make sure it was zipped to the top. She shoved her hands deep into her pockets and walked faster, hoping to generate heat. Seconds later, she moved her hands to put them over her ears, but that caused her jacket to lift and expose her midriff to the cold.

Tori didn't hear the car pull up beside her. Seeing a large silver fender from the corner of her eye, she dropped her hands and came to an abrupt halt. Apprehension coursed through her.

The car stopped, and the driver opened his door and stepped out, peering over the roof at her.

"*Est-ce que je peux vous aider?*"

Tori didn't answer, taking an involuntary step backward. Deep down, she recognized that her fear was unreasonable. She wanted help, and help had come in the form of this person. He was of medium build, in his mid-thirties, with curly blond hair and what seemed like blue eyes from this distance. He struck her as being clean-cut and harmless, but Tori had been through so much today, the sight of anyone, no matter how harmless-looking, frightened her.

The man circled the front of his car and approached her.

"*Avez-vous un problème? Est-ce que je peux vous être utile?*"

His voice, even though the words were incomprehensible to Tori, was filled with concern. She took two more steps backward, and the man stopped in his tracks.

"*Mademoiselle, êtes-vous blessée?*"

Realizing this man was determined to help her, Tori found her voice.

"I don't speak French."

"Oh."

Comprehension crossed the man's face, followed by a small frown as he obviously searched for words.

"May I help you?"

Tori hesitated, but shook her head. For some reason, she couldn't bring herself to put her safety into this man's hands. She couldn't even make herself walk the few steps it would take to reach his car.

The stranger studied her as if she was someone who had just escaped from an insane asylum. He reached into his jacket pocket and retrieved a cell phone.

"I will call the police, and they will come to get you," he said, in halting English.

"No." she shouted, too quickly and too loudly. Seeing his expression, Tori softened her tone. "That won't be necessary. I'm just lost, you see. I have to find out how to get back to the city."

"What city?" the man said.

Tori glanced around her. What other city was there? How far had she gone?

"Quebec City."

"Oh, *la rive nord.*"

"What?"

"You need to go to the north shore."

"The north shore?"

"Yes, the other side of the St. Lawrence."

The other side? She'd crossed the river?

"I can take you there. I'm on my way to Québec now."

Tori considered it for a moment. She'd be foolish to refuse his offer. Besides, the longer they stood on the side of the road discussing it, the more frozen her extremities became.

"Thank you. That'd be very nice."

He opened the passenger-side door for her, and Tori slid in before she had time to change her mind. The man settled into the driver's seat, and as he fastened his seat belt, he glanced over at her.

"My name is Sébastien."

"I'm Tori," she said.

She felt certain she must look like quite a sight. Sebastien, besides being a knight in shining armor, was also very tactful by not mentioning that fact.

Few words were exchanged as they drove toward Quebec City, and Tori was thankful for the extended silence. She couldn't bring herself to answer questions. She didn't know if Sébastien was always the strong, silent type, or if he didn't have a solid-enough grasp of the English language, but she wouldn't look a gift horse in the mouth.

Crossing the bridge to go back to Quebec City, Tori heard and felt the rhythmic bumps caused by the joints in the floor of the bridge, the same sensation she had experienced lying in the back of Yvon's car. She was angry with herself for not realizing they'd crossed a bridge at the time. Then again, what good would it have done for her to know? Everything had been out of her control.

Despite her limited knowledge of the layout of the city, Tori directed Sébastien to Chantal's apartment with surprising ease. As they pulled up in front of the building, Tori took a deep, steadying breath. Her acting skills would be put to the ultimate test when it came to convincing Chantal she'd been involved in nothing more than an 'innocent' mugging.

After thanking Sébastien for his help, she climbed out of the car with surprising difficulty. Her sore muscles had cramped, and she couldn't suppress a grimace.

"Do you want me to help you?" he asked, his voice laced with concern.

"No, I'll be all right. Thank you again."

With that, she shut the door of the car and waved a cheery goodbye to her savior, a feeling of utter dread weighing her down.

Chapter 14

Tori dragged herself up the stairs of the building, relying on the railing to stay upright. Ringing the bell for the apartment, she waited several seconds before the door opened, but that short amount of time allowed her to gather her thoughts.

"Tori! *Mon Dieu*, what happened to you?"

Chantal's reaction made Tori appreciate Sébastien as being the epitome of tact.

Without waiting for a response, in typical Chantal fashion, Tori was tugged into the apartment and submitted to a close examination of her face by her new roommate. All the while, she was subjected to a lecture in incomprehensible French. When the stream of words stopped, she realized Chantal stared at her expectantly. Now was the time for the test.

"I was mugged," she said, bluntly.

"Mugged?"

"Yes, someone tried to rob me, and when they saw I didn't have any money on me, they roughed me up a bit."

Even to her own ears, her story sounded stilted and fabricated. Chantal drew back and considered her doubtfully.

"I'll call the police," she said, reaching for the phone.

"No."

Seeing the look of surprise on her friend's face, Tori changed her tone.

"There's no need. I'm fine."

She wished people around here didn't insist on calling the police every time something went wrong.

"You don't look fine. And even then, we should always call the police. You can give them a description."

"No, please, Chantal. I don't want to involve the police. Besides, I didn't get a good look at anyone. They...they pulled me into a dark alley...and...and they wore masks."

"*Mon Dieu*, it must have been terrible. You could have been raped. You weren't raped, were you?"

"No, I'm not hurt. Like I said, they just roughed me up a bit, and I could never identify anyone, so it's no use calling the police."

Chantal stared at her uncertainly for several moments before she acquiesced.

"What can I get for you? What can I do?"

"Nothing. I'm just cold and shaken up a bit," Tori said, fighting to keep the misery out of her voice.

"Then I'll run a hot bath for you, and you can relax."

"That'd be great. Thank you."

The idea of letting a bath soak the chill from her bones was appealing.

Tori was soon alone in the bathroom with a steaming tub full of bubbles in front of her.

Stripping off her clothes, she inspected the new blackish-blue colors that had been added to her body. In a few days, they'd be a wonderful greenish-yellow. Her face was covered in small scratches, and there was a large bruise on her right cheek where Danny had hit her. She didn't care. She was alive, and nothing was broken. The physical scars would heal and disappear. The emotional ones would be much harder to handle.

Tori reclined in the tub and closed her eyes, hoping to relax, but images floated before her closed lids like a movie projected on a screen. Regrettably, a horror movie played in the theatre of her mind. As she relived the events of the day, from her trip in the back of Yvon's car to the return in Sébastien's, her body trembled.

She'd come treacherously close to being killed again today, and knowing she'd been involved in another person's death, albeit accidentally, made her stomach roil in distress. She sat up in the tub and wrapped her arms around her knees. Her limbs continued to quake.

Tori lifted her head when she heard the unmistakable sound of voices coming from the living area of the apartment. She couldn't make out the words, but she recognized the deep rumble of Mario's voice. That explained Chantal's incongruous willingness to drop the subject of Tori's supposed mugging. She wanted to leave it in Mario's hands.

Tori wondered how long she'd have to hide in the bathroom before he gave up and left, but the thought was shoved aside. Mario wouldn't give up.

She was right. Minutes later, a hand rapped on the door.

"Tori, I want to talk to you."

He sounded calm, but Tori wasn't looking forward to seeing Mario. She'd have more difficulty facing him with her contrived story than she had with Chantal.

"I'm in the bath," she said.

"You've been in there a long time. You should be getting out soon, don't you think?"

He sounded very pleasant. Tori was encouraged by his tone.

"I won't be long. I'll be out in a few minutes."

Heavy footsteps strode to the living room, and her eyes widened in surprise when the front door slammed. Had Mario left so soon? Maybe she'd escape an interrogation, she thought.

The bath had felt good, but getting dressed reminded Tori of all her aches and pains. She knew she'd feel worse in a day or two. For the time being, she'd have to put on a brave front.

In the living room, Mario stood beside the window, with no sign of Chantal, and any hopes Tori had of avoiding his questions were dashed. His eyes narrowed as they traveled over her face, and his jaw hardened. He took a few steps toward her until they stood a foot apart.

"What happened?" he said.

She focused on the opening of his shirt where dark chest hairs peeked out. She shrugged nonchalantly.

"Well, I guess I was in the wrong place at the wrong time. This guy came out of nowhere and tried to take my…"

"Tori."

The unexpected sharpness of his voice startled her, making her look up into his eyes. What she saw was a new Mario. Gone was the Mario who was laid-back and charming. Instead, here was a man with an expression of barely-controlled anger and frustration.

"Tell me what really happened," he said. "You're a terrible liar."

She considered forging onward with her concocted story, but she felt certain he wouldn't buy it, and she'd just make him angrier. She owed him more than that.

Again, she lowered her eyes, but she shook her head resolutely.

"I can't, Mario."

His hands came up and grabbed her upper arms, making her gasp in pain as he lightly squeezed her bruised flesh. He cursed softly in French, took hold of her right hand and pushed up the sleeve of her bulky sweater until he exposed the vivid discoloration of her skin.

Gritting his teeth, he did the same to her left arm, appearing relieved to see it was all right. He ran his gaze over her and, anticipating where his deliberations might lead, she crossed her arms over her chest, barring his way if he thought to continue his investigations any further.

"Who did this to you? Tell me."

"I can't," she said.

"Why not? If you're in trouble, I can help you. I *will* help you."

"I know you would. And I appreciate it, but I don't need your help. I can take care of myself."

"Take care of yourself?" he said. "Do you call this taking care of yourself? You've been beaten black and blue."

Tori opened her mouth to argue with him, but realizing it'd be futile, she settled onto the sofa, staring at the floor and rubbing her arms to wipe away the chill that had returned. She knew the shivering had nothing to do with the temperature. The trauma of the day and having to face Mario's inquisition had set her nerves on edge.

Mario's feet moved into her line of vision. He knelt in front of her, placing his hands on her knees, and stared at her with concern in his eyes.

"Why can't you tell me? I'm your friend. I want to help you."

Tori closed her eyes and tried to calm her frayed nerves. She didn't have a firm grip on her emotions at the moment, and his gentle tone of voice could be her undoing. As it had been with Ben, the temptation to lay all her troubles at Mario's feet was considerable, but she refused to give into it. She wouldn't endanger anyone else's life. Danny had proven, once again, he conducted business with ruthlessly dangerous criminals.

She faced Mario with eyes filled with unshed tears. She placed her palm on his cheek, rough with five o'clock shadow.

"Mario, please don't ask me for anything more. I can't tell you."

"I can't stand by and watch you be hurt. There has to be something I can do."

She smiled feebly.

"No. There isn't anything anyone can do."

The despair she felt was evident in her voice, even to her own ears. Her body slumped in defeat and fatigue. She was not only physically tired but mentally and emotionally wrecked. She couldn't go on any longer, fighting a fruitless fight. It broke her heart to give up and leave Danny, even though she'd leave him to a destiny of his own making.

Mario, undoubtedly sensing her distress, sat beside her on the sofa and tugged her into his arms. As he rubbed her back, he crooned soothing words to her in French. Although she didn't grasp their meaning, her body slumped against him. After several minutes, he put his hand on her cheek and used his thumb to lift her face to his.

His kiss was gentle and inviting. The last of the tension left her body as she circled her arms around his neck and pulled him closer. His arms tightened, and what had started as a gesture of comfort soon grew into a flare of passion. Tori wanted to drown herself in Mario. She needed to have the terrible memories and images replaced by something special. She instinctively knew it would be special with this man.

His hands roamed her body, and her breathing was shallow and labored. When he put his hands on her waist and gently but determinedly set her aside, she looked up at him in dazed confusion.

"What's wrong?" she said.

"Nothing's wrong," he answered. "I just don't think we should take this any farther."

She blinked at him in bewilderment.

"You don't?"

When he shook his head, Tori composed herself and straightened her clothes. Mario diligently avoided her eyes.

"You know, I'd still respect you in the morning," she said.

He smiled sheepishly.

"I'm glad to hear that. For now, I think I need to check on supper."

Tori couldn't help but chuckle. The roles were definitely reversed.

"You made supper?"

"No. Fortunately for you, Chantal did the cooking. But she decided to go out at the last minute and left the food for us to eat."

Tori knew why Chantal had chosen to 'go out at the last minute', and she felt guilty for driving her friend out of her home. But, she didn't want to resurrect the subject and invoke another series of questions. She'd apologize to Chantal later.

Tori followed Mario into the kitchen toward the source of the delicious aroma drifting from the room. She peered over his shoulder as he checked the contents of the oven and couldn't hide her curiosity.

"Mmm. What is it?"

"Pork tenderloin, marinated in a sauce made with maple syrup. She put in some baked potatoes and made a salad for us."

"She did all that?"

Tori's feelings of guilt were compounded many times over. Chantal had gone to a lot of trouble preparing the meal and had left the apartment so Mario and Tori could hash through the events of the day.

"Don't worry. She's having a good time. She's meeting up with some girlfriends, and they're going to hit the bars. There's a lot of partying in the city during Carnival."

Tori wasn't convinced he told her the truth, but she kept her doubts to herself. She'd question Chantal the next day.

Mario didn't bring up the earlier subject of Tori's injuries or the awkward few moments they'd experienced after their burst of passion. Instead, he concentrated his efforts on taking her mind off her problems, telling her anecdotes about Quebec and its culture. She was glad for the respite, but was aware she'd pay for it later. She didn't think either Mario or Chantal would give in so quickly.

When the meal was over, and Chantal's kitchen was returned to its usual pristine condition, Tori realized she had to discuss her plans with Mario. Her mood somber, she stared out the living-room window, wondering how to broach the subject. Mario took the first step for her.

"What's bothering you, Tori?"

He stood right behind her.

"I have to leave, Mario."

"What do you mean?"

"I mean I have to go home."

"To Florida?"

She nodded.

"When?"

"Soon. As soon as possible."

It'd take her a couple of days to get some funds together. At the moment, she was broke. Taking time off work without pay and traveling to Canada hadn't been kind to her bank account. She had yet to contact the garage, but she was certain there was nothing to be done about her car. Even if it could be salvaged, the cost of repairs wouldn't be negligible. She'd have to borrow money from a friend. She couldn't call on her mother for help, not at this point.

He stepped closer to her and laid his hands on her shoulders.

"I don't want you to go."

"I have to."

She didn't trust herself to say more than a few words at a time. Her throat was clogged with tears. She wouldn't miss the terror she'd been subjected to while she was here, but she'd undoubtedly miss Mario. He'd been a good friend, and he could easily become much more than that. But, she wouldn't allow it to go further. She had a life elsewhere and a mother who needed her. The fact that she'd go home alone added to her grief.

Mario put his arms around her and pulled her back against him. He lowered his head until it rested alongside hers.

"Couldn't you stay a little longer?" His voice was soft and low in her ear.

She couldn't speak. Her silence was her answer.

"Are you running from someone or something?"

She tensed. Yes, she was running from danger, but she had responsibilities in Florida, and she had a life to resume, putting the past behind her. She turned and slid her arms around him, resting her cheek on his chest.

"I have to go, Mario. My mother is very sick, and I have a job that's waiting for me. I have no choice."

He hesitated for a moment.

"It's very sudden."

She shook her head.

"It isn't sudden. I've already been here almost two weeks. It's time to go now."

She was surprised to see the pained expression on his face. She reached up to pull his mouth down to hers, and he didn't set her aside.

Chapter 15

The next morning, Tori awoke to the sound of voices coming from the direction of the kitchen. The words weren't shouted, but the tone of the conversation sounded angry. She was afraid she was, once again, the subject of the sibling's argument.

Chantal didn't approve of Mario and Tori having a relationship, except perhaps as friends. Of that she was certain. Yet, Tori had the impression Chantal liked her as a person. Was it because she was from out of town and wouldn't be settling down in Quebec? Did she truly believe her brother's heart would be broken?

At this point, Tori was more concerned about the state of her own heart. Her feelings for Mario were strong, perhaps too strong, and leaving him would be much more difficult than she'd assumed.

A few minutes later, the door slammed heavily, and Tori understood at least one of the siblings had left the apartment. As she climbed out of bed, she braced herself to face the remaining one.

"Good morning," she said, seeing Chantal, with her back to her, ferociously scrubbing an already immaculate countertop.

Tori jumped in alarm, her heart pounding, as her friend swung around, holding a large carving knife that had appeared out of nowhere. When her gaze met Tori's, Chantal dropped the weapon on the counter and leaned back against it, taking a shaky breath.

"I'm sorry, Tori. I didn't mean to scare you," Chantal said. "But, you scared me first." Her laugh was forced. "Come and sit. I'll get you a coffee."

As Chantal took care of the coffee, Tori took a few breaths and attempted to control her heart rate. She was shocked at how menacing Chantal looked with a dangerous weapon in her hand. She'd be a force to be reckoned with if ever confronted by a real enemy. Tori shook her head. She had seen so much violence over the past several days she was beginning to discover it in the most innocent of situations.

"I heard you and Mario arguing before."

Chantal's hands hesitated before resuming their constant motion.

"Yes, well… brothers and sisters argue a lot."

Tori wouldn't let her wiggle out of it so easily.

"Was it about me?"

"No. Why would we argue about you?"

Again, Chantal scrubbed at the countertop, avoiding Tori's look.

"Maybe because you don't approve of what happened between us last night."

Chantal stopped her scouring and sighed.

"It's none of my business. You're both adults and old enough to make your own decisions."

"But you don't like it."

Chantal faced Tori with sadness in her eyes.

"You're not going to stay here. You're going to go home."

"Yes, I am. Very soon, probably."

Mario's sister shrugged her shoulders as if to say, 'That's what I mean'.

Tori stood and crossed over to Chantal.

"I know it may have been a mistake – for both of us – but it happened, and I have no regrets. I really care about your brother, and I don't want to hurt him. But I'm leaving soon, and at least I'll have a few good memories to take with me. Besides, I don't think I'll be breaking Mario's heart, so you shouldn't worry about it."

Chantal nodded unconvincingly.

An hour later, after Chantal left to go work at the boutique she managed, Tori considered her next move. She knew she had to make arrangements to go back to Florida. The cheapest form of transportation would be the bus. It would also be the most time-consuming, but Tori didn't think she had much choice. As it was, she'd have to borrow the money for the bus fare and, when she got home, she'd get a loan to buy another car.

The first step was to learn how much a bus ticket would cost. Without her phone, and having forgotten to ask Chantal for the password to her computer, she'd have to rely on an old-fashioned telephone directory to call the bus station.

Tori had never been in Chantal's office. It contained a small desk, complete with computer, printer, scanner, and telephone. She assumed it'd be the ideal place to store a phone book.

She didn't find it on top of the desk, so she searched the drawers, hoping a directory existed in this electronic world. She drew a blank with the first two drawers and, without much optimism, she opened the third and last one. It was a much smaller drawer and less likely to contain a bulky book. She was about to close it after a cursory scan, but something caught her eye.

Feeling guilty for snooping, Tori removed the object and smiled as she recognized two of the many faces in the glossy framed photograph. She caught sight of another familiar face and her brow creased in puzzlement. Her focus was drawn to the background of the picture. Her eyes widened in horror as it dawned on her what it all meant. She dropped the picture on the floor as if it had burst into flames. Tori whirled and ran from the room.

CHAPTER 16

The group was gathered in a small room, furnished with nothing more than an oblong table, a half-dozen chairs, a coffee maker, and a telephone. The physical atmosphere of the room was dull and impersonal, in sharp contrast to the personalities of the five people it contained. Without exception, they were all young and dynamic, and all committed to their chosen career. At the moment, they were in the midst of a heated discussion about their next move. Pros and cons were measured, but everything was weighed against the element of risk involved.

One man stared unseeingly out the window, a cup of coffee in his hand, and many troubled thoughts swimming in his head. When his cell phone rang shrilly, the others didn't react. But, the man's response to the caller drew everyone's attention.

"What? She's gone? Where? How?"

His voice was loud and became louder with each word spoken. His expression was fierce as he listened to the person on the other end of the line.

"Where was René? He was supposed to be guarding the front of the building. How did she get past him?"

The answer didn't please him. He disconnected the call without another word, set down the phone with barely-controlled movements, and slammed his fist on the table.

He didn't need to explain anything to the other occupants of the room. They'd heard enough to understand the gist of what had happened, and they knew they had to give him a few moments to cool off. The bravest – or the most foolish – of the group spoke up.

"How did she get past René?"

"Out the back. Apparently, she discovered he was watching her," he said in a growl. "God knows where she is now."

"Jeff, we're going to have to tell the boss."

Before anyone could answer, the door opened, and the subject of the last statement strode through the door. He stopped abruptly when he saw the faces before him, and a frown creased his forehead.

"What's wrong?"

All eyes shifted to the man named Jeff, leaving the burden of explanations on his shoulders.

CHAPTER 17

Tori slipped into the crowded corner store with two purposes in mind. Firstly, she needed to get warm, and secondly, she had to find a phone to call a taxi.

She'd roamed for at least an hour, frequently stopping along the way, going into boutiques or fast-food restaurants to warm up for a few minutes. She couldn't stop for long. They'd be searching for her and, although she didn't think she'd been followed, she wanted to be extra careful.

She'd spotted the lone man sitting in a car on the street in front of the apartment. She didn't know if he was there to spy on her or not, but she didn't want to take a chance. She'd slipped out the back door of the apartment building and found her way to Cartier Street through an alleyway.

Tori went to the back of the store to find the pay phone and punched in the number of the taxi company that was printed on a sticker on the wall. She spoke to the dispatcher in English, but had no trouble making him understand where she was. At this point, her concern wasn't communication. It was if she had enough cash in her pocket to pay for the trip. She'd stolen the small amount of money she had from Chantal's night-table drawer, but refused to accept any guilt for the crime.

Tears sprang to her eyes as she thought about the deception that had been played out against her. Tori may have suffered physically over the past two weeks – and she had the aches and bruises to vouch for it – but nothing could ever hurt as much as the pain that had been inflicted on her heart and spirit.

First, it had been Danny who'd turned against her, and now the two people she had come to trust and care about had proven to be as false as a three-dollar bill. On top of all the lies and deceptions, she had the added humiliation of being exposed as a fool. She understood she tended to be naïve, and she trusted too easily, but no one had ever taken advantage of that fact to such an extent, until now.

Tori set aside the hurt and concentrated on surviving. She needed to get help and shelter with someone trustworthy, and the only person who came to mind was Ben. He'd helped her once, and Tori hoped he'd help her again if she asked him. The problem would be finding him. She had to get to the cabin, and she worried her memory wouldn't be sharp enough to lead the taxi driver to the small snow-covered road where she'd crashed her car, seemingly a lifetime ago.

In the warmth of the taxicab, Tori relaxed marginally. She felt safer in the back seat of a vehicle with a stranger at the wheel than she had wandering the streets of Quebec, repeatedly looking over her shoulder. She wasn't a suspicious person by nature, and it was a terrible sensation to skulk around studying everyone as if they meant her harm.

She did her best to tell the driver where she wanted to go. She knew she mangled the names of the towns and streets that would lead to her destination, but he smiled kindly and nodded his understanding. He didn't make conversation, obviously realizing how frustrating it would be to attempt it.

As they drove, Tori saw the landscape change, becoming more rural. Optimism blossomed as she recognized familiar territory, and she used those welcome sights to smother the horrible feeling of betrayal that lingered in her mind.

Approaching the street where her car had crashed, Tori sat forward in her seat. When she asked the driver to stop the car in the middle of the deserted road, he looked at her curiously, perhaps speculating where she intended to go from there. She knew her request was bizarre, to say the least, but she was so thankful to have arrived, she didn't care what the man thought. As a bonus, she had a small amount of money left in her pocket after settling her taxi bill.

Tori waited for the driver to leave, with a last doubtful glance sent her way, before searching for the snowmobile trail to Ben's cabin. It'd be the most direct route and there'd be little danger of getting lost.

It didn't take her long to find it. Even though the track had a fresh layer of snow on top of it, the well-worn indentation was still clear. Without hesitation, Tori climbed the snowbank onto the trail, dragging her small bag of possessions, and headed in the direction of the cabin. She was more warmly dressed this time, since she had 'borrowed' Chantal's winter wear. It helped to make the trek much less arduous.

Despite her relief at being close to reaching Ben, Tori couldn't hold back the tears. She was bitterly hurt that a woman she'd taken a liking to, and a man she'd come dangerously close to caring for, had both deviously worked against her behind her back. Every direction in which she'd turned brought her face-to-face with someone who wanted to hurt her in some way.

She'd driven thousands of miles on what she considered to be a mission of mercy and, instead of being greeted with open arms, two attempts had been made on her life by people associated with the very man she wanted to help. Then, to add hardship to misery, she discovered she'd been tricked, deceived, and blatantly used by experienced imposters.

After thirty minutes of trekking through the snow, Tori thought she should've reached her destination, but she spotted no traces of human footprints or those of a large dog. There were rabbit prints, but nothing larger. That either meant she wasn't close enough, or she'd gone in the wrong direction after all.

Coming over a small rise in the snow, Tori saw the roof of the cabin in the distance. She smiled in relief, but it was short-lived when she noticed there wasn't any smoke coming from the chimney. It couldn't be, she thought. He had to be there.

She hurried as swiftly as her booted feet and the deep snow would allow. Reaching the cabin, she stopped and stared in dismay. It looked deserted. The porch was covered in fresh snow, free of footprints, and there definitely wasn't any smoke coming from the chimney.

Tori's shoulders slumped. She'd come all this way for nothing. Ben wasn't here. She'd have to go back to the road and find some other way out of the city. She had twenty dollars in her pocket, and an almost-full credit card that she was afraid would be traced. She couldn't afford even the cheapest motel room in town.

It was too much. She dropped her head into her cold hands and sobbed. How could this be happening? She had to be the most naïve, most impulsive creature on earth. This whole endeavor, from start to finish, had been a farce of her own making.

Drying her tears, she decided she'd have to come up with a solution. She was cold and hungry. She stood in front of a structure that could give her shelter, at least until tomorrow. She wouldn't prove how stupid she was by turning around and traipsing back along the trail to face God-knows-what when she reached the road.

The decision made, she climbed onto the porch and hunted for a key. She was much shorter than Ben, but if she stretched on her tiptoes as far as possible, she could run her fingers along the top of the door. She came up empty-handed. She searched for rocks or objects on the porch under which he could have hidden a key, without success. Glancing around, she spotted the ice house and bogged through the snow to investigate.

After a few minutes Tori shouted in triumph. She found a key under a can just inside the door. She grinned with satisfaction when the door of the cabin swung open. As she stamped the snow off her boots, she had a strange sensation, as if she'd come home. The interior looked the same as when she'd left it, making her wonder if Ben had ever returned after taking her to the city. She realized she'd never asked him how long it'd be before he'd go back to his cabin.

Tori's breath fogged in front of her, and she knew she had to light a fire in the wood stove. Her Girl Scout training was long ago, but she'd make a good attempt. Luckily, the wood bin was full, and there was a healthy supply of kindling and newspaper at hand. She found some matches and set to work. Shortly, she sat back to admire her efforts.

Tori dragged a chair close to the stove and stayed there until the numbness left her extremities, and she could remove her coat. She explored the cupboards for something to eat and was happy to find a supply of canned goods. Further searching unveiled a manual can opener, which was difficult to master, but she was finally able to open a can of beans. She set the can on top of the stove and had a simple, much-appreciated, hot meal.

CHAPTER 18

The man didn't say a word as he listened to Jeff. The story didn't take long. Tori had come across the damning evidence, realized what had gone on, assumed she was being watched, and slipped out the back of the apartment building unseen. They could only speculate how long she'd been gone.

It was Chantal who'd found the framed photograph lying on the floor of her office, the glass shattered. There was no sign of Tori, nor her bag of meager possessions. Chantal also noticed her warmest coat and boots were missing. Searching further, she discovered some cash from her night-table drawer had disappeared.

Chantal didn't mind that she'd been robbed. On the contrary, it comforted her to know Tori had warm clothing and a bit of money in her pockets. Chantal's insides were gnawed by guilt and worry. She felt it was a small sacrifice to make if it helped to protect Tori from the harsh winter elements and keep her safe.

The dominant emotion among the people in that stark, impersonal room was anxiety. Everyone grasped that it was essential to find Tori as soon as possible. There was no telling what she might do in her present state of mind. She could fall into the wrong hands, and everything they'd worked so hard to achieve would slip through their fingers.

There wasn't any shouting or finger-pointing. It was too late for that. They had to keep their emotions under control and decide how best to get their hands on their escapee. She had up to a three-hour lead on them. Had she left the city? Was she on her way back to Florida? Was she hiding somewhere until she found the opportunity to make her next move? All they knew was that she was angry and emotional, and that transformed her into a volatile weapon.

Upon the discovery of her disappearance, they'd searched the train and bus stations, along with the airlines. Much as expected, their efforts were fruitless. They knew her funds were limited, thus decreasing her chances of leaving the city.

The boss shifted his cool, blue eyes to Jeff.

"So, where would she go?"

He spoke in French, calmly and fluidly, but the people in the room recognized that he was anything but calm. He was disappointed they had again allowed something to go wrong. Heads would roll if this last mistake meant the downfall of the operation to which they'd devoted so many months of work.

Jeff leaned against the windowsill, his hands in his pockets, staring at the floor in front of his feet. He shook his head.

"She doesn't know anyone here, and I can almost guarantee she doesn't trust anyone here."

As the last words fell from his lips, his eyes sharpened, and he lifted his head to encompass the gathering in the room. They all waited expectantly, knowing he had a plan.

CHAPTER 19

With some effort, Tori dragged the mattress off the twin bed in the back bedroom and settled it in front of the wood stove. She didn't like the idea of sleeping in the small, dark room by herself. The last time she'd been there, Ben had slept in the other bed and Riley had been with her. Now, the one place that gave her warmth and comfort was the stove, so while there was still a bit of daylight, she set up a small living area for herself in one corner of the cabin.

She refused to dwell on what she'd do the next day or the day after that. She knew she couldn't stay here indefinitely. Ben could fish and hunt for food. He had the experience to survive for weeks at a time in the bush. But, Tori was aware that she had neither the knowledge or the physical strength required to live in the wilderness, despite the many amenities available to her. She didn't even know how to light the propane stove or lanterns. For the moment, all she had was a kerosene lamp and a few candles to provide light, and she used them sparingly.

There was a limited supply of canned goods on the shelves and, although she realized there was meat in the ice house, she'd eat it only as a last resort. Knowing she'd been betrayed by Chantal made it easier to steal from her, but she didn't want to deplete Ben's inventory of food and supplies while she hid in his cabin. She'd have to find another solution to her problem. In the meantime, she took advantage of her solitude to lick her many wounds.

As night descended, Tori added another log to the stove and burrowed underneath the covers. There was nothing else to do here, alone in the isolated woods, and she wondered again about the man who chose to spend so much time here with just his dog for company.

Sometime later, Tori opened her eyes to see it was still dark in the cabin, with a faint sliver of moonlight sneaking in through the curtained windows. She didn't know what had caused her to awaken. It wasn't cold - there was a warm glow coming from the stove - and there hadn't been any sharp noises.

Then she heard it. A distant buzzing. Tori sat up, her heart pounding. She recognized the sound. It was a snowmobile. She felt a surge of relief, but she grabbed hold of it and reined it in. It was possible it wasn't Ben. The trail was visible and accessible to anyone, and she'd been followed here by Danny's friends before.

She'd have to be careful. Tori fumbled her way to the corner of the room to hide out of sight behind the sofa. She wished she had a weapon, but there wasn't time to find one, and she couldn't see her way around the cabin without lighting a candle and drawing attention to herself.

The sound of the machine grew louder until it spluttered to a stop outside the door. Heavy footsteps climbed the stairs onto the wooden porch, accompanied by other lighter, faster steps, and her heart leapt with hope.

A current of cold air wove its way into the room as she was confronted by an excited Riley. She wrapped her arms around his neck and gave him a quick hug before she lifted herself from the floor and faced the tall man framed in the doorway. The moonlight was behind him and cast his face in shadow. She sensed his stillness, knowing he was surprised, but hopefully not disappointed, to see her.

"Ben, I'm so happy you're here. I didn't know what I was going to do."

She took several steps toward him but stopped when his face came into focus, faintly lit by the moonlight. She gasped, her hand going to her throat.

"No!"

CHAPTER 20

Chantal had joined the group, willing to do her part, but after a few moments, the boss pulled her aside.

"You're going to have to calm down, Chantal."

"I am calm," she said, but she knew the combination of guilt and worry for Tori had carried her energy level to a new high.

He laughed without humor.

"Yes, you're calm. Calm like a rabbit thrown into a wolf's den."

"It's my fault she's gone. I have to find her."

"It's not your fault. It's not even René's fault, and he was the one who was supposed to keep track of her. We all made mistakes. Now we all have to fix them. The next time we get our hands on her, she won't be getting away again, and we won't be handling her like she's precious china. I'm not taking any more chances with her."

Chantal grimaced, but she was in agreement. This had gone far enough. They were at a point where they had to get much tougher with Tori. Time was running out.

Chapter 21

Tori gathered her thoughts and forced her limbs into action. Without caring that she wore neither coat nor boots, she skirted the large, silent figure and headed for the open door. Her progress was abruptly halted. An arm clamped around her waist and picked her effortlessly off the floor, her arms and legs flailing.

"Let me go. Put me down."

Tori aimed for his face with her swinging elbows, but he reached around and held her arms to her sides. She kicked at him and had the satisfaction of hearing his muffled grunts of pain as her feet connected with his body.

The next thing she knew, she lay face-down on the sofa with his heavy weight on top of her body, her legs and arms pinned.

"Stop it. You're the one that's going to get hurt, not me. You're not going anywhere, Tori. Not this time."

His voice was gruff and familiar, yet somehow different. Tori was driven by fury. She wasn't conscious of fear or anxiety. Her mind couldn't sort out why he was here, or how he'd found her. She trembled with anger.

"I know you're upset, but you have to understand you have to give us what we want. There's nowhere for you to go, and I've got all the time in the world. It'd be a lot easier for both of us if you calmed down and cooperated."

"Easier? Why should I make it easier for you? You're just a lying, cheating, two-faced bastard. I will never in my life do anything for you."

"Fine. Don't do it for me. Do it for the rest of the world."

As he spoke, the man loosened his grip on the prostrate woman and moved away from her, putting enough distance between them to avoid being kicked or beaten again.

She glared at him malevolently, watching as he lit the lanterns on the wall.

"The world needs to be protected from people like *you*," Tori retorted.

When Riley came over and put his head on her knee, she absentmindedly stroked the top of his head. Then, in sudden realization, she stared at the animal, and a hundred questions whirled through her mind.

"Why do you have Riley? How did you know I was here? You got to Ben somehow, didn't you? Did you hurt him?"

The expression on the man's face softened with both chagrin and sympathy.

"Tori...," he said softly.

She understood what it was about his voice that was both familiar and different. He spoke without a French accent. She focused on him, taking in his build, the color of his eyes, and the absence of eyeglasses.

Tori heard the clicking noise in her head as pieces of the puzzle snapped into place. Her eyes widened in horror, both at the shock of the truth and the depth of her gullibility. She couldn't speak. She shook her head in useless denial, but there was no denying the evidence that lay before her. And, the monumental size of the betrayal that had been erected around her.

The man she knew as Mario took a few steps toward her, his right hand outstretched. She moved farther away from him, again trembling with rage.

"Don't touch me. Don't you ever touch me again."

"I know you're angry, and I don't blame you. I'd like to talk to you about it. I'd like to explain."

His voice was calm and soothing, but she'd have none of it.

"Angry? Angry doesn't even come close to what I'm feeling. I...I can't believe it. Right from the beginning, it was you."

Abruptly, Tori swiveled, grabbed her coat and hat from the rack behind her, and through tear-filled eyes, searched for her boots. Spotting them near the door, she took two steps toward them before he grabbed her arm.

"I can't let you go."

Without breaking her momentum, she swung around with her arm raised. Her clenched fist hit him accurately across the jaw. Caught by surprise, his head snapped sideways, and his grip momentarily loosened. Tori didn't miss her chance.

Grabbing her boots as she passed, she threw open the door and ran onto the snow-covered porch. At some level, she felt the shock of the cold on her feet, but she didn't care. She ran, knowing he wouldn't be far behind her and she had to put distance between them.

An unintelligible shout came from the direction of the cabin, and Tori was soon flat on her stomach with her face in the snow, four large paws on her back. She had a terrible sense of *déjà vu* and knew she'd been defeated by the last living being she thought she could trust.

She was yanked to her feet and thrust toward the cabin with such force she stumbled and would've fallen if not for the hand that grabbed the back of her coat and righted her. She spun around on him furiously.

"Stop pushing me around," she said through clenched teeth.

He didn't say a word, but Tori saw by his expression he was no longer in the mood to be calm and soothing. His face, complete with reddened cheek, was etched with anger, his jaw locked shut. She knew he fought to control himself. Stupidly, she chose to ignore all those signs.

"I have never in my life met anyone more despicable than you. You...you are the lowest of the low. I hate you. I despise you, and if you ever touch me again, I'll kill you."

Tori was driven by both loathing and anger. She hesitated for a moment to catch her breath, but when she opened her mouth to yell at him, her words were cut off. The wind was forced from her lungs as his shoulder sank into her stomach, and he picked her up and carried her to the cabin.

Tori didn't want to go without a fight. She couldn't kick him because of the grip he had on her knees. But, she battered his back with her fists until she realized he perceived little or nothing of her efforts through the protection of his heavy coat. Determined not to give up, she twisted her body to the side to grab his hair, but she was rewarded with a painful twist to her ankle as soon as she moved. It served to infuriate her all the more.

From Tori's upside-down view of the world, she saw the cabin loom closer and watched powerlessly as he climbed the steps to the door. She realized he wouldn't let her escape again, and because she'd angered him, he wouldn't show her any mercy.

She was right. He set her down, none too gently, in a hard, wooden chair, and bent until his face was a couple of inches from hers. She met his eyes, glare for glare, but when he spoke, his voice was deep and ominous.

"If you ever try anything like that again you'll regret it, Tori. I promise you that. I've never condoned violence toward women, but in this instance, I'm beginning to think it may be justified."

She opened her mouth to respond indignantly, but he reached up and grabbed her chin in his hand with a viselike grip.

"No. You're going to shut up. I mean it. You're going to listen to me, whether you like it or not."

Tori knew she was no match for Mario, or whoever the hell he was, but he could talk until he was blue in the face, and she'd never be taken in by him again. She'd never trust him or feel anything but contempt for him.

She responded to his remarks by clamping her mouth firmly shut and staring at a spot on the wall over his left shoulder. If he was put off by her attitude, he gave no indication.

"First of all, you have to realize I was just doing my job."

At this, she bristled with rage and shoved her hands under her thighs to resist the urge to scratch out his eyes. She couldn't hold back her rebuke.

"That's some job you have there. Is it written in your job description that you have to sleep with your victims? Do you get worker's comp if you happen to pull a groin muscle while fulfilling the demands of your *job*?"

"That isn't what I meant, and you know it," he said, running his fingers through his hair.

She turned a venomous glower on him.

"I know nothing about you, absolutely nothing. Except that you're a lying piece of shit."

She saw him draw a deep breath and stare up at the ceiling. Ignoring her last comment, he spoke in a low voice.

"We've been working on this operation for a long time, and when you fell into my lap...I mean, when you came here, and I grasped the connection between the two of you, I had to pursue it. I was obliged to. You have to realize that. What happened between us should never have happened. I don't mean I didn't want it to happen," he hastened to add, "but I shouldn't have let it go so far. I'm sorry if I hurt you, and I can understand you're angry about it, but I wasn't using you. You have to trust me when I say everything I've done has ultimately been to protect you."

She swung her disbelieving glare to his face.

"It's true," he said. "Yes, I did what I had to do for the sake of my job, but I was also watching out for you and trying to keep you from danger. That's why I stayed so close. That's why I had you set up with Chantal. That's why I arranged to be with you as much as I could. And if I couldn't, Chantal was there."

"Don't forget Sébastien," she said, her voice dripping with sarcasm. "And maybe even the Bonhomme Carnival was in on the whole thing. You guys must have had quite a laugh at my expense."

"Of course not," he said. "Do you think I enjoyed this? Do you think I got a kick out of lying to you? I would've preferred to be straight with you up front."

"Then why weren't you?" she said.

"Because we didn't know which side of the fence you were sitting on."

"And now you do?"

He hesitated.

"I don't believe you're directly involved in the illegal drug trade," he said.

"Well, thank you for that enthusiastic vote of confidence," she said acerbically.

He ignored her biting remark and continued, "However, we know there's a connection between you and Danny Wilcox, and we'd appreciate whatever help you could give us."

She grunted.

"In other words, the cops are getting nowhere, and they want little old me to hand over Danny on a silver platter."

His eyes narrowed on her face.

"It isn't true that we're getting nowhere in this case, but we've been spinning our wheels for too long. Things would be much easier if we had your full cooperation."

"Really? Like you gave me your full cooperation when you tricked me into believing you were a nice guy named Ben, coming to my rescue and taking care of me for a few days. Then delivering me to the city where you and your friends could keep an eye on me. And I suppose that was what you considered full cooperation when you transformed yourself into a sweet guy named Mario, so ready to show me the delights of Quebec City while setting me up in his 'sister's' apartment. What is Chantal to you anyway? Is she just another cop, or is she your girlfriend? That's it, isn't it? That's why she was upset when you kissed me and when she found out you'd slept with me. Or is she so used to your *job requirements* that she's able to ignore them? You're a consummate actor, you know. You missed your calling. You could've had a wonderful career in Hollywood. You and all your friends. You managed to pull the wool over my eyes."

"We have to be good at what we do. When we're dealing with people like Wilcox and his gang, we have to work well undercover, or we wouldn't survive very long." He hesitated for a moment. "You had us worried when you took off like that, Tori."

"Did you expect me to hang around after seeing that picture of you with Chantal and a whole group of people at a police function?"

"You could've given us the opportunity to explain. Leaving like that was a dangerous choice."

"In your view, perhaps. In mine, I have no desire to conspire with the police."

He opened his mouth to respond, but before he had a chance, Tori continued.

"And Sébastien? It wasn't a coincidence that he picked me up on the side of the road that day. You knew I was there."

"Yes, we followed you. We were preparing to move in when we were spotted by someone. Everything fell apart after that."

"Fell apart? I was almost killed."

"I know, and I'm sorry you had to go through that, but we underestimated Danny's surveillance team. We were still far from the actual location when we were sighted. We knew something had gone wrong, and pulled out as quickly as possible. I was worried sick about you."

She snorted derisively.

His expression was wary, while hers remained angry and suspicious. She broke the silence.

"What is your name, anyway? Ben or Mario?"

"Neither. My name is Jean-François Lafond, but people call me Jeff."

Tori drew her brows together.

"That sounds familiar to me."

"You saw it on some mail I had on my kitchen counter that day in Valcartier."

Her eyes widened in dawning comprehension.

"That was your house. Of course."

It all made perfect sense to her now. She folded her arms over her chest and leaned back in her chair, crossing her legs.

"Why didn't you tell me your real name when you pulled me out of that lake? Surely, you didn't know who I was before that happened."

"No, I didn't know who you were. But after the visit from your two friends, I knew you were connected to Danny Wilcox."

Her eyebrows rose at the mention of the two thugs on the snowmobile. She waited as he continued.

"At first, I didn't appreciate having my privacy invaded, and I used an alias as a means of protecting it. I was taking some time off after a long undercover case."

She glared at him, shaking her head.

"You pulled a good one on me. I never made the connection between the nice, hairy, gentle man who helped me out and the clean-shaven Clark Kent who took me under his wing. You even managed to acquire a French accent."

Before he started to think she had complimented him, she burst his bubble.

"You are a bastard. I didn't think it was possible for me to hate anyone this much. Of all the terrible things I've experienced in the last two weeks, what you did to me was the absolute worst."

"Tori, you have to understand I didn't do this because I wanted to…"

"I don't care," she said heatedly. "I don't care about your reasons for doing what you did. It was wrong. And you can dress it up whatever way you want, it's still going to be ugly. Don't *ever* rationalize it to me."

CHAPTER 22

Jeff was taken aback by the intensity of Tori's words, but he realized, in her eyes, he could never justify what he'd done. That realization was a bitter pill to swallow. He'd never wanted to hurt her, but he had. And not only had he hurt her, but he'd turned any sentiments she may have had for him into bone-deep hatred and mistrust. He experienced the dreadful and disheartening confirmation that he'd reaped what he'd sown and, for the first time in his career, he really hated what he did for a living.

Nevertheless, Jeff had a duty to perform, and even though he might hate the means, the end was a noble cause. He knew he couldn't change Tori's perceptions about what she felt had been done to her, but he could and would continue to protect her to the best of his ability. He also wanted to make her understand the need to capture the top drug lord in the province of Quebec.

"Tori, we want your help. We need you to lead us to Wilcox."

"You can't do that on your own?" she said, not bothering to hide her disdain.

Jeff sighed.

"As you know, he's elusive. Every time we get close, he picks up and pulls out before we can get hold of him."

He saw a glimmer of satisfied triumph in her eyes before she hid it behind an angry mask. He had a question to ask her, and he mentally braced himself. He was certain he wouldn't like the answer.

"What's your connection to Wilcox?"

He could see the ice chips shoot from her eyes.

"That's none of your business," she said firmly.

"All right, then. How about this? Can we count on your full cooperation?"

He asked this question with an air of resignation. Her answer was obvious before the words were out of her mouth.

"Go to hell."

It was daylight when Jeff fell into a deep sleep in his bed in the back bedroom. He needed to get some rest. He'd been up for almost twenty-four hours. The first part of his day had been spent with his co-workers devising a strategy to find Tori. Then, he'd traveled through the bush in the darkness to reach the cabin before having his disturbing and futile encounter with Tori.

"I'm going to lie down and catch some sleep," he'd told a sulky-looking Tori. His statement was met with stony silence.

"You're going to have to come to the bedroom with me."

"I will not," Tori said, her body stiff with outrage. "If you think…"

"No, that's not what I'm thinking. I just want to keep an eye on you, that's all."

"How do you expect to do that and sleep at the same time?" she said with a smirk.

Her expression morphed to shock, closely followed by anger, when he slid a set of handcuffs out of his back pocket.

"You're not serious."

"Very serious," he said with a grimace.

•   •   •

Jeff was the recipient of a stream of verbal abuse. Nevertheless, he accepted it as his due and resigned himself to the fact that he'd fallen from his pedestal, breaking every bone in his body on the way down.

Fortunately for him, after Tori's initial wrath was spent, he could shut out the occasional invective she hurled at him and get some much-needed rest. When he woke a couple of hours later, he was momentarily disoriented until he twisted his head toward the other bed and saw Tori glowering at him.

Jeff smiled at her warily, hoping to see some softening on her part. He received a look of such anger he decided he'd never let her have access to a sharp object. She'd be happy to cut out his heart and feed it to the fish in the frozen lake.

"I want you to take me back to the city," she said in a voice that was as hard as the metal frame of his bed.

"I intend to do just that," he said, pushing himself into a sitting position.

Tori nodded, appearing to accept his words at face value, but he knew he needed to clarify them. He was sure she wouldn't appreciate him keeping her in the dark again.

"Tori, when I take you back to the city, I'll be taking you to police headquarters."

She reacted as he'd expected. She pierced him with a glare and clenched her fists at her sides.

"You will not," she said.

"I have to."

"You have no reason."

"I do have a reason. You've been associating with a known criminal, and it's within our rights to take you in for questioning."

"I also have rights," Tori said indignantly.

"Yes, you do. If you want to have a lawyer present, it's your right to have one."

"A lawyer? I'm innocent. I haven't done anything against the law."

"I didn't say you had. We aren't accusing you of anything. We just need to ask you a few questions."

"With the goal of capturing Danny," she finished for him.

He spread his hands out by his sides.

"Of course, that's our goal. He's a dangerous felon wanted by the authorities for a number of crimes ranging from drug trafficking to murder. We've been working to get this guy for two years, ever since he first came on the scene, and you could be the one to give us our big break."

"It's time you understand I don't want to help you. As a matter of fact, I have no intention of ever helping you... not ever."

"In that case, you should understand you could be brought up on charges of obstructing justice, and aiding and abetting a wanted felon."

"Are you threatening me?"

"No, I'm warning you."

•   •   •

Jeff prepared something to eat before they left for their return journey, but he was careful not to turn his back on Tori. He'd removed the handcuffs and given her the freedom to roam the cabin, but he didn't trust her not to attempt something foolish. She wouldn't be able to get far on foot, but he couldn't allow her to blindside him with a heavy frying pan, or some other weapon, and have the opportunity to steal his snowmobile.

Even Riley seemed to perceive a change in the atmosphere, and Jeff was pleased to see the dog had retained his loyalty to his master. The animal no longer approached Tori to be petted. Instead, he kept a close eye on her, as if he knew she could escape again.

Tori refused to speak to either of them. She picked at her meal while gazing out the window in stony silence. Jeff abandoned any notion of carrying on a conversation with her. The set of her jaw and the coldness of her eyes showed feelings that had gone beyond anger into the realm of bitter hatred.

It was a relief for him when it was time to get dressed for their departure. Soon, they were ready and, with a last scan of the cabin to reassure himself everything was in order, Jeff led Tori outside and headed for the snowmobile.

He started the ignition and sat down, leaving plenty of room for Tori to be seated behind him. When she didn't sit, he looked up to see her staring at the seat in distaste. It took him a moment to comprehend it was the idea of having to hold onto him that caused the look. The realization angered him.

"Sit down and hold onto me, or I'll put you in front of me and handcuff you to the handlebars."

Tori gave him a toxic glare before she sat on the seat and gingerly grasped the sides of his coat, being careful not to make contact with his body. Out of spite, Jeff gritted his teeth and pressed his thumb down on the accelerator, making the machine jump ahead like a racehorse out of the starting gate.

Her shriek echoed in his ear, and her legs lifted into the air until she grabbed hold of his coat and righted herself. She wrapped her arms around his midsection, and he smiled with satisfaction, even though he knew what he'd done was childish and petty.

They took the same route they'd taken the last time, arriving at his house in Valcartier and using his pickup truck to make the trip into the city, leaving an exhausted Riley behind. Jeff expected a silent trip into the city but was surprised by a string of questions from Tori.

"So? Who is Chantal? She isn't your sister, is she?"

"No, she isn't."

"Is she your girlfriend?" she asked, returning to her unanswered question.

He threw her an affronted look.

"No, she isn't. How low do you think I am? Never mind, don't answer that." He should never have given her an opening like that. She'd love to tell him what she thought of his morals. "Chantal is my partner."

"She's a cop."

It wasn't a question; it was an affirmation.

"Yes."

"An undercover cop, like you?"

"Yes."

"Were you working undercover when you were disguised as Ben and stayed at the cabin? Whose cabin is that?"

Jeff sighed. He'd rather not go into long explanations about his life, but guilt drove him to answer her questions as honestly as possible.

"No. I told you. I wasn't working. I was enjoying some peace and relaxation after a long case." He added a thick layer of sarcasm to the words 'peace and relaxation'. "And, it's my cabin, by the way."

"But you made up the name 'Ben'?"

"Benoit is my father's name, and yes, I decided to use it instead of my own, for privacy's sake."

"What were you doing there?"

"Relaxing." He didn't know how many ways he could say it.

"Relaxing?"

Tori's idea of relaxing obviously didn't involve holing up in a cabin in the wilderness having to survive on wild game and fish pulled from a frozen lake.

Jeff could hear the uncertainty in her voice.

"Yes, believe it or not, I find it relaxing to spend time at the cabin. It makes a nice change from my normal routine."

"Your normal routine being...what? Dressing up as a bad guy, or a good guy, depending on the situation? Sleeping with women along the way if you judge it'll advance your investigation?"

"Stop it. That wasn't the way it was."

"Well, that's the way it looked. And that's the way it felt."

She swung her head to the window to hide the tears that sprang to her eyes, but he heard them in her voice.

Jeff ran his hand through his hair. He was at a loss as to what to say to reassure her. He had to remember that he now dealt with her in a professional capacity, and it would be that way until the case was over.

"Is Chantal in love with you?"

Her question took him by surprise.

"No, of course not. Why would you say that?"

"Why was she angry with you?"

Jeff hesitated. He didn't know how to phrase the answer without incriminating himself.

"What I did was wrong – from an ethical point of view. I should never have been…intimate with a…potential suspect."

"Potential suspect?" Tori's brain evidently snagged on those two words.

"Like it or not, Tori, that's what you are. As far as the police are concerned, you could very well be an accessory."

She opened her mouth to respond before clamping it shut. She'd apparently realized it wouldn't help for her to lose her temper and say something she'd regret, in particular if she was a 'potential suspect'.

Tori maintained a stern silence for the rest of the trip to the city, probably mulling over the information Jeff had given her. He understood she had trouble coming to terms with the man sitting next to her.

He'd gone from the kind, scruffy-looking Ben to the bespectacled, amiable Mario to the tough, accusing cop. Not only had he changed his appearance at every turn, but his personality had undergone a remodeling each time. It was part of his job to make those changes seamlessly. He'd have to work hard to convince her he was really a combination of all of the above.

Within half an hour, they pulled into the Sûreté du Québec headquarters. The Sûreté was the police force for the entire province of Quebec, but they worked with the municipal police forces and the Royal Canadian Mounted Police when the need arose.

Jeff shut off the truck and twisted in his seat to look at Tori, despite the fact his view was of the back of her head as she determinedly stared out the window. He sighed in exasperation.

"We can do this the easy way by walking in there together and getting this over with. Or, we can do it the hard way, and I can cuff you and haul you in like a common criminal. How do you want to do it?"

She didn't speak. She pivoted her head to glare at him with contempt, but he saw the gleam of tears in her eyes before she pushed her door open and stepped out of the truck. He felt a sharp stab in his heart. He preferred her railing at him and throwing heavy objects than having to endure her bitter silence.

Chapter 23

Tori sat stoically on the bench in police headquarters. It was in a hallway with several closed doors on each side. She was alone except for a bored-looking police officer at a desk, so she took advantage of the privacy to study her surroundings. She'd never been inside a police station before, her knowledge limited to what she'd seen on television.

It was much quieter than she'd expected. She'd pictured phones ringing incessantly and people bustling around chasing after bad guys. Instead, everyone went about their business with a minimum of fuss.

Tori closed her eyes and leaned her head back against the wall. The stress of the past several days went straight down to her bones. She took a deep breath and relished the few minutes she had to herself, out of Jeff's presence.

She couldn't keep her emotions under control when she was near him. She was angry and hurt. The worst of it was that she knew it was her fault. It's true he was doing his job, something he'd been trained to do and was paid to do. She could admit it to herself, even though she strongly disagreed with his methods.

She, however, had been stupidly naïve, unable to see through his carefully-constructed act. When Tori set out on her undertaking, it had been a very personal one. She'd been determined to do it on her own, without involving or becoming involved with anyone else, but she'd allowed herself to be distracted, and that was a mistake for which she was solely responsible.

Now, she had no choice but to strengthen her resolve tenfold and resist any pressure that could be and would be put on her.

On the heels of that thought, one of the doors along the hallway opened, and Jeff emerged, followed by an older man. He was at least six inches shorter than Jeff and had the beginnings of a paunch that strained his belt. His expression was grim as he advanced toward her. When he reached her side, and they made eye contact, his piercing blue eyes softened with a smile that appeared, at least on the surface, to be genuine.

"Hello, Mademoiselle Anderson. I'm Captain Bouchard. I'm pleased to meet you."

His voice was heavily accented but pleasantly deep and warm. Tori responded with a faint smile. She couldn't bring herself to state she was also pleased to meet him, because, in truth, she'd rather be anywhere else but in this police station.

"If you wouldn't mind, I'd like to take a few moments to ask you some questions."

Bouchard gestured toward one of the closed doors as if inviting her into the drawing room for afternoon tea. He turned and sauntered away, evidently expecting her to follow, which she did. She felt Jeff's presence behind her, but she refused to acknowledge it. Inside the room, Tori sat in the chair across from Captain Bouchard's heavy wooden desk and folded her hands together in her lap, mentally preparing herself for the upcoming inquisition.

"First of all," he said. "I want you to realize you're not under arrest at this moment. You're here for questioning as a possible witness. However, if you'd like to have a lawyer present, you're free to call one."

"I don't want a lawyer, thank you," she said stiffly. She was aware of Jeff sitting in the chair next to her, although she made an effort to shut him out of her thoughts. His chair was pushed back. All she saw in her peripheral vision were his feet stretched out in front of him, crossed at the ankles.

"As you wish," Jeff's boss responded. Tori thought she detected a flicker of relief in his eyes. She was quite certain the police derived no pleasure from dealing with lawyers.

"I'd like to know the nature of your association with Danny Wilcox," the captain asked.

Tori steadied herself. From now on, she had to be strong. She had to resist whatever they'd throw at her. She set her jaw stubbornly.

"I refuse to discuss that subject."

Out of the corner of her eye, Tori saw Jeff's legs unfold as he set his feet flat on the floor, and he leaned toward her, putting his elbows on his knees.

Her resolve stiffened further.

"Mademoiselle Anderson, I must inform you that your cooperation would be greatly appreciated, and it would be much easier for everyone, yourself included, if you answered our questions."

"Then I'm sorry to disappoint you, but I should inform you I have no intention of answering your questions."

She felt rather than saw a sharp movement to her right, but any other action on Jeff's part was stopped by a quick glance from the senior police officer.

Captain Bouchard sighed resignedly and forced a smile.

"Surely you understand we're dealing with a dangerous criminal. Wilcox is wanted for a long list of offenses, including murder. It's my job, and my deepest wish, to remove him from the streets of Québec and see him brought to justice." He paused to let his words sink in. "I believe you're an intelligent woman. I also believe you have a sense of morals. If you could answer a few simple questions that may lead us to Wilcox, you'd be doing a great service for the security of a lot of people."

His expression was pleasant and expectant. Tori sat in front of him, unmoved.

"Mademoiselle Anderson?" Bouchard said.

"I can't help you," Tori replied in a flat voice.

"I think you *can* help us."

"All right then, I *won't* help you."

His eyes narrowed on her face, and Tori sensed Jeff shifting restlessly in the chair beside her.

"I believe you had certain business dealings with a man by the name of Yvon Picard," the captain said.

Tori bit her tongue. She wanted to assert she'd never had any kind of *business* dealings with Yvon, but she was determined to remain silent. The captain didn't give the impression that he noticed.

"We know you met with him on at least one occasion, that being two days ago when he transported you to Wilcox's latest hideaway." He paused to give Tori an opportunity to respond but continued after a moment. "As you know, our attempt to apprehend him failed on that day. He is very adept at disappearing."

Again, he paused and cleared his throat before going on.

"Unfortunately for him, Yvon was not able to escape."

Tori eyes widened in surprise and focused on Bouchard's face. What did he mean? She couldn't bring herself to ask the question, but she didn't have to.

"You see, we found Picard. We found him in the forest, not far from the building Wilcox had been hiding in. And his throat had been...what is the English word?...slit?"

Bile climbed up her throat, and she closed her eyes to shut out the image. Instead, it became clearer in her mind's eye. She'd disliked Yvon. He'd been able to make her skin crawl with a single glance, but the fact that he was dead – had been murdered – shocked her to the core. She didn't resist when Jeff took her hand and held it. She was almost unaware of the act.

Two men. Two men had died that day. They'd both been criminals, but she was indirectly responsible for the deaths of both of them. Tori wavered in her chair. One of Jeff's hands came across her shoulder to support her, and she was incapable of resisting. Her thoughts swam, surging from Yvon to the nameless man who had tumbled into the white-water river. He hadn't been mentioned by the captain, and she could no longer hold back the information. She felt as if she would implode.

"There was another man," she whispered, her attention fixed unseeingly on the table in front of her.

Chapter 24

"Another man? Who? What do you mean?"

Jeff asked the questions in a soft voice. He saw how the news about Yvon affected her and didn't want to make this any more difficult than necessary. But his mind leapt with the hope that she'd come across with a snippet of information that could lead to a breakthrough.

Jeff was desperate to put an end to this case and the subject of Danny Wilcox, although the reasons for his desperation had gone from being professional to being very personal. It didn't matter, as long as they could put it all behind them and move on with their lives.

"He...he tried to kill me...I swear."

Tori's face was a mask of anguish and pleading. She reached out to Jeff for the first time since she'd discovered his true identity, and his heart twisted, feeling her agony. He forced himself to concentrate on what she said.

"Who, Tori?"

"I don't know his name. I just know he was going to throw me into the river. But...but he fell. So did I, but I rolled into a tree." She shook her head numbly. "I didn't do it on purpose, I swear."

Jeff stared at his boss and received a nod in response. Jeff understood what the nod meant, but it didn't make it any easier.

"Tori, we're going to have to take a statement from you about what happened that day."

Tori came to life then, the haze clearing from her eyes. She was sharp enough to understand they could use this information against her, and he knew she wanted to be careful not to fall into any of their traps.

"Yes, I'll make a statement about what happened between myself and that man."

Captain Bouchard interrupted.

"We'll need a complete statement about everything that transpired that day."

"I won't give it," Tori replied, stubbornly.

"That would constitute an obstruction of justice." Again, he paused. "I could have you arrested. I don't know if you've ever spent time in a jail cell, but it's not considered to be very pleasant."

Tori didn't respond, but Jeff saw a muscle tightening in her jaw. He decided he'd been silent long enough.

"Tori, please cooperate. A few questions, that's all. All we're searching for is a lead, any kind of lead."

Her gaze spun to his face, and he was taken aback by the coldness in her eyes. Jeff experienced a fresh wave of frustration. He wanted to shake her. She once again focused on the desk between her and Bouchard. Jeff shifted to face his boss.

"Maybe we should think about house arrest," he said. This earned him another hate-filled look from Tori.

Captain Bouchard considered this suggestion for a moment and nodded.

"Yes, perhaps that would be the best idea for now. We can set her up in a safe house with Chantal again."

"No."

Both men stared at her, surprised at her sudden outburst.

"I won't have anything more to do with Chantal or him," she said, tossing her head in Jeff's direction. "And I won't stay in any safe house, as you call it."

The captain leaned forward, resting his elbows on the table in front of him, piercing her with an intense glare and speaking in a steady, low-pitched voice.

"I'm afraid you have two choices. It is that, or a jail cell that you can share with some of our less desirable citizens."

Chapter 25

Tori sat in the front seat of the car, with her arms folded across her chest, fighting to contain the rage that coursed through her. She wanted to scream and rant at the man who sat in the driver's seat. Although it might make her feel better, it'd serve no purpose. He'd proven to be just as stubborn as she.

Both Jeff and Bouchard insisted they had no intention of releasing her, declaring she had the two choices offered to her. When she stated she wanted a lawyer after all, they were quick to oblige her. A lawyer was summoned, and after a long talk with Jeff and his boss, he politely informed her it'd be in her best interest to accept the offer of a safe house, both as a question of personal security and as a gesture of cooperation from the police department. Scornfully, she accepted defeat. She hated it, but she accepted it.

Now, Tori was on her way to her place of confinement with the man who was her new nemesis. She desperately wanted to be rid of him and this city. For all its beauty, it had brought her nothing but misery. Even when she'd enjoyed herself with 'Mario', it had all been a sham, created by Jeff and his circle of treacherous friends. Now, she had to endure their company even longer. They may have won the first battle, but she'd hope to win the war.

Tori hadn't paid attention to their journey so far, not caring about her destination. When Jeff slowed for an exit, she saw the name 'Stoneham' on the sign. She checked out her surroundings as they drove through the town, seeing its quaintness, a mixture of old and new. There were family farms that had survived many generations nestled side-by-side with modern houses. There was an old church and cemetery rubbing elbows with a bank, a pharmacy, and a grocery store.

As they drove along a side road, she saw something she'd only ever seen on television. On her left, there was a ski hill with a smattering of log buildings at its foot. People were carried up the hill on lifts like a human assembly line. Skiers and snowboarders descended the long, white slopes, some at a leisurely pace, crisscrossing the hill, while others came down at astonishing speeds.

Jeff slowed the truck, undoubtedly noticing her fascination.

"Would you like to try it? I can take you if you like."

Tori heard the vein of hopefulness in his voice. He'd enjoy a truce, if not a full-blown reconciliation, between them, but he should know from the start he'd set himself up for a big disappointment.

"No, I would not like, thank you very much," Tori said.

Again, she folded her arms across her chest and stubbornly turned her head to stare out the window, seeing a row of condos and ski chalets on the side of the street opposite the hill.

Tori didn't have long to wait to discover their destination. Jeff pulled into the driveway of one of the condos, and Tori realized she'd have a full view of the ski station while she was confined. Maybe it was the best choice after all, she reflected. She doubted the view would've been as nice from a jail cell.

Jeff carried her bag into the condo, and she couldn't help noticing he carried a small overnight bag of his own. Despite her vow to speak to him as little as possible, she couldn't stop herself from blurting out the question.

"You're not staying here, are you?"

"Part of the time, I will be. Chantal and I, and maybe someone else, will be taking shifts staying with you."

"Watching me, you mean."

He looked at her sharply.

"Yes, we'll be watching you – for your own good."

She laughed humorlessly.

"For my own good? You mean, to make sure I don't escape."

He shrugged and took off his outerwear.

"That too."

"Why you? Why couldn't they have found someone else? And why here? Surely this place must cost a fortune. The Quebec police force must have a very healthy budget to be able to keep places like this as a safe house."

Jeff answered her last question first.

"Not at all. It belongs to a friend of mine. He offered it to me. I presumed it'd be more pleasant for you."

She didn't know how to respond to that statement. Was she supposed to thank him, her jailer?

"And as for why me? Because I volunteered. Of course, I have other duties, but when I'm able, I'll be here."

"Why?" she said again.

Tori didn't know why she asked. She wasn't sure she'd be happy with the answer.

"Because I want to see this through. Because, no matter what you think of me, I want to make sure you're safe. Safe from Danny and all his thugs. And because I'm hoping I can convince you to do what's right."

She stiffened in outrage.

"I *am* doing what's right. You're the one who's in the wrong."

Fury flashed in his eyes. She didn't flinch as he came up to her and grabbed her by her shoulders. She didn't make a sound as he jerked her off her feet until her face was a few inches from his.

"I'm in the wrong? How can you say that when I've dedicated the last two years of my life to getting that murderous criminal off the streets? How can you say that when you're preventing me from doing so? How can you defend him?"

Tori didn't answer him. She couldn't. She stared at him wide-eyed, astounded by the force of his anger. She saw it in his eyes, a mixture of rage and disbelief.

He dragged her against him, pressing his mouth to hers. She wouldn't call it a kiss. It was more of an assault. It was as if he wanted to force his beliefs on her through sheer will and the pressure of his mouth. She didn't resist, nor did she surrender. She didn't make a sound or move a muscle. She stood there, her arms aching from the force of his hands digging into her flesh, and let him vent his feelings. She knew what his reaction would be when he came to his senses.

He pulled away from her. She'd been right. His eyes were filled with guilt and self-loathing. She didn't have to punish him for his behavior. He would punish himself enough. All she did was turn and walk away, down the hallway, searching for a room she could claim as her own for the time being.

CHAPTER 26

That evening, Chantal arrived, having the grace to look sheepish when she greeted Tori and received nothing but a cold glare in return. She came bearing groceries, for which Tori was wordlessly thankful. She was famished, but after exploring the kitchen earlier to find it empty, she refused to ask Jeff what he intended to do about supper.

They hadn't spoken to each other all afternoon. He'd morosely watched television, changing channels without appearing to have any particular goal in mind. She'd come across a bookshelf that was well-stocked with suspense thrillers and mystery novels. She chose one and settled into an easy chair to read, acting as if Jeff didn't exist, which was no easy feat.

The condo was modern and comfortably furnished with black leather couches and chairs. Full-length windows in the living room gave an unrestricted view of the ski hill in front of them.

Tori continued to read while Chantal and Jeff carried on a low-voiced conversation in the kitchen. She was curious about what they talked about, but she avoided making any move that would let them see her interest. Since they spoke in French, she couldn't understand them anyway.

The sound of pots clanging, water running, and drawers opening and closing drifted from the other room. Chantal obviously prepared a meal with her usual gusto. The ultra-modern kitchen was well equipped with stainless steel appliances and all the gadgets and gizmos anyone could want, especially someone who loved to cook as much as Chantal.

Tori wanted to help with the preparations, but the intensity of her stubbornness was stronger than her need to be helpful. She remained in the chair, feigning indifference whenever anyone entered the room.

The atmosphere during the ensuing meal was awkward and stilted. Chantal and Jeff discussed an array of mundane subjects ranging from the weather to ski conditions. Any attempt to draw Tori into the conversation was met with remote silence. The meal was finished without another word spoken, the atmosphere heavy. Jeff and Chantal cleared the table and cleaned the kitchen while Tori returned to her easy chair and her book.

When she was certain she was alone, Tori gazed out the window, enthralled by the brightly-lit ski hill and the people gliding down the slopes, making it seem so easy. The instant one of her captors entered the room, she shifted her attention to her novel, hoping to appear riveted by the story. She'd held it in her hands for hours, and she hadn't made it past the first chapter.

Jeff took his leave shortly after supper, leaving the two women alone. With the exit of her partner, Chantal's mood was unusually guarded and contemplative. Tori was the recipient of many speculative glances. She braced herself for what would come.

"Tori, I have to talk to you about what happened. You need to understand. I was just doing my job. We all were. That doesn't mean we didn't become personally involved, it's just …. Where are you going?"

"To bed. I'm very tired."

Tori knew she was rude, but she couldn't face this now. Her emotions were still too raw, and if she heard one more time that they were 'just doing their job' she'd scream.

"I wanted to talk to you," Chantal said, bewildered.

"There's nothing to talk about. I've listened to the same speech from Jeff. I don't want to hear another version of it from you," Tori said.

Chantal crossed the room and stood face-to-face with Tori.

"You may have heard the same speech from Jeff, but it didn't have the right effect on you. I was hoping you'd see reason if you heard it from me."

Her words angered Tori.

"What makes you assume it would make a difference coming from you? You're no better than he is. What you did was even worse. At least as a woman, I would've expected more from you. I would've expected you to understand. But it was just as easy for you to betray me as it was for him, and I'll never forgive you for that."

Tori spun on her heel and marched into her bedroom, slamming the door behind her. She half-expected Chantal to follow her and insist on continuing their conversation, but all was quiet.

The next morning, Tori woke to the smell of coffee, bacon, and eggs. For a moment, she forgot where she was and why she was here. When her memory returned, she allowed herself a minute of self-pity before she climbed out of bed and got dressed.

As usual, Chantal bustled about, setting the table, draining the bacon, flipping the eggs, and buttering the toast. Neither of the women spoke to each other.

Tori felt a stab of guilt. She was certain Chantal and Jeff weren't expected to wait on her hand and foot, yet she hadn't lifted a finger since coming here. But, she told herself, they were part of the system responsible for holding her against her will. She should be free to go back to Florida.

Breakfast was eaten in uncomfortable silence, and Tori was relieved when it was finished. But, the end of the morning meal signaled the time for the changing of the guard. Tori was dismayed when the front door creaked open and heavy boots stomped on the mat in the entranceway. Jeff had arrived for his shift.

CHAPTER 27

Jeff came into the kitchen with a smile on his face, but it vanished when he saw Tori's glum expression and Chantal's impatience to leave the condo. His partner stood, left the dirty dishes on the table, and rushed to get her coat. She never left a room unless it was pristine. It was a sign that the past twelve hours had been strained, to say the least.

After the door slammed behind Chantal, Jeff turned and saw Tori clearing the table, loading the dishwasher, and cleaning the kitchen counters. At least, that was something. It was better than watching her sit and stare into space, or pretend to read a book.

"How did you sleep?" he said.

"Fine."

"Were you warm enough?"

"Yes."

"Chantal's a great cook, isn't she?"

"Yes."

"Did you two have an argument?"

"No."

"She didn't look very happy."

"Oh."

Jeff thrust his hands into his pockets to prevent said hands from grabbing her and shaking her. He'd never experienced such a depth of frustration with a woman. For that matter, he didn't think he'd ever felt such frustration with another human being, and in his job, he met all kinds.

Jeff went into the living room to watch TV. Listening to the morning news would be a distraction. When Tori walked into the room and sat on the couch, he didn't acknowledge her presence. Two could play at that game, he decided.

As the day wore on, they both became restless. Tori paced between the chair and the window, staring at the ski center across the street. Jeff paced between the living room and the kitchen. He'd open the fridge, peer inside, and close the door again without touching any of the contents. The condo was much too small for two people who didn't get along, he realized.

"So, do you want to do it?" Jeff said.

Tori's eyes widened, and she stared at him with a mixture of shock and incomprehension.

"What?"

"Do you want to try it? Skiing, I mean."

"Skiing?" She let out her breath. "Well...I don't know...I assumed I had to stay in the condo."

Jeff shrugged. "Not necessarily. I don't see any harm in doing a few runs."

"What will Captain Bouchard say?"

"I don't think he'll have a problem with it."

Tori hesitated, biting her lip and staring at the white slopes. It was obvious to Jeff that she'd been entranced by the ski hill since her first glimpse of it.

Her decision made, Tori stood up and faced Jeff.

"Why not?"

"Great," he said, encouraged by her attitude. "I'll check out the equipment."

Jeff disappeared into a storage room and came back several minutes later carrying two sets of skis. He stood them by the door, returned to the room, and came back with boots, poles, and goggles. Tori frowned at the equipment uncertainly. He realized she wouldn't know where she was supposed to start.

"All right, these look like they should fit. Try them on."

Jeff dropped a pair of blue and grey ski boots on the floor. They had a collection of straps and buckles attached to them. Seeing her confusion, he loosened the attachments and set one of the boots in front of her. She slipped her foot in and watched while he adjusted the straps to hold her foot snugly.

"How does that feel?"

"There's something wrong. I can't straighten my leg."

He chuckled. "You're not supposed to straighten your leg. The boot purposely bends your shin forward to give you the proper posture on your skis."

"It's not very comfortable."

"Maybe not, but you'll get used to it. The important thing is whether the boot fits or not."

"Yes, it fits all right."

"Good. We're lucky that Pierre keeps an extensive stock of equipment here. Otherwise we'd have to rent everything and have the bindings adjusted to fit the boots. This way we save a lot of time."

He stood and gestured toward a set of skis and poles.

"These should be the right size for you, and the boots are already fitted for them, so that's perfect. My equipment was here. All we have to do is dress, and we'll be ready to go."

Jeff saw Tori was excited about the ski adventure and unable to keep it hidden. For his part, he was happy he'd found something to break through the rigid shell she had built around herself.

CHAPTER 28

They were at the outdoor kiosk buying lift tickets. Jeff hadn't wasted any time, perhaps afraid Tori would change her mind. She had no intention of doing so. She may never have another opportunity to try this sport.

She was led into the building that housed all the amenities of a ski center, including an equipment rental area, storage lockers, a *casse-croûte* (a counter restaurant in Québec), a more upscale restaurant, a bar, and a ski shop selling everything from mittens to ski boots. The building was built of logs, giving it a rustic appearance, but the conveniences were modern and efficient. And, business was brisk. Although it was a weekday, the place was busy.

With help from Jeff, Tori donned her ski boots, finding them awkward for walking. She lumbered across the room like a Tyrannosaurus Rex, attempting to get used to them. Outside, Jeff adjusted the goggles for her and fit them into place on her head.

"Why do I need these things?" she said, her voice muffled by the thick scarf she'd wound around her face.

"They're tinted, so they act as sunglasses shielding your eyes from the glare off the snow. They help protect your face from the cold, and lastly, they keep the snow out of your eyes."

She pondered this last point as he moved off. How would she get snow in her eyes?

With much difficulty, she made her way over to the ski lift, struggling to imitate Jeff's technique of pushing his skis out to the sides to propel his body ahead. It was a laborious task, and by the time she reached the lift, sweat ran down her back. She didn't think she'd suffer from the cold temperatures today.

As they lined up for the lift, Jeff gave her instructions.

"When it's our turn, follow me, move forward, and place yourself at the line painted on the floor. Put your poles in your right hand, use your other hand to hold onto the seat and get your balance. As soon as you feel the chair at the back of your knees, sit down."

"It sounds complicated. What if I fall off?" she asked.

"You won't, don't worry. And even if you do, they'll stop the lift right away."

"What? But, what if…"

They had reached the front of the line. Tori's attention was drawn to the couple in front of them. They glided ahead smoothly and sat on the slightly-swinging metal chair, chatting animatedly as they were lifted into the air. Jeff grabbed Tori's elbow and urged her into place. She inelegantly slid to a stop, her skis in position on the line. Her mouth dry, Tori glanced behind her at the chair that swung around the corner and moved steadily toward them. Obediently, she had her poles in her right hand, and she sat as soon as she felt the chair behind her.

"Oh, my God," she exclaimed, as the chair lifted off the ground. She felt like she had boarded a thrill ride at an amusement park, except there was nothing to hold her in.

"It's all right. Here, place your feet on the lower bar."

Jeff had lowered the safety bar that prevented them from falling out of the chair, and Tori relaxed, feeling more secure. The chair climbed the hill. From her vantage point, she admired the scenery surrounding her, from the rolling snow-covered hills to the picturesque village nestled in the valley.

She also understood the need for the goggles and scarf. What little skin was exposed to the elements felt the effects of the ascent. They were out of the protection of the trees, and the air became colder the higher they climbed.

"When we get to the top, I'll lift the bar. As soon as your skis touch the ramp, stand up and push yourself off."

Tori gaped at Jeff with dawning horror.

"Oh God, that's true. I have to get off this thing."

"No problem. It's easy. Just remember to stand up. All right?"

Tori nodded, unable to speak. She saw the summit approach. There was a small shack at the top and a man who doubtless helped inexperienced skiers disembark. Panic rose in her chest. She should never have agreed to come here, she thought.

Jeff lifted the bar, removing the barrier between her and the ground many feet below, and her fear increased. She stared straight ahead, her eyes wide. As they reached the ramp, her skis made contact with the wooden floor beneath them. Jeff stood and left the chairlift behind. Tori, however, sat frozen in place. The chair continued to move, gently swinging around the shack until it faced the bottom of the hill. A strangled squeal escaped her throat, and her mittened hands clutched the seat on either side of her. Gradually, the lift came to a stop, bobbing in mid-air.

Without moving her head, Tori directed her gaze downward to gauge the distance to the ground. She was at least six feet in the air. She was afraid she'd break something if she jumped. There was also the fact that her boots were attached to skis and she had no idea what to do to control them when they touched the ground.

A strange, choking sound came from her left, and she swiveled her head to see Jeff shaking with mirth. Tori was stunned. How could he find anything funny about the situation? When he made a remark to the dour-faced lift attendant, who then let out a snorting laugh, she wanted to kill him.

Tori's face burned with embarrassment under its cocoon of winter paraphernalia as she realized she was the butt of the jokes among the people sitting in the other lift chairs, waiting for the mechanism to resume its course.

Jeff removed his skis and made his way over to her, accompanied by the lift attendant. She decided she'd wait for him to get her off the chairlift and to safety before killing him.

"Enjoying the view, Tori?"

"Go to hell," she said through gritted teeth. She refused to make a scene in front of the ski center's employee and embarrass herself further.

As each man removed a ski from her boots, Jeff made a remark in French, inciting another burst of laughter from the stranger. It was squelched when the man glanced up at Tori's face and saw her expression. He said something to Jeff, nodding in her direction. Jeff shrugged good-naturedly, obviously accepting his fate.

When the skis were removed, Jeff reached his arms up toward Tori.

"Jump down. I'll catch you."

Tori didn't hesitate, and she didn't hold back. She hoped to flatten him underneath her, but he caught her effortlessly and set her on the ground, not bothering to hide his grin. Her humiliation was complete when the sound of applause rose from the watching crowd.

Without looking at Jeff, Tori picked up her skis and made the short climb to the top of the hill. Watching Jeff retrieve his skis and put them on, she tossed hers to the ground and placed her boots in the bindings, pressing down until she heard the click telling her they were securely attached.

"How about we start down?" Jeff said.

"Have you finished laughing at me?" Her voice trembled with indignation.

Jeff's eyes widened with false incredulity.

"I wasn't laughing at you. I was laughing *with* you."

"No." She raised a pointed finger to his face. The effect was largely lost by her thick mittens. "No. If you were laughing *with* me, I'd have to be laughing too and, in case you didn't notice, I wasn't laughing."

"Well, you should've been. That type of thing happens to everybody, and it's very funny."

"If it happens to everybody, why didn't you tell me about it?"

"I did tell you. I told you to stand up and push off when your feet touched the ramp."

He had a point, but Tori was in no mood to admit it. Instead, she dug her poles into the snow on either side of her and pushed herself forward. She immediately regretted the move. She moved much faster than she expected, and with a screech of surprise, she barreled into a male skier in front of her. One of her legs went between his and knocked them both to the ground in a tangle of limbs and skis.

She was mortified. Tori struggled to apologize, not knowing what to say in French. Two strong hands came underneath her arms, lifting her to her feet. With an apologetic grin and an evidently amusing remark, Jeff helped the other man to his feet. The skier left them with a smile and a quick wave to Tori.

She swiveled to face Jeff.

"Do you have to keep making jokes about me?"

"Oh, come on, Tori honey..." He stopped and grimaced.

"Don't you dare call me 'Tori honey'. I am not now and never will be 'Tori honey' to you. Do you understand?"

"Yes ma'am," he replied, acting suitably admonished.

"Let's get down this damn hill."

The joy and pleasure Tori had imagined skiing would bring her had dissipated. All she wanted to do was get to the bottom of the hill and take off her skis.

"Are you willing to let me show you what you should do?" Jeff said.

"Yes," she said. Tori understood that if she wanted to achieve the goal of reaching the bottom she'd need at least a bit of his advice.

"To start, I have to show you how to slow down or stop if you have to."

"That would be a good place to start," she said wryly.

Jeff demonstrated the basics of skiing. He taught her how to bring the tips of her skis together to slow down or stop; how to redistribute her weight on her skis to make turns and how to use her legs as springs to carry her over the bumps and uneven surfaces. Before setting off, Jeff explained that she had to crisscross the hill on her way down. It would help to keep her from going too fast, but she had to remember to weave from one side to the other.

"You don't want to fly into the bushes. Meeting a tree at thirty kilometers an hour is not a smart thing to do."

Tori wasn't sure how fast thirty kilometers an hour was, but it didn't sound smart to come face to face with a tree no matter what speed you went.

They set off down one of the easier hills, Tori following Jeff as he angled across the slope. As she approached the trees lining the hill, she found she couldn't turn her skis, and the bushes came closer and faster. She made the only decision that came to mind and threw herself onto the snow, bringing her descent to an abrupt halt. Jeff was soon beside her, again lifting her into an upright position.

"That was a good move, but you're going to have to get the hang of turning, or it'll take us a while to get to the bottom."

"I tried, but it didn't work."

"Okay, let's try something else."

He moved behind her, placing his skis on either side of hers, and folding his arms around her waist.

"What are you doing?" she said, alarmed.

"I'm going to guide you down for a bit, let you get a feel for what you should be doing."

"All right," she said, "but no funny stuff."

"It's pretty hard to do any funny stuff through all these layers of clothing in the middle of a ski hill in broad daylight," he said.

The combination of the topic of conversation and his proximity sent Tori's thoughts into dangerous territory. His breath warmed her cheek, and she was sure her goggles would soon fog up. She planted her poles in the snow and stiffened her spine.

"Let's go."

Despite her misgivings, the plan worked, and Tori learned to control her turns, if not master them. Jeff released her and let her use her new skills on her own. Tori held herself stiffly, without the easy grace of most of the skiers, but she felt she made progress. Jeff stayed close beside her, crossing in front of her and shouting instructions along the way.

"Will you stop that?" she shouted at him.

"What?" he said, as he crossed in front of her again.

"All that whooshing around. You're making me nervous. And I don't need to be distracted by all your advice right now. Couldn't you just go down to the bottom and leave me alone?"

"Sure, I can do that. Just take your time and relax. And remember, it's all downhill from here."

With a laugh, he sped toward the bottom of the slope, missing out on Tori's glare.

With Jeff out of her way, Tori noticed he wasn't the only one who liked to speed down the hill, missing the other skiers by a hair's breadth. She constantly glanced over her shoulder to see who was behind her.

Frightened by a man coming toward her on a snowboard at a breakneck speed, she panicked, certain he'd plow into her. Both her concentration and her balance were lost, and she fell to the ground in a heap of skis and poles until she resembled a modern art exhibit.

"Je m'excuse. Je n'aurais pas dû passer si proche de toi. Es-tu blessée?"

Tori looked dazedly up into the concerned face of a young man, the snowboarder. She struggled to get up, but she was hopelessly tangled.

"Attends. Je vais t'aider."

Seemingly wanting to be of help, he unhooked her skis, letting her legs flop to the ground. He grasped her elbow and tugged her into a sitting position.

"C'est correct. Je m'en occupe."

Jeff had appeared out of nowhere and bent to help Tori stand. The snowboarder looked apologetically at Jeff and made a remark in French that was inaudible to Tori. Jeff's response brought a bark of laughter from the other man. He smiled and waved to Tori before turning to retrieve his snowboard and continue his descent.

"You did it again. You laughed at me."

"Not at all. I wanted to make the poor guy feel better."

"Make him feel better? What about me? I'm the one he almost killed."

"Don't exaggerate. You're not even hurt," he said.

"You should have seen how fast he was going. He was heading straight for me."

"Yeah, I saw the whole thing. You panicked and fell, that's all. You're not supposed to pay attention to the people behind you. All you have to worry about are the people in front of you."

"That's easy for you to say," she said.

Tori made it to the bottom of the hill with a sense of accomplishment, and she agreed to another run. She made it off the lift and down the slope without incident and had to be coaxed into the chalet for a rest and some refreshments.

The next time they went out, they did three consecutive runs before taking a rest. Jeff's cell phone rang, and he grimaced when he glimpsed the display.

"Oui." He paused and listened to the voice on the other end for a moment. *"Non, on est..."*

Jeff stopped talking, winced, and moved the phone from his ear. An angry voice sprang from the device, and Tori had a feeling she knew who it was. When she saw the expression of guilt on Jeff's face, her suspicions were confirmed.

"Okay, je comprends. On s'en va tout de suite."

He disconnected the call and glanced at Tori, who returned his gaze with raised eyebrows and an I-told-you-so look.

"We have to go."

"I guess Bouchard had a problem with it after all, didn't he?"

"Yeah, I guess so."

"I also guess you're in big trouble now, aren't you?"

"Don't sound so happy. Bouchard will get over it. You see, deep down he loves me."

CHAPTER 29

The enjoyment of the afternoon faded when they arrived back at the condo. Tori was reminded of her true status as the door shut behind her and Jeff removed his coat. His gun peeked out of a shoulder holster, something he'd worn all afternoon, but had been forgotten by Tori during the excitement of trying a new adventure.

Jeff's attitude didn't help. He was grim-faced, either because of the dressing-down he'd received from his superior or because he felt chafed by the objectionable task of babysitting. They lapsed into silence, finding separate means of passing the time.

After absentmindedly scanning a magazine for a half hour while Jeff watched television, Tori got up to explore the contents of the refrigerator. Suppertime approached, and she felt certain working in the kitchen would serve the dual purpose of giving her something to do and removing her from the disturbing presence of her captor.

Jeff came into the room as she peered into the refrigerator. Her back was turned to him, and his entrance was silent, but Tori sensed his presence. The knowledge she could do so bothered her more than the fact he intruded upon her time in the kitchen.

"I can help you with that."

"That's not necessary," she said.

"I don't expect you to wait on me."

"I'm not waiting on you. I have to eat too, you know. It's no more trouble to prepare a meal for two as it is for one."

There were a few moments of silence as Jeff frowned at her rigid back.

"Tori, how long is this going to go on?"

"I don't know what you mean," she said.

"You *do* know what I mean. It's this...this attitude of yours. It has to stop."

She whirled on him, her eyes narrowed, her voice harsh, forgetting her determination to ignore him.

"My *attitude*? My attitude has to stop? Yeah, sure. Why not? Maybe I should fall all over you, telling you what a wonderful, brave man you are, how it doesn't matter that you lied to me and used me. Maybe I should drag you into the bedroom to show you it doesn't bother me to know you slept with me to soften me up and get me to tell you something about Danny. Maybe you'll get lucky, and I'll blurt out dates, times, and places while I'm overcome with passion."

Tori stabbed his chest with her finger as she spoke. His face hardened into an angry mask.

"Well, let me tell you something, Mr. Big Important Cop, if you don't like my attitude, then that's just too damn bad. You're stuck with it, and the only way you're going to avoid it is to get out of my sight and out of my life."

She swivelled back to the counter, picked up a knife, and chopped green peppers with a vengeance. She felt Jeff's gaze boring into her back, and the silence was heavy with strain.

When she heard him walk away, she set down the knife and gripped the counter with both hands. She was torn between apologizing and throwing the utensil at him.

An hour later, the doorbell chimed. Jeff approached the door, his weapon at his side, to reveal a tall, blond-haired man on the doorstep. Tori saw by the way Jeff visibly relaxed that he recognized the man who strained to look past him.

"*Jean-Pierre, c'est toi qui prends la relève?*"

"*Oui. Bouchard m'a envoyé.*"

Jeff stepped aside to let the younger man in, and Tori wondered at the slight frown on Jeff's face. Who was this new guy? Why was Jeff annoyed with him?

"Tori, this is Jean-Pierre Rincourt. He'll be taking over for me tonight."

The young cop enthusiastically shook her hand.

"Mademoiselle Anderson, it's a pleasure to meet you. I know we will get along very well."

Tori couldn't suppress her smile. The combination of his charming accent, his puppy-like eagerness, and his boyishly handsome face was impossible to resist.

"I'm pleased to meet you also, Jean-Pierre, and I'm quite sure we'll have no problem getting along."

She cast a meaningful glance at Jeff and saw her words had hit their mark. His look of annoyance transformed into a full-blown scowl.

"Why is Chantal not here?" Jeff said in a gruff voice.

"*Quoi?* Oh, she was called out on another assignment."

"I assume Bouchard filled you in on all the details. You're aware of your responsibilities?"

"*Mais oui, Jeff.* I think I'm capable of handling this."

Jean-Pierre had picked up on Jeff's annoyance, and he pivoted to face his fellow officer with a slight frown of his own. Jeff apparently decided it was time to back off. With a shrug, he gathered his belongings, and after a few grumbled words of farewell, he left the condo.

Tori enjoyed the evening with Jean-Pierre. He was likeable and, in Tori's view, he was innocent of any wrongdoing. He hadn't been involved in the series of organized deceptions against her, and was at the condo because he'd been assigned the task of watching over her. As a result, she spent the evening on the couch with her feet curled underneath her, having the first decent conversation with another human being since her days with 'Mario'.

During the evening, he inquired about her job and family. Tori answered him in vague terms. She reminded herself Jean-Pierre might be the Quebec police force's secret weapon, using his charm and apparent guilelessness to extract information from a reluctant witness. When his questions led to a subject she judged too personal, she maneuvered him into talking about himself. He did so without hesitation, eagerly sharing the details of his life.

Tori told the story of her skiing adventure earlier in the day, both the good and the bad. Seeing the experience through someone else's eyes, she realized how funny it had been, and she wondered if she may have been a bit harsh toward Jeff.

When the conversation stalled, Tori glanced at her watch and discovered it neared midnight. With a smile and a friendly goodnight, she made her way to bed, exhausted from her day of skiing, but untroubled by the usual stress of spending her evenings with Jeff or Chantal.

Several hours later, Tori groggily awoke from a deep sleep. She squinted at the night-table and saw it was seven o'clock. The sky had just begun to lighten. She settled back under the covers until she heard the ominous sound of heavy footsteps pounding down the hall toward her room. She sat up in alarm, clutching the covers to her chest. Something told her Jean-Pierre wouldn't make so much noise unless there was an urgent problem. She swung her legs out of bed as the door was thrust open and two men charged into the room.

Tori's heart tripped. She knew these men had nothing to do with the police, at least not from the outside of a jail cell. They were disheveled, unshaven, and hostile-looking. The gun pointed at her head was the clincher.

CHAPTER 30

Jeff didn't sleep well. His slumber was disturbed by worries, and the bulk of those worries concerned Tori. It frustrated him that she refused to collaborate with the police, and she was stubbornly unwilling to admit Wilcox was a danger to either her or society in general.

Tori seemed to live with the fantasy that Danny Wilcox was someone who merely skirted along the edge of the law, and she'd be able to drag him back from that edge and reform him. He'd heard of sensible women who were habitually attracted to the 'bad boy' type, always needing to be their saviors, even as their hearts were trampled in the process.

That thought led to another that made Jeff feel even more angry and frustrated, but the feelings were aimed toward himself. Why couldn't he shake his attraction to her when it was obvious she was willing to risk her life for a worthless criminal? He should run as fast as possible in the opposite direction.

Even with that thought in mind, he was in the car making an early start to the condo. For some reason, he had an uneasy suspicion.

Last night, Jeff had been surprised to see the rookie cop at the door instead of Chantal. He knew Jean-Pierre was a good officer, although inexperienced, and Jeff admitted guard duty was not a rigorous task demanding any special skills other than vigilance.

What Jeff hated to admit to himself was that he was jealous. He didn't like Tori's reaction to Jean-Pierre's good looks and enthusiasm. It'd been too long since she'd looked at him like that, and it irked him to no end. He reminded himself it was his problem to deal with, and he shouldn't take it out on Jean-Pierre.

He'd feel better when he saw Tori was safe and rested after a good night's sleep alone in her own bed.

Traveling on the highway toward Stoneham, he called ahead to see if they needed him to pick up milk, bread, or other essentials along the way.

By the third unanswered ring, Jeff checked the display on his cell phone to be sure he hadn't dialed the wrong number. By the fifth ring, he was more than a little worried. By the seventh, he experienced real fear. He hung up and called 911, identified himself, and instructed them to send the closest SQ squad car and an ambulance to the condo.

He hoped neither of them were necessary, but he had to prepare for the worst. He was at least ten minutes from the safe house, but there was a possibility he'd arrive before the patrol car. The town was far from headquarters, and the Sûreté du Québec had a large area to cover. There wasn't always a car near the outlying areas.

Jeff raced to the condo and, as he'd suspected, the authorities hadn't yet arrived. Jean-Pierre's Jeep Cherokee sat in the driveway, a light coating of snow covering most of the red paint. Seeing it there did nothing to tamp down Jeff's fears. If the cop was at the condo, he should've answered the phone.

He pulled over to the curb and scrutinized the outside of the building for a few moments. He couldn't see any movement in the windows, and there weren't any suspicious-looking vehicles or people in the area. All outward signs indicated everything was quiet. Had he been overreacting? Could both Rincourt and Tori be so sound asleep they couldn't hear the phone ring?

Jeff removed his gun from its holster and held it at his side as approached the house, keeping an eye out for intruders.

Before ringing the doorbell, he tested the handle and was dismayed to discover it was unlocked. Rincourt should've locked it last night. Had he forgotten, or had he already been out this morning?

Jeff shoved the door open, keeping his back to the wall of the building and his gun raised. The door opened and stopped when it nudged up against something heavy. Jeff saw a pair of legs lying on the floor, the upper body hidden behind the door. A man.

His heart pumping, Jeff peered into the condo to make sure no one was in the room with a weapon. He stepped through the opening and kneeled beside the body of Jean-Pierre. Keeping his gun pointed in the direction of the living room, he fumbled for a pulse with his left hand and was relieved to find a weak one. The police officer appeared to have been the victim of a serious blow to the head, but he was still alive.

That was the good news. The bad news was his worst fears had been confirmed. Someone had broken into the condo to get to Tori. Jeff's breath faltered as several scenarios flew through his mind, the majority of them bad, few of them positive.

His training as a cop didn't desert him. He made his way through the living room toward the kitchen, keeping his back to the walls. Nothing seemed to be disturbed in either of those rooms. As he made his way toward the staircase, a noise to his left alerted him, and he swung with a raised gun to face two uniformed police officers in the same stance.

"Drop your weapon," he was ordered, in rapid but clear French.

"I'm a cop, Detective Jean-François Lafond. I'm working on a case, and there's another possible victim in the house. I have my ID in my back pocket."

"Remove it."

Jeff bit back his irritation. He understood their need for caution. After all, he stood with a gun in his hand, but Tori could be fighting for her life right now, as was Jean-Pierre, and every second was precious.

Reassured by his badge, the officers joined him in his search of the condo. Within minutes, they were certain the rest of the apartment was empty. Tori had either escaped or been abducted. Jeff ardently wished for the former.

Placing a quick phone call to Bouchard at headquarters, Jeff told him about the situation and asked for a forensics team. Meanwhile, the ambulance arrived to transport a still-unconscious Jean-Pierre to the hospital. Jeff hoped that the young man would survive his injuries, and he could help them find out what had happened to Tori.

Even as Jeff tried to quell his panic, he looked for a hint of what could've happened in the past couple of hours. He was sure it was no longer than that, perhaps even less than an hour. Rincourt had been fully-dressed, prepared for the day ahead of him. The coffeemaker had a pot of freshly-brewed coffee in it, and a clean mug sat beside it, ready to be filled. Jean-Pierre hadn't been surprised in his sleep.

Tori appeared to have been pulled from her bed. Literally. The covers lay on the floor as if they were dragged off and, if he wasn't mistaken, one of them was missing. He was sure there had been a light blue quilt as the uppermost bedcovering, and it was no longer anywhere to be found. Her clothes seemed to be all accounted for, although he couldn't be sure, and her slippers were on the floor beside the bed.

Jeff was relieved that there was no sign of blood on the bed or in the rest of the condo, except where Jean-Pierre had been left lying on the floor. A quick scan revealed her coat and boots were in the closet, as was her handbag. If she'd escaped, she wouldn't be far, without any warm clothes or money, but the evidence weighed greatly on the side of the theory that she'd been removed by force.

Jeff didn't have long to brood over this fact as Bouchard and Chantal arrived. He filled them in on whatever details he'd discovered so far, striving to keep the alarm out of his voice. Chantal stared at him with concern, and he knew what she thought. Holding onto his emotions, he faced Bouchard.

"We have to find her. We'll have to revert to our original plan, the one we were working on before Tori came into the picture."

Captain Bouchard tightened his lips and shook his head.

"We haven't worked all the kinks out of that plan yet. We didn't have enough time. You can't go in there blind."

"I wouldn't be going in blind," Jeff said. "I have information under my belt. Anyway, we must hurry. They have Tori, and they've already attempted to kill her twice. You can be sure they didn't drag her out of here to attend a social event."

The senior police officer considered his words for a moment. Jeff was desperate for his boss to grasp the urgency of the situation. He knew him well enough not to interrupt his thoughts, even though each second that passed increased Jeff's panic level by a notch.

Bouchard nodded.

"You're right. We have no choice at this point. We'll have to move in."

Jeff caught Chantal's speculative glance. He silently urged her to set her protest aside. When she looked away without speaking, he knew she understood his unspoken request, but she gave in grudgingly.

CHAPTER 31

Tori suppressed a groan as she strove to find a more comfortable position on the hard cement floor. Her fidgeting attracted the scrutiny of her two 'charming' captors. Their gazes simultaneously left the playing cards they held in their hands, glanced toward her, saw it was a case of her being miserable, and resumed their game.

Tori stared at them with revulsion. They were disgusting-looking creatures. They both had dirty, shaggy hair, worn T-shirts and jeans, and large steel-capped boots. One of them was skinny, and she suspected he suffered from crabs as he regularly scratched his crotch area.

The other man didn't seem to have the same problem, but his crotch was covered by the belly that hung over his belt and rested on his lap. His T-shirt had given up working to cover the excess fat, leaving his belly button and body hair exposed.

Tori leaned her head against the damp wall and closed her eyes. Her shoulders ached from having her wrists tied behind her back, and she no longer felt her fingers. Her ankles were also tied, but loosely enough to let the blood circulate in her feet. The benefit was negligible. They were still bare and numb from the cold emanating from the cement floor. Physically, she felt wretched.

Emotionally, Tori was furious. It was the third time Danny's cronies had mistreated her, and they'd gone so far as to try to kill her on the first two occasions. If she saw Danny now, she'd strangle him with her bare hands. At the very least, she'd give him a piece of her mind.

After coming face-to-face with Little Dog's gun – Tori had privately nicknamed her jailors Big Dog and Little Dog – she'd made a last-ditch effort to escape, planning to crawl across the bed and jump out the window. Big Dog had proven himself to be remarkably quick in spite of his size. He grabbed her ankles and hauled her back across the bed. Clutching the covers, she kicked at him to no avail. He deftly attached her hands behind her back, tied her ankles, and gagged her. He then rolled her up in the quilt and threw her over his shoulder like a rag doll.

Tori realized they were outside the condo the instant they stepped out the door. Despite the tight shroud of the quilt, she felt the chill of the air. She was tossed into the back of a vehicle, presumably a van of some sort. She didn't struggle during the long drive that followed. It'd be pointless. Her bonds were too tightly and expertly done, and she preferred to save her strength for whatever might face her when they arrived at their destination. She hoped Danny would see what they'd done to her, and he'd step in to help.

After a long, rough ride, Tori was carried into this desolate building, which was nothing more than a shack, and left sitting on the cold cement floor with her back against the wall. She was somewhat covered by the quilt, although it had slipped from her shoulders and her bare feet peeked out the bottom. Whenever she tucked her feet under her for more warmth, the quilt opened and further exposed her to the cool air.

Her pajamas were simple and made of cotton, but they covered her fully and decently. She wouldn't have wanted to sit here half-naked.

After Tori spent hours observing the unending game, and unsuccessfully checking out the shack for possible escape routes, Big Dog must've decided he was hungry. He rose from the table and crossed the room to a small bar fridge, removed some sandwiches, beer, and bottled water, and carried them back to the table. Despite her discomfort and the unappetizing surroundings, Tori realized she was famished. She watched the men and hoped some food would come her way.

The two men ate their lunch, washing it down with beer, and acting like they didn't have a hungry, half-frozen woman trussed up on the floor beside them. Their lack of compassion angered Tori even further, but venting it would get her nowhere, so she pretended indifference. She'd rather starve to death than beg for anything from these detestable people.

Finally, Little Dog approached her with one small sandwich in his hand and a bottle of water. He set them on the dirty floor beside her while he untied her hands. Wisely, she didn't speak. She took the sandwich from the floor and wiped off the dirt before swallowing it in two bites. She guzzled the water thirstily, and her meal was complete.

Chapter 32

Captain Bouchard paced the floor in front of Chantal and Sébastien, his hands joined behind his back. Chantal fidgeted in her seat. She'd also love to pace, dissipating some of her nervous energy. She'd prefer to escape the small office altogether, but her boss would order her to sit still if she so much as moved a muscle.

She didn't remember the last time she'd been so worried about a case. She liked Tori and felt guilty about having lied to her the way she had. Now that the woman was missing, Chantal was unable to concentrate on anything else.

Her mind wandered to a conversation she'd had with Jeff an hour earlier. She'd caught up to him in the corridor and had to force herself not to comment on his appearance. He seemed to have grown older by several years in the past few hours.

"Any news?" she said.

"Nothing. They're still waiting for communication," he said, running his hands through his hair.

Chantal realized her partner had strong feelings for the American and, at first, she'd reproached him for it. He knew better than to become personally involved with a suspect or a witness in a case. But that didn't change the fact it had happened, and Chantal was aware sometimes things were out of your control.

"It'll come in, and we'll get him. We have to be optimistic."

"With every minute that passes we're less likely to find her."

"That's not true. Tori's smart. She's gotten away from them before. She can do it again."

Chantal realized her words sounded empty to Jeff. His face was twisted in anguish, and she'd give anything to wipe it away.

"I won't give up," he said, his voice trembling with emotion.

Her partner had been excused from this forced vigil in Bouchard's office, probably because his emotions were too volatile at this point. As Bouchard glanced at his watch for perhaps the hundredth time, Chantal wished she'd been given the same exemption.

The captain glared at the phone as if willing it to ring. Chantal had rarely seen her superior so agitated. She understood he had a lot depending on the outcome of this case, but normally he kept his sentiments tightly locked away.

The authorities had worked to arrest Danny Wilcox for the past two years, and he always evaded them. They'd worked on a plan to infiltrate his circle, but when Tori came along, they'd set the plan aside. Everyone knew the Floridian could be an important link for them.

The Sûreté were unable to trace Wilcox's identity any earlier than the point at which he'd first appeared on the scene in Quebec. It was as if he'd never existed before then, but Tori had a connection to him and could provide them with some crucial information about his past, and possibly his future plans.

"This has to work," Bouchard said, breaking the tense silence in the room.

"There's no reason for it not to," Sébastien said.

The captain snorted.

"With Wilcox, there's always a reason for something to go wrong. Victoria was our best bet, and now…"

He shook his head and thrust his hands into his pants pockets.

Chantal was aware her boss was anxious on several levels. He wanted and needed to penetrate the drug gang. He had to arrest the leader and make a dent in his operations, but Chantal knew he also liked and respected Tori, despite her reluctance to help them. Perhaps more importantly, they'd concluded that Danny Wilcox had someone inside the police force helping him by providing inside information.

When they'd followed Picard and Tori to her meeting with Wilcox on the south shore, their plan to infiltrate the building was ruined when the police presence was detected. That time, they'd chalked it up to bad luck. This time, however, it was too big a leak to dismiss. The fact that they had Tori in a safe house had never been made public, and the knowledge of the actual location was limited to a relatively small group of people.

"I've always put my faith in everyone in my department," Bouchard said, slamming his fist into his other hand. "I never felt the need to withhold information from the officers reporting to me. Now, I have someone on the force who's shared confidential information with a criminal."

Chantal and Sébastien exchanged a glance. There was nothing they could add to make him feel better. The facts were glaringly obvious.

The door to the office swung open, and Luc Fortier entered, another officer working on the case. He found himself the target of three concerned pairs of eyes. There was no doubt he had their full attention.

"Well?" barked Captain Bouchard.

"Wilcox has made contact with the people who took Tori."

"Good. And you've traced the calls?"

"Yes, and everyone's been informed. But, we have two problems."

"What are they?" Bouchard asked.

"First of all, Wilcox is sending someone to pick up Tori, so we don't have much time. Secondly, the call originated in Trois-Rivières."

CHAPTER 33

Tori remained motionless, hoping they'd forget her and leave her untied, but her hopes were destroyed when Big Dog shuffled over and retied her hands behind her back.

The afternoon dragged on, and with every minute that passed, her nerves were more tightly strung. She had no idea what her fate was to be, but she wished something would happen, no matter what, instead of this endless waiting.

Even her captors were obviously more restless and apprehensive as the day progressed. What little they said to each other was undecipherable to her, but she sensed by the tone of their conversation that they were disturbed by something. She assumed it was the lack of communication from their boss. As did they, she looked forward to the opportunity to talk to Danny. Once and for all, she wanted to straighten out this mix-up.

All the occupants of the shack were startled when the jarring sound of a cell phone broke the uneasy silence. Little Dog grabbed the device from the counter and answered the call.

"*Oui.*" Silence. "*Ça va.*" End of conversation.

The phone clattered on the table, and the man glanced at Tori before speaking to his companion.

"*Il va envoyer quelqu'un la chercher.*"

"*C'est bien. J'ai hâte que ça se termine.*"

Tori saw the relief on their faces, and she knew a turning point was about to be reached. She hoped it was a turning point that would be to her advantage.

The atmosphere was noticeably lighter as the two men resumed their card game, joking and smiling. Tori waited it out. As the minutes ticked by, she convinced herself it was Danny who'd called, and he was on his way to her. That was the best-case scenario, because deep down she was certain Danny wouldn't harm her, and they'd be able to talk.

After the long hours of sitting on a cold cement floor, with nothing to do but think, her anger had dissipated, and she understood Danny's intentions. He wanted to punish her, and he thought scaring the life out of her and making her wait so long would serve the purpose. He hoped the whole experience would make her turn tail and run.

In a way, he was right, because Tori had every intention of leaving Quebec as soon as possible, but it wouldn't be before she made one final effort to convince him to come with her. Satisfied everything would end well, Tori closed her eyes and relaxed for the first time in several hours.

Half an hour later, she was alerted by a shuffling sound. She watched the two men move to peer out the grimy window. Someone had arrived, but she wasn't comforted by the sight of her keepers drawing their guns and standing back from the door, poised for action. They wouldn't act this way if it was Danny who'd arrived, would they?

There was a perfunctory knock on the door before it was shoved open, and a large man strode in. He didn't carry any obvious weapons and appeared amused to see two guns pointed in his direction. Glancing around the room, he spotted Tori on the floor. He leered at her for a few seconds before turning to face her companions.

Tori assessed the newcomer and wasn't pleased with what she saw. He was tall, with longish, dirty hair, and a scruffy beard. His tattered bush coat was open to reveal a large belly hanging over his belt, but it was covered by a heavy khaki green shirt. His jeans were torn at the knees, and his large black boots were unlaced. His leering smile had revealed yellowed teeth with a few noticeably missing. All in all, his appearance was repulsive, and she didn't hold much faith that his character was much better.

After an exchange of words in French, during which both Little and Big Dog continued to stare at the new man with suspicion, Tori's eyes widened as the stranger approached her, a wide grin on his face.

"So, this is the package I am to deliver, eh?"

His English was clear enough to understand. It was his manner that was frightening and all too expressive. He looked Tori up and down like she was a piece of cheese and he was a starving rat. Tori cringed, drawing her legs up underneath her. She didn't know why he was here, but she was afraid if he laid a hand on her, she'd throw up the tiny sandwich she'd eaten a few hours ago.

"Come on. Get up. Our friend Danny wants to see you."

Those were the words Tori had wanted to hear, but hearing them come from this creature's mouth lessened the excitement she'd normally have experienced. Nevertheless, she made an effort to stand up, if only to avoid the possibility of him helping her.

However, she'd been so long on the cold floor her limbs wouldn't cooperate. The large man frowned, and she recognized from his hand motions, if not his words, that he wanted the other men to untie her.

Little Dog babbled in French. It was obvious he objected.

"Do I look like a donkey? Untie her, and she can walk."

The man's response was spoken in English, but its meaning must have been understood. The skinny thug continued to chatter and wave his arms.

"Her feet are bare. She can't run. They'll freeze as soon as she steps outside, and I intend to hold her very close."

With those last words and a disturbing smirk, he threw his arm across Tori's shoulders and pulled her up against him. She had no defense, her hands and feet still bound, but she tried to right herself and push away from him.

His body exuded a rank smell, and his bulging stomach pushed up against her, but she felt the strength in his grip and knew she'd be no match for him if he wanted to hurt her. Her heart pounded in fear. She wondered if she was jumping from the frying pan into the fire.

When his words failed to get a response from either of the men, the newcomer yanked a knife from a leather holder attached to his belt and set to the task himself. Neither of the men argued with him. Perhaps they were afraid of him. Or, perhaps, they felt the decision had been taken out of their hands, and they were no longer responsible for the consequences.

Tori held her breath as the knife cut through the thick ropes, and her pulse skipped as he hesitated before slipping the knife into its holder, all the while keeping his eyes locked on hers. She recognized the move as a threat, and had no intention of putting him to the test. She trembled to think of the damage he could do to a person with such a weapon in his hands.

Tori rubbed her wrists before gathering the quilt around her and taking a few steps toward the door of the shack. She gasped when the man's arm circled her waist and dragged her up against his side. Risking a quick peek upward, the lecherous look on his face made her recoil. She tore her gaze from his and focused on the door, laboring to calm her ragged breathing. Hopefully, she thought, Danny had instructed this heathen not to harm her.

Awkwardly, they made their way the short distance to the door, hampered by the quilt encasing Tori's legs and the fact that his strides were much longer than hers. He showed no signs of adjusting his pace to accommodate her.

They were hit by a blast of frigid air as they paused on the threshold. The man seemed unaffected by the cold even though his coat hung open, but it easily cut through the quilt and flimsy pajamas. Tori was relieved to spot a large blue pickup truck with a white cab over the box parked twenty feet away. Her feet wouldn't freeze during the time it took to cover that distance, she decided.

As she stepped outside, she changed her mind. Her feet numbed the instant they touched the snow, and she wanted to sprint to the truck. Again, she was hampered by her chaperone. He didn't appear to be in a hurry.

"My feet are cold," she said, having endured a few seconds of the sensation of bare skin on snow.

"I'll warm you up," he said, as he laughed and swung her around in front of him, lifting her off the ground to hold her tightly against his chest, his face mere inches from hers.

Over his shoulder, Tori saw Little Dog and Big Dog in the doorway, looking uncertain, and for a moment, she debated calling out to them for help. The notion was dismissed. At least she was on her way to Danny, she reasoned. And, she was unbound and free of the cabin. Her chances of escaping had increased.

They reached the truck, and the grip on Tori's waist loosened for an instant as he pulled the door open and tossed her onto the passenger seat. She braced herself for an unpleasant interlude as he reached across her to fasten the seatbelt, but was surprised to see his lewd expression was replaced by a serious one. Incongruously, that fact alarmed her even more.

Shutting the door, he crossed in front of the truck to climb into the seat beside her. He swung the vehicle toward the road, and accelerated. Tori stared at him, measuring his change in mood and wondering what it meant for her.

"Are you all right?"

It was a simple question and, under normal circumstances, wouldn't have evoked anything besides a simple answer. But it wasn't the question that made Tori's heart jump into her throat. It was the voice that delivered it.

CHAPTER 34

Tori had mixed and oscillating feelings. Her first reflex was shock and disbelief. It couldn't be, could it? Then, when she realized it could very well be, she was flooded with relief, and, a second later, rage. Her fist lashed out and landed squarely in his solar plexus.

"Ow! What was that for?"

"You...you scared me half to death."

"I got you out of there, didn't I?"

"Yes, but did you have to terrify me in the process?"

Jeff glared at her, but his expression softened as she trembled with reaction.

"I'm sorry, but I had to be believable. I couldn't let them suspect I wasn't legit, or we'd both be dead now."

She nodded her head in agreement. If she opened her mouth, she'd cry. As it was, she had trouble blinking back the tears. The strain of the day and the fear she'd experienced at the hands of Jeff – before she knew he was Jeff – had gotten to her, and her emotions were raw and jagged.

"Are you all right? Did they hurt you in any way?" Jeff said.

"I'm fine," she muttered.

"Good. We're not out of the woods yet. And I mean that both literally and figuratively," he said, as he glanced in his rear-view mirror. "They may decide to check with Wilcox and realize I'm an impostor. Then they're going to be after us."

"How did you know where to find me?"

"We've been watching these guys for a long time, and we know some of their usual spots. Before you came along, I'd prepared to infiltrate the group undercover, so we'd already done some of the legwork. We were scanning the cellular communications in a few specific areas to close in on the exact location where they could be hiding you. We intercepted Wilcox's phone call to your two friends."

"You did? It was Danny that called? Do you know what he said to them?"

"It doesn't matter what he said. What matters is we had a small window of time to get to you before someone else did, and we were able to do it."

Tori focused on his first sentence.

"What do you mean it doesn't matter what he said? I want to know."

"I don't have time for that now. We have to get rid of this truck and get out of here, because either we're going to meet the people who were originally assigned to pick you up, or those other two will come after us."

"What are we going to do? Have you got a plan?"

At that, Jeff grinned, revealing his ugly teeth, and reminded Tori that she'd have to ask him how he'd pulled off such an excellent disguise.

"I always have a plan, sweetheart. My problem is getting you to cooperate with me so that I can implement it."

"Very funny. What do you want me to do?"

Despite her desire to meet Danny and resolve their problems, the events of the day had taken their toll. Now, all she wanted was to put distance between her and Danny's underlings.

"Reach behind your seat and pull out the boots and clothing I brought for you. Put it on while I take care of the truck."

Tori unfastened her seat belt and twisted in her seat to find a coat, snow-pants, and boots lying on the floor behind her. As she reached for them, she suspected they were a few sizes too large for her, but they were better than what she presently wore. As she scrambled into the outerwear, Jeff swung the truck crossways on the road. He backed it up until it was wedged against the snowbank behind them.

"What are you doing?"

"Don't worry about it. Just get dressed and meet me outside."

Jeff climbed out and headed toward the back of the truck. Tori finished dressing and jumped onto the road. As her feet touched the ground, the familiar whine of an engine reached her ears. Her eyes widened in disbelief when Jeff backed his bright red snowmobile out of the rear of the truck onto the snowbank before swinging it around to face the woods. The truck was then parked on a small path between some trees, making it almost invisible from the road. Returning to the snowmobile, he motioned for Tori to climb on behind him.

Tori didn't look forward to another trip through the forest on the back of the noisy machine, hanging on for dear life, but she had no choice in the matter. She positioned herself behind Jeff and wrapped her arms around his waist.

That was when Tori encountered a problem. She couldn't reach all the way around his middle because of the extra padding he had inside his shirt. Jeff grabbed her hands and placed them underneath the false stomach. She clasped them together and had the double advantage of the warmth of his bare skin and the coverage of the bean bag stomach to protect her bare hands from the cold.

They progressed bit by bit through the woods. There was no existing trail, and Jeff had to negotiate the snowmobile past the trees and outcroppings. After ten minutes, he found the path he wanted and picked up speed.

Within the hour, they pulled up to Jeff's house in Valcartier and climbed off the snowmobile. Tori stood for a moment and stared at the house, recalling the first time she'd seen it and naively believed it to be the house of Ben's friend, Jean-François.

So much had happened since then it would always be bittersweet to come back here. No matter how happy she was to be off the snowmobile and in a warm, comfortable house, it reminded her of the way she'd been betrayed, not once but twice, by the same man, all in the name of duty.

Nevertheless, when Jeff pressed a cup of hot coffee into her hands and sat her in a cozy armchair, she didn't refuse. Tori watched as he made the phone call to police headquarters to let them know they were both safe and sound. She saw him frown and shake his head in dismay, and she wondered what development caused such an expression.

Did it have to do with her? Or Danny? Was it about another unrelated case? She waited while he finished his conversation and hung up. Then she waited a few minutes longer while he prepared his own cup of coffee. Her patience came to an end.

"What did they say?"

"Who?"

She glared at him. If he assumed he could avoid answering her questions, he'd have to think again.

"Them. Your boss. Your co-workers or partners, or whatever you want to call them. The people you were talking to on the phone."

"Oh, them. They were just giving me an update."

"And? What is it?" she said, rolling her eyes in exasperation.

"Not much."

"Stop it. I have as much to do with this case as you do, and I don't appreciate being left in the dark. What did they say?"

Jeff leaned ahead and fixed her pointedly with an intense stare.

"I need to correct you. You don't have as much to do with this case as I do. You don't want to have anything to do with this case. You won't cooperate with us, remember? So, why now, all of a sudden, should I start volunteering confidential police information to you?"

Tori shrank into her chair, taken aback by his attitude, but knowing he had a point. She'd refused to collaborate with the police at every turn, and now she demanded information from them. He had every right to refuse her, and although she felt angry and frustrated, she pushed those feelings aside.

She lowered her eyes to her coffee for a few moments before she spoke. She would eat humble pie, but just a small portion.

"You're right. It's none of my business."

She glanced up to gauge Jeff's reaction to her statement, but his face was carved in stone. Whatever he'd heard on the phone had put him in a bad mood.

"Can I ask you one other question?"

"What is it?" he said.

"Jean-Pierre. Is he okay?"

Tori braced herself for the worst.

"Jean-Pierre? Yeah, he's okay. He took quite a blow to the head, and he'll be off duty for a few weeks, but he's going to be fine."

"Good. I was worried about him. I couldn't see him when they carried me out of the condo, and I was afraid he'd been badly hurt...or worse."

"No. He's fine, although I hope it was a lesson for him. He made a big mistake at the condo. He never should've opened the door without identifying the person on the other side." He shook his head. "And Bouchard never should've assigned a rookie to stand guard. Not when he knows the kind of people we're up against."

Tori still wore the coat and pants she'd arrived in, although her feet were again bare. Despite the heavy layer of clothing, a violent shiver shook her as she thought about the men who'd crashed into her bedroom that morning. Jeff must have discerned her reaction. He got to his feet and helped her out of the coat.

"Here, we'll get you out of these things and into something warm enough to take the chill out of your bones. Take off those pants while I go find something."

By the time she was down to her cotton pajamas, he had reappeared with a large sweatshirt, and matching sweatpants emblazoned with 'Sûreté du Québec' in large, white letters.

"They're going to be a bit big, but the pants have a drawstring waist, and we can roll up the legs and sleeves. I got you a pair of warm socks too."

Uncaring that she'd look ridiculous in the oversize clothes, Tori readily tugged them on over her pajamas and snuggled into their warmth. She settled on the couch with her mug of coffee and reflected on the difference in her circumstances from just a couple of hours ago when she didn't know her fate.

Her reflections were interrupted by the shrill ringing of Jeff's cell phone. He was in another room, but the unmistakable sound of alarm in his voice made Tori jump out of her chair. In the kitchen, phone to his ear, his eyes were wide with distress. He spoke in French, but the apprehension in his tone couldn't be misinterpreted. Tori understood something had gone wrong. She hoped it didn't have anything to do with Danny.

When Jeff glanced in her direction and mentioned her name, her body stiffened with tension. She watched him finish the conversation and look at her, but she knew he didn't truly see her. Some other horrible picture passed before his eyes.

"What's wrong?" she said.

"Chantal," he whispered.

"What's happened to her?"

Tori didn't like the tone of his voice or his demeanor, and she experienced a jab of fear for the woman she'd once considered a friend.

"She's gone, disappeared."

Momentarily speechless, Tori didn't know what it all meant. She realized Chantal worked in a dangerous profession, as did Jeff, but she knew nothing about the cases on which they worked, or the types of situations in which they found themselves. She drew her conclusions based on Jeff's reaction to the news that Chantal had disappeared, and she found nothing encouraging there. He was genuinely worried, and she felt a flash of sympathy for him and a wealth of dread for Chantal.

"What...what happened? Where could she be?"

Tori knew her questions were senseless. If they had the answers to those questions, there wouldn't be any need for concern. They'd find her.

At any rate, her enquiries didn't receive a response. She was convinced Jeff's mind raced with a thousand thoughts about what had to be done to retrieve his partner. Shaking his head, he seemed to focus on the here and now, and grabbed Tori's elbow.

"Get dressed. We have to go."

Tori responded to the urgency in his voice and rushed to gather her coat and boots.

Chapter 35

As they sped toward the city in Jeff's truck, Tori dared to question him further about Chantal.

"Do you have any theories about what happened to her?"

Jeff glanced at her and grimaced.

"Yes, but I don't know if you want to hear them."

"You believe it has something to do with Danny," she said in a low voice. It wasn't a question.

"It's probable," Jeff said.

"How can that be?"

"When we were tracing the cellular calls, narrowing down the possibilities of where you were hidden, we discovered Wilcox had called from Trois-Rivières."

"Where's that?"

"It's a town west of Quebec City, on the way to Montreal."

"What does that have to do with Chantal?"

"She went with Sébastien to join up with the Sûreté in that area. They were going to make an attempt to close in on Wilcox."

Tori frowned. She remained silent, preparing for the rest of the story.

"There are a couple of spots we suspect he uses as hiding places. Chantal went to check out one of them while Sebastien investigated the other. He never heard back from her again."

"She went alone?" Tori asked, disbelievingly.

"No, she had another officer with her, but he was found unconscious at the scene."

Tori heard the tension in his voice even though he tried to hide it. She laid her hand on his arm.

"She'll be all right, Jeff. She seems very capable."

To her own ears, her words sounded hollow and inadequate. Tori could imagine the small amount of comfort they brought Jeff.

"I thought you couldn't find Danny. If you can trace his phone calls, why have you never caught him?" Tori said.

"We got lucky this time. Or, maybe he got sloppy, one or the other. He doesn't keep a cell phone long enough for it to be traced, but our computer geeks managed to close in on a conversation that was probably his. We thought we'd caught a break, but it backfired on us."

Tori could hear the bitterness in his voice, and despite their differences, she felt for him.

An hour and a half later, they arrived in Trois-Rivières and made their way to the local headquarters of the Sûreté du Québec. There, they found Sébastien and a group of other officers holed up in a room with maps and computers, piecing together what could've happened to their fellow officer, Chantal Pouliot.

Everyone fell silent as Tori and Jeff entered the room. Tori saw a number of eyes sweep over her accusingly. She knew they considered her an accomplice to Danny, or, at the very least, an uncooperative witness.

Even though she knew the latter to be true, she was aware, from their standpoint, one was not much better than the other. She was also aware, when it came to the safety of one of their own, their distrust of her would be increased tenfold. She wasn't surprised when she was escorted from the room to be left on her own in another smaller one. When she tested the door she found it locked from the outside.

CHAPTER 36

"There was no sign of a struggle...no blood...no evidence at all?" Jeff said.

"None. It was like she went up in smoke," Sébastien said.

"She must've gone to investigate something, perhaps in the woods nearby. Did you have a large-enough search area?"

"We did. And the dogs are out there now, but they haven't turned up anything."

Jeff stared out the window, a fist pressed to his chest.

"They were ready for us, ready and waiting. Somehow, they knew we were coming, and set up a plan to take Chantal," Jeff said, his voice rough with anger.

Sébastien nodded in agreement.

"I think you're right, but the question is why. What do they have to gain by picking up Chantal?"

"Maybe they're seeking revenge. Maybe they want to use her as a bargaining tool. Maybe they're just out for a few kicks."

As he spoke, Jeff became more discouraged. None of the possibilities were good. Chantal was a cop and a woman, and the people who'd taken her had no respect for either species.

Jeff and Chantal had often posed as brother and sister while undercover. The reality was that he thought of her as he would a sister. She was a partner and a good friend. They'd watched each other's backs for five years now, and they knew each other so well they could communicate with just a look. He was worried sick about her, but he had to set his worrying aside, so he could focus all his efforts on finding her. One of the other officers broke into his thoughts.

"Do you think they'll communicate with us?"

"Do I assume they'll want to bargain with us, you mean?" Jeff said.

The other cop nodded.

"I hope so. It'd mean Chantal could still be alive and able to be used as a bargaining tool," Jeff said.

Captain Bouchard strode into the room, his natural energy making everyone bristle with awareness.

"So, what do we have?"

"Nothing yet," Jeff said. "We have no leads and no clues as to which direction we should head."

"Roadblocks?"

"They're in place, but so far nothing has been discovered. Either they moved faster than we anticipated, or they found a hiding place in the city."

They all turned as the door opened again and a tall, thin man in his mid-fifties entered the room. Jeff recognized him as Captain Simon Meunier, the local head of operations in the Trois-Rivières region of the province. He shook hands with all the officers from Quebec City and spoke of his distress over Chantal's abduction.

The group reviewed the case. Meunier and the rest of the team in Trois-Rivières were acquainted with Danny Wilcox and the drug operation he ran in the province. The quantity of drugs in circulation had risen markedly since Wilcox's arrival on the scene, and there was hardly a region that wasn't affected in some way.

"Where did you leave Victoria?" Captain Bouchard asked Jeff.

"She's in the other room," he said, distractedly.

"She's here?"

Alerted by the alarm in his boss' voice, Jeff dragged his thoughts from Chantal and focused on Bouchard's face.

"She's in the next room," he repeated.

"Why didn't you leave her in Québec City?"

"There wasn't time. I would've had to find someone I could trust to leave her with, and I wanted to get here as soon as possible."

"You could have left her in a jail cell. She'd have been safe there."

Jeff winced. "I don't think that would have gone over very well."

CHAPTER 37

After what seemed like hours, the door to the room opened, and Jeff came in, carrying a cup of coffee.

"Oh, good, a coffee," Tori said.

Jeff raised the cup to his lips, took a long, slow sip, and looked at her with false innocence and raised eyebrows.

"Oh, did you want a cup of coffee, too?" he said.

When she narrowed her eyes, he smiled and handed her the cup.

"Sorry. I just took one sip."

She glared at him and pointedly turned the cup to avoid putting her lips where his had been. The action didn't go unnoticed and evoked a smile from him. Tori squelched her irritation and concentrated on the reason they were here.

"Do you have any news about Chantal?"

Her words wiped the grin from Jeff's face.

"No. Nothing."

"All this time and they haven't found anything?"

She had paced the floor while she waited for an update, afraid Jeff had left to go hunt for his partner without telling her. Tori felt a wave of disappointment at the news that they were no more advanced in their investigation. She saw an equally disappointed look on Jeff's face, and her heart softened toward him.

"Is there anything I can do?"

Tori said the words without thinking, but when Jeff's eyes sparked with anger, she realized she'd opened herself up for attack.

"As a matter of fact, Tori, there's a lot you could do. But you've known that from the very beginning," he said, his voice harsh. "If you'd asked me that question days ago and been prepared to carry through, Chantal would be alive and well now. As it is, we don't know where she is. And, if she's alive, God knows what kind of shape she'll be in. Is it worth it? Is *he* worth it? Christ, Tori, how many more lives are going to be destroyed before you clue in? I swear to God, if anything happens to Chantal, I'll...I'll..."

He whirled away from her and raked his hands through his hair. Tori knew he couldn't finish the sentence because he didn't know what he'd do if anything happened to Chantal.

Jeff put his hands on his hips and took several deep breaths before swinging around to face her again. It was obvious his anger simmered beneath the surface.

"I'm sorry, Tori. I..."

"No, don't say you're sorry, Jeff. You've every right to be angry with me. I understand your loyalty to Chantal is what's driving you, and I respect that. All I ask is that you have the same respect for my loyalty to Danny."

His eyes widened.

"You're comparing Chantal to Wilcox?" he said, shaking his head in denial. "Whatever you do, Tori, do not *ever* compare Chantal to him."

He pivoted and stalked out the door, slamming it soundly behind him.

Chapter 38

Two hours later, the call came in. The group was huddled in the conference room, poring over maps and fielding calls from police officers patrolling the area. A young female cop burst into the room, telling them she'd received a call from someone claiming to be Danny Wilcox. He'd left a message to say he'd call back in five minutes, and they should be prepared to take his call.

Energy charged the atmosphere in the room. No one knew if the news from Wilcox would be positive, but at least it'd be something, and hopefully they could devise a plan of some sort.

Captain Meunier instructed that all other calls be held, and only the call from Wilcox should be transferred to the conference room. Some sat, many paced, but no one spoke as they waited for the phone call.

In precisely five minutes the phone in the center of the table jangled, and despite the fact it had been expected, the shrill sound sparked a united jump to attention from everyone present. Captain Meunier pressed the hands-free button.

"Meunier here."

"Ah, hello, Captain." The voice on the other end of the line was deep and insolent.

"Wilcox?"

"Maybe."

Glances were exchanged among the group, but no one was in any doubt that it was Danny Wilcox on the other end of the line.

"Where is our officer?"

"Right here, and if you want her back, you'll cooperate."

"What do you want, Wilcox?"

"Tori."

A stab of alarm pierced Jeff's heart. He hadn't expected that. He'd assumed the request, if there was one, would be for money or free passage to another country, but not this. He stared at Bouchard to gauge his reaction to the demand, but his boss' expression was stoic. When Jeff opened his mouth to speak, he was silenced by Bouchard's hand on his arm and a warning look.

"How?" Bouchard said.

"You'll meet me in the parking lot at the foot of the bridge at eight o'clock, beside Le Bar Crystal. We'll do the switch there."

"How do we know Chantal is okay?"

A chortle sent shivers down their collective spines.

"Don't worry. She's okay." A pause. "Oh, and Captain, don't try any funny stuff. I want Tori's face to be visible, and don't even think about putting a wire on her. She'll be searched, and if we find anything, there'll be no telling what we'll do to her."

The line went dead.

"Okay," Bouchard said, glancing at his watch, "it's six o'clock. We'll have to get ready for the switch."

"You're not seriously considering it?" Jeff said.

"We have to get Chantal back," Bouchard said.

"So you're going to give him Tori?"

"Excuse me," interrupted Captain Meunier, "but what interest does Wilcox have in this person you call Tori?"

Jeff faced the man who'd spoken, but before he had time to respond, Bouchard answered his question.

"They used to be involved in some way, or perhaps they still are. We're convinced she has information that can lead us to him. But, she's staunchly loyal to Wilcox and refuses to cooperate. There's been a complicated game of cat and mouse going on between them since she arrived in Quebec City a couple of weeks ago."

"It isn't a game." Jeff hissed. "He's been trying to kill her. That's why he wants her; so he can get rid of her once and for all. I can't believe you're going to sacrifice a human life without a second thought."

"Jeff, calm down. I…"

"Calm down?" he said through gritted teeth. "You're sending a lamb to the slaughter without even blinking an eye."

Jeff knew he drew curious looks from the other occupants of the room, but he didn't care. He couldn't let this happen. He was about to start on another tirade when his superior raised his voice to interrupt him.

"Jean-Francois, I will not allow Tori to be killed, just as I will not allow Chantal to be killed. I'd expect you to know me well enough by now to realize that. But, for the moment, we have to play his game, and I need you to have your wits about you if we're going to play to win. Do you understand?"

Jeff took a deep breath and waited a moment for the red haze to clear from his eyes. Bouchard was right, and he should've realized it from the beginning.

CHAPTER 39

Tori was startled out of her trancelike state when the door swung open. She'd been left in the dreary room for too long, and she'd stared at a badly-done painting of Old Quebec City until the colours had blurred and the images were even more misshapen. She'd used the occasion to think, and she was convinced Chantal's disappearance was a random act, a case of being in the wrong place at the wrong time. How could Danny be involved? What would he have to gain by harming a police detective?

When Jeff entered the room, he had Tori's immediate attention. She was impatient for news of Chantal, and she stood, wringing her hands, waiting for him to speak. His hesitation puzzled her. Did he have bad news and not know how to break it to her? Was something else happening of which she should be aware?

Apparently getting over his indecision, with a small movement of his head, he urged Tori to follow him to the conference room. The door was ajar, and the room hummed with the low murmur of voices. Moving over the threshold, silence descended on the group of people gathered around the table.

Their number had increased by a few, and a dark cloud of gloom hung over them. Tori assumed the worst and waited for someone to tell her Chantal had been found dead.

Captain Bouchard broke the silence, asking her to sit down. She did so warily, as if someone might pull the chair out from underneath her at the last moment.

"Miss Anderson, I'll get straight to the point, because we have no time to lose. We've heard from Danny Wilcox."

This information came as a surprise to Tori. Lacking an appropriate response, she remained silent and waited for the other shoe to drop. The police captain continued.

"He said he has Chantal with him."

Tori managed to find her voice through a fog of confusion.

"He does? Is she okay? Why is she with him?"

"He abducted her, as we suspected."

"What? Why?"

She scanned the room, hoping for an explanation, but everyone gaped at her with expressions ranging from curiosity to cynicism. She returned her attention to the man in front of her.

"Why?" she repeated.

Captain Bouchard cleared his throat before continuing.

"He wants to make a trade," he said, watching her face closely. "Her for you."

There was a moment's silence as Tori absorbed this information.

"Okay," she said.

"Tori...," Jeff began, but his words were forestalled by the upraised hand of his boss.

"Miss Anderson, I must explain to you the implications of what I just said." He spoke as if he talked to a small child. "Danny Wilcox said he will give us Chantal if we hand you over to him and step back, leaving you at his mercy."

"I understand that."

"Yes, but do you understand the danger involved?"

"I don't believe there's any danger," she said matter-of-factly. Her words provoked astonished looks from a few of the occupants of the room who hadn't witnessed Tori's loyalty to Wilcox.

"Victoria, you've had a few attempts made on your life since you've arrived in Quebec, have you not?"

Tori stared at him wordlessly, her lips tightening in determination. She knew where he was headed with this, and she had no intention of falling into his trap.

"Wilcox has repeatedly tried to hurt you, and even murder you, and yet you have no fear at the idea of being at his mercy?"

"Danny had nothing to do with those attacks against me. They were caused by a misunderstanding between him and his men, that's all."

Tori's eyes flashed with anger, and her gaze never wavered from Bouchard, but a sound of exasperation came from the man behind her. Palpable waves of frustration rolled off of Jeff, and she willed herself not to glance in his direction.

"Danny would never willingly harm me," she said.

Bouchard continued.

"That may be, but I have a responsibility to ensure your safety. I also have a responsibility toward a fellow police officer who finds herself in danger. We have a difficult decision to make."

"It isn't difficult at all. I'll go, and Chantal will be given back to you," Tori said.

"Yes, I'm afraid that's what will have to happen. I can't sacrifice Chantal's life. You'll have to go."

Tori experienced a mixture of relief and disappointment. She was happy Chantal would be returned, and that she'd have another opportunity to see Danny. But, she couldn't help feeling resentful that they were so willing to hand her over, even though they perceived the risk to be high.

What hurt the most was that Jeff, the man who'd always so stridently criticized Danny, had made only a token protest. It was that fact, above all others, that took away the pleasure she would've felt about escaping the clutches of the authorities and being given the chance to see Danny.

Chapter 40

Captain Bouchard was correct when he said they didn't have a lot of time to prepare. Tori was again led back into the neighboring room, accompanied by Jeff, who lowered his head and took up his pacing. Tori didn't interrupt his deliberations. Her head also swirled with the realization that something important was about to happen.

Tori had hidden it well from the group of police officers, but she had a healthy dose of fear creeping through her veins. She was aware there was an element of danger involved with the upcoming trade, but she resolutely shoved the fear aside and concentrated on the advantages of being handed into Danny's hands. If she could get him alone, she'd be able to explain her intentions to him.

Even that was secondary compared to knowing Chantal would be returned to safety. Tori now realized the female cop had been abducted and perhaps hurt because of her, and she'd do anything to make up for that.

Her musing was interrupted when the door opened, and an officer entered the room carrying a tray of food that he placed in front of Tori before leaving. Tori stared at it without interest. She hadn't asked for anything to eat, and she had no appetite at the moment.

"You should have something before you leave. God knows when you're going to have a chance to eat," Jeff said.

"I'm not hungry."

"I don't care," he said testily. "You're going to eat."

"What difference does it make to you if I eat or not?" she said, hurt by his apparent indifference to the fact she'd soon leave his life permanently and join the man he insisted was a dangerous criminal.

He fixed her with a sharp glare.

Tori returned her attention to the plate in front of her. The hamburger looked like it had been cooked yesterday and reheated in a microwave oven, and something resembling a salad sat limply beside it. The more she stared at it, the worse it appeared. She pushed the plate aside only to have it pushed back toward her. She glowered at Jeff mutinously.

"I don't want it."

"Eat it."

"No."

"Tori, you're going to eat it. If you don't, I'll force it down your throat."

"Why do you care?" she asked again.

"I don't, but I'm under orders to make sure you have something to eat, and I'm going to do it. So, we can do this the easy way, or I can force you to eat it. Believe me, I'm in the mood right now to do something violent, so if I were you, I'd eat the damn hamburger."

Tori could see he was in a horrible mood. She assumed it was because of his fear for Chantal. To keep the peace, she resolved to eat the food that rapidly congealed on the plate in front of her.

Once Tori started, it wasn't as bad as she'd expected, and soon the burger and a small portion of salad had disappeared. Jeff's grim expression never changed, but he didn't complain about her efforts.

"Put on your coat, and we'll get going," he said.

When she was ready, he grasped her by the elbow to escort her from the room. Tori shivered at the touch and experienced an echoing tremor in the pit of her stomach. She didn't know if it was caused by fear or anticipation, or maybe a combination of the two, but she'd made a decision, and she had to stand by it.

They met Captain Bouchard in the corridor, who smiled encouragingly and introduced her to another police officer by the name of Robert Lagacé, a man in his late forties with a no-nonsense manner about him. He'd been chosen to accompany her to make the trade.

Tori, Jeff, and Officer Lagacé left the building and went to the parking lot. Tori's heart sank when Jeff marched to his pickup truck while she got into an unmarked car with his colleague. She'd assumed he'd come with them, but he'd walked away without a word of goodbye. The sense of disappointment and grief took her by surprise. The man by her side glanced at her face and hurried to reassure her.

"He's coming with us, but he'll follow in his truck. You don't have to worry. You're not on your own."

Relief flowed through Tori but she was puzzled by the fact Jeff wouldn't ride in the same car as her. Had he decided to distance himself so completely that he refused to have anything but the most basic contact with her?

Officer Lagacé explained to her that the rendezvous was to take place in a parking lot on the outskirts of the city, located behind a bar that had gone out of business a few months back. When they arrived, there were a few other cars in the lot, and Tori glanced around nervously, searching for signs of Danny. Jeff's truck pulled up and parked alongside them. Within a minute of their arrival, Lagacé's cell phone rang, focusing Tori's attention as he answered it.

The ensuing conversation was short and to the point. By the time the officer disconnected, Jeff stood by the open window of the driver-side door. The two policemen spoke in French, and Tori had the impression they were dismayed by the information gleaned from the telephone call.

No other explanations were given as Jeff climbed into his vehicle and waited for Lagacé and Tori to pull out ahead of him.

"Where are we going? Why isn't Danny here?" Tori said.

"He's changed the meeting place. We expected he would. There are too many places we could hide a sniper here, and he's enjoying the opportunity to send us on a joyride."

Tori took a moment to digest this information.

"So, where are we going?" she repeated.

"He wants us to head out of the city, and he'll call with further information," he said with a frown.

She could see Lagacé wasn't pleased with the plan, but they both knew Danny held the upper hand, and he'd continue to do so as long as he had Chantal. Tori didn't condone Danny's tactics. Kidnapping and blackmail were unscrupulous means to achieving an end, and she realized Danny was already in enough trouble without adding to it by resorting to this.

He was desperate, persistently hunted and hounded by the authorities, and he used whatever method he believed would work in his favor. Why he went to such lengths to get Tori by his side was another question, one she had become afraid to consider.

The side mirror of the car reflected Jeff's vehicle. Tori held her gaze on that image and thought about everything that had happened between them in the past weeks. Their relationship – or whatever it was they had – was about to come to an end. She was aware she wouldn't see Jeff again after today, and she felt a heaviness in her heart, even while she knew it was foolish to feel that way. There never could've been anything between them. Apart from the fact they lived in different countries, there'd been too much deception and duplicity between them. She wouldn't be able to push it under the mat.

She sighed and returned her attention to the road. They left the highway and drove on a little-used side road. Officer Lagacé's cell phone rang once more. He answered it gruffly, received his instructions, and hung up with hardly a word being spoken. He glanced at Tori and answered the question he saw in her eyes.

"It won't be long. Another few minutes."

Her heart thumped.

He was true to his word. Three minutes later, he pulled into what appeared to be an abandoned service station. Jeff followed behind. They parked the vehicles to form a barricade between them and the vacant building. Following the cop's orders, Tori crouched on the floor of the car. As far as she could tell, there was no other sign of life in or around the building, and Tori assumed they waited for another phone call with instructions.

Lagacé drew his gun and exited the car, using the vehicle as a shield. From her position, she saw Jeff do the same. Noticing the two men were alerted by something behind her, Tori raised her head and peered out the window.

A man of medium height and dark hair come from the direction of the building. He wasn't holding a weapon, but Tori knew he could have one under his leather jacket. He shouted something at the two police officers, but she couldn't make out what was said. Tori looked at Jeff and saw him glare at the stranger before exchanging a glance with Lagacé. Jeff opened the car door.

"Get out," he said.

"Who is he?" Tori said, as she crawled across the console and out of the car.

"One of Wilcox's men," he said gruffly, moving her behind him, cutting off her view of the thug.

"Where's Danny?" she said, her heart racing.

"I don't know."

"Hand her over," shouted the man.

"Not until we get Pouliot," said Officer Lagacé.

A nauseating laugh made Tori's skin crawl.

"No, you first."

"Let us see her," Jeff said.

Tori couldn't hide any longer. Kneeling behind the car, she peeked over the hood. The man shouted an instruction over his shoulder without taking his gaze from the police officers. Another larger man appeared, carrying a body slung over his shoulder.

Tori gasped. She stared at the two men beside her to gauge their reactions but saw no change in their expressions other than a tightening of their lips. Obviously, they'd been more prepared than she was for this outcome.

"You told us she wasn't harmed," Lagacé yelled across the several yards separating the two groups.

"She's all right. She's just a little sleepy," the man said with a grin.

"Bring her over here."

"No, we're going to set her in the middle, and little Miss Tori will come over to us."

The sound of her name shook Tori out of her daze. Her thoughts had been centered on the fact that Chantal had been abused. Now, she knew she was expected to trek across that expanse and take the other woman's place. The danger had become very real. She'd agreed to be traded for Chantal, and she was still willing to do so, but she was also terrified.

Tori stared at Jeff imploringly, seeking comfort, encouragement, anything he could offer to help her deal with whatever awaited her. Her stomach clenched. His face was a mask of impassivity.

Jeff touched his hand to the small of her back and gave her a gentle shove. She stumbled before circling the car and crossing toward the abandoned building. Chantal lay unconscious on the snow-covered asphalt in front of her. As Tori shuffled past the prone form, her gaze was drawn downward, and she saw the outward signs of mistreatment; the bruised and swollen face, and the matted hair. Tori's heart went out to the woman. She may have felt wronged by Chantal, but she never would have wished for something like this. It was barbaric.

She looked at the evil, smiling faces of the men in front of her, and tremors reverberated through her body. Glancing over her shoulder at Jeff and Officer Lagacé, she saw they stood behind their vehicles, their expressions unreadable.

Tori's breath was raspy. With another peek at Chantal, she pulled her concentration back to her original mission. She told herself these men may appear sinister, but they were her connection to Danny, and she couldn't let this opportunity slip from her grasp. When one of them seized her by the arm, she almost lost her self-control, desperately wanting to spin around and run back to the relative security of Jeff and the police.

Tori missed her chance. She was dragged behind the building to be shoved onto the back of a four-wheeled all-terrain vehicle behind the larger man. When the machine jumped forward, she was forced to search for something to hold onto other than the man in front of her. She wrapped her hands around bars intended for that purpose, and again questioned the wisdom of what she'd chosen to do.

Despite her best efforts, she was thrown up against the driver at regular intervals. He didn't react. He had the single-minded purpose of delivering her to whatever destination he had in mind.

The speed of the machine was enough to create a wind-chill factor that penetrated the protection of Tori's jacket. Her hands were encased in woollen mittens, but they were numb in minutes. To top it off, it had started to snow, and large, wet flakes plastered themselves to her head and body, forcing her to close her eyes to avoid being blinded.

Several minutes later, the man pulled the ATV up to a house located on a deserted stretch of snow-covered lane. The trees and the high snowbanks made the building almost invisible from the road, which was no more than a wide path.

Numbly, Tori slid off the machine and followed the driver into the house. They'd been followed by another machine driven by the other man. Her thoughts returned to Chantal, and a quiver of revulsion snaked through her insides. She studied the house in front of her from a different perspective. Perhaps it wouldn't provide her with her expected reunion with Danny. Perhaps she'd have a much more threatening and appalling meeting within its walls.

CHAPTER 41

The house wasn't heavily furnished. There was a couch, an armchair, and a television in the living room, along with a table and two chairs in the kitchen. Tori hoped she wouldn't see what was in any of the other rooms of the dilapidated bungalow. She already wished she'd never seen it at all, or the people who'd brought her here.

"Take off your jacket and boots," the driver of the ATV said.

Tori contemplated refusing, but when the other man removed a gun from under his jacket, she decided it'd be best to cooperate. After she'd removed the items, the larger man grasped her arms from behind. Her squeal of protest was squelched and replaced with a gasp of indignation when the other thug ran his hands over her body, probably searching for electronic devices.

When he yanked up her sweater and plunged his hands in her bra, Tori roared in outrage, struggling to kick her way out of their hold, but her efforts were ineffectual. She was forced to submit to their examination no matter how much she fought them. By the time he'd finished his exploration, her breathing was ragged, and her eyes were wild with fury.

Ignoring her, the man picked up her jacket and inspected it carefully.

"Too bad we don't have more time, *chérie*. I would like to continue what I started, but I'm afraid Danny has other plans for you."

Tori thought of many answers to that comment, but she held her tongue. She'd inflict her revenge when she faced Danny.

Heavy footsteps and loud banging noises shook the structure. No one knew where to turn, the racket coming from both sides of the house, until a tall, dark shape smashed through the front door.

"Get out of the way," Jeff shouted.

Tori dove for the corner nearest the open doorway as two more police officers entered from the back. The man in the leather jacket followed her and, within a couple of seconds, she was draped across him, being used as a shield with a gun held against her temple.

Everyone in the room froze. Tori's gaze connected with Jeff's, but she couldn't read his thoughts. She was at the mercy of the man with the gun. He dragged her to her feet and backed toward the door, yelling at the policemen in French. She didn't have to understand the words to grasp the meaning. She was being taken hostage, and they could do nothing to stop him. She was on her own.

Luck was with her. As the man backed down the outside stairs of the house, he missed his step, and tumbled to the ground, loosening his grip on Tori. She reacted instantly. Twisting out of his arms and getting her feet under her, she ran at full speed toward the end of the driveway where Jeff's familiar truck was parked.

It was like a lifeline to Tori, and each step of her bootless feet brought her closer to it. Behind her, heavy footsteps thumped on the hard-packed snow, and she knew the man was close. Hopefully, not close enough.

She whimpered when a bullet whizzed past her head. He was shooting at her, she thought. It spurred her to run faster, and she chanted in her head as she ran. *Please be unlocked. Please let the keys be in it.*

Tori circled the truck to reach the driver-side door and pull it open, gasping with relief. She jumped into the truck and slammed and locked the doors almost in one movement. Seeing the keys in the ignition, she offered up a silent prayer of thanksgiving.

Her spirits plunged when she twisted the key, and nothing happened. Searching for a reason, she jerked away from the door when someone pulled on the handle, and she saw the face of her assailant inches from her on the other side of the window.

"Damn it, Jeff. Where are you?" she said.

It was a matter of moments before the man would break into the truck, and she wasn't sure if she could fight him off.

It dawned on her that the truck had a manual transmission. She wasn't totally ignorant about how to drive such a thing, but it had been many years, and her experience was limited.

Tori fumbled for the clutch pedal with her left foot and cursed Jeff for his long legs. She didn't have time to find the lever to adjust the seat. She slid down as far as possible and stretched her cold, wet toes until she could start the ignition.

She winced as the man smashed the butt of his gun against the window, trying to break through the glass. Again, Tori wondered why Jeff hadn't come to her rescue. She thrust the transmission into first gear and held a ragged breath. Her foot slipped off the clutch and the truck stalled.

She was showered with tiny fragments of glass. A hand reached into the cab of the truck to grip her shoulder. She screamed in panic and threw herself sideways, pulling herself from his grasp.

The man's hand groped inside the door, looking for the inside door lock. Tori gathered her strength and used her left foot to smash his hand against the door. He howled in pain and yanked his hand away. She righted herself, pushed in the clutch, and started the truck.

Tori gave it some gas before she popped the clutch, and the truck leapt forward with a wild bucking movement, but it didn't stall. Unfortunately, she didn't lose her passenger. He had his uninjured arm wrapped around the side mirror, and he stood firmly on the running board.

Tori gunned the gas and ignored the fact she was still in first gear. She was too preoccupied with keeping the vehicle on the road while she sat low in the seat, scarcely able to see over the steering wheel. To make matters worse, the windshield was partially covered in snow. She drove blind.

The man recovered enough to reach in and try to grab hold of Tori. While avoiding his clawing fingers, she fumbled for the windshield wiper control. Finding it, the snow was removed from the windshield with one large swipe, and the thug was blindsided by a build-up of heavy, wet snow. Forced to put his hands to another use, he clung to the side of the truck and wiped the snow from his face.

Tori's reprieve was short-lived. She was able to center the truck in the middle of the road before he reached inside the cab again. As one of his hands closed around her throat, Tori had a flashback to the last time someone had tried to strangle her. Panic welled up inside her chest. Tori had to suppress it long enough to get rid of the man hanging on to the side the vehicle. She jerked the steering wheel to the side and back again, hoping to dislodge him, but his hand tightened around her throat.

Tori saw stars. Removing a hand from the steering wheel to tear at his, she tried without success to break his grip. In desperation, she drove the truck to the opposite side of the road and headed toward a telephone pole. She planned to graze it, knocking him off the side, without smashing into it head-on. As she neared the pole, the stars overtook her vision, and she was afraid she'd miss her mark. Metal scraped against wood, followed by the dull thud of a body connecting with a pole, and she fought back the rising bile in her aching but suddenly-free throat.

The truck was wedged into the snowbank alongside the telephone pole. Tori didn't dare glance back to see what had happened to her erstwhile passenger. This wasn't a time for compassion. Instead, she pressed the four-wheel drive button on the dashboard, restarted the stalled truck, and pressed on the gas pedal. With a roar, it lurched onto the road, and Tori was on her own.

Reaction set in. Her legs trembled, and her breathing was rapid and harsh. She whimpered as the adrenaline rush subsided. Shifting the truck into second and then third gear, Tori realized she had no idea where she was. She drove without any destination in mind, feeling safer if she was mobile. Unable to think ahead to her next step, she focused her concentration on keeping the truck on the road.

Tori suffered from a case of snow blindness. Everything was white; the road in front of her and the banks on either side. The wind had picked up, and the falling snow gusted and twirled in front of the truck. She was forced to slow down, and she strained her eyes to see the road in front of her, hoping she was headed in the right direction and not into a snowbank.

The broken window didn't help. The snow blew in against the side of her face, and she had to regularly wipe away the frigid wetness.

Tori didn't know how long she drove under those conditions, but the sound of sirens broke through her concentration. When she realized they were behind her and steadily coming closer, she moaned in relief. It was the first time she'd treasured police sirens.

Tori pulled the truck over to the side of the road and brought it to a stop.

The trembling took over her entire body. She lowered her forehead to the steering wheel and hoped the police would cart her off to jail for stealing a vehicle. It sounded like an appealing prospect at this point.

The truck door was flung open, and she was hauled into a pair of strong arms. Tori didn't have to look to see who it was. She knew. As he held her, she burst into tears of pent-up fear and relief.

Chapter 42

After several minutes, Jeff slid Tori over to the passenger side of the truck and settled behind the steering wheel. He nodded at the two other cops who'd waited by the side of the road while Tori gave way to her emotions. They returned to the scene.

Jeff had no intention of taking Tori back to the place he'd just left, wanting to downplay the outcome of her wild ride. It hadn't been a pretty sight.

He cursed the sequence of events that had prevented him from getting to her more quickly. When Jeff had seen the man drag Tori down the outside stairs of the house, using her as a shield, his mind had raced, searching for a way to circumvent his escape without bringing harm to Tori.

He was proud of her quick reaction when they fell to the ground after tumbling down the steps, and he was about to follow at a sprint when he was startled by the explosion of a gunshot coming from behind him. Assuming the shot was from the other criminal who was left behind, Jeff dropped to the floor and rolled behind the couch. He prayed Tori would reach the truck and be safe until he could get to her.

Peering from behind the safety of the couch, he was shocked when he saw the gun in question was held by one of their own, a rookie cop. The look on the cop's face said it all. It was fixed in an expression of stunned horror.

"What the hell are you doing?" Jeff said, disbelievingly.

"I wanted to stop him."

"Jesus Christ. Stop him? You could've killed Tori."

"I'm...I'm sorry. I wanted to stop him."

Jeff grabbed the gun out of the other man's hand in disgust and shoved it into his own waistband. He glared at the second cop who restrained the other thug.

"Cuff him and get him out of here. I'm going after Tori."

As he swung around to leave, he heard a loud grunt. Before he could react, he was tackled from behind and found himself lying on the floor with the felon on top of him, trying to wrestle the gun out of his waistband. He would've succeeded if Jeff hadn't moved swiftly. He grabbed the man's arm and twisted it out of reach, wrapped his leg around the man's thighs, and manoeuvred him into a debilitating position face-down on the floor.

"Bring me the cuffs," Jeff said.

When the cuffs were in place, and the scene was secure, Jeff jumped to his feet and bounded out the door. His anger was spurred by his frustration. Because of the comedy of errors, he'd lost precious minutes. By now, the other guy would've caught up to Tori, and God knew what kind of situation she was in at this moment.

Racing toward his truck, he saw it pitch clumsily onto the road and was relieved to know Tori had made a clean break. Even with that thought in mind, he didn't slow his pace. He expected to find the other man nearby, and he'd no intention of letting him get away.

Jeff was stunned when he reached the spot and found it deserted. Staring after the retreating pickup truck, his heart tripped in terror to see the man hanging onto the driver's side, reaching through the window. Jeff spun around and ran to the nearest police cruiser.

He reached it panting for breath, saw the keys in the ignition, and thanked God for small blessings. He used the radio to call for backup, and accelerated to follow his pickup truck.

The road twisted and turned, but there weren't any connecting roads onto which they could branch off, so Jeff was confident he'd catch up to them. The rapidly-falling snow wasn't helpful, forcing him to slow down or risk running into the back of his own truck in the blinding wind.

Turning a corner, there was a brief respite from the snow, and Jeff saw the vehicle pull out from the left-hand side of the road, lurching once again. As he passed the spot from which the truck had left, he saw a dark shape on the snow.

With his heart in his throat, assuming the worst, Jeff stopped the patrol car and threw it into reverse. The car had just rolled to a stop before he ran toward the telephone pole, his pulse beating double-time.

Reaching it, Jeff drew in a sharp breath and closed his eyes for an instant, before kneeling to get a closer look at the damage. Glancing at the telephone pole, he saw the blood and brain matter clinging to the wood. A shiver of horror swept through him. He hoped Tori hadn't seen what had happened to her aggressor. If she had, she'd have a long road ahead of her before getting over the shock.

At the thought of Tori, he stood, intending to go after her, just as Lagacé pulled up accompanied by another patrol car.

It was several minutes before Jeff could leave the scene, several minutes during which Tori drove in an almost catatonic state. How she kept the truck on the road, he had no idea, given the fact she'd never adjusted the seat to accommodate her shorter legs.

Jeff didn't want to let her go. They clung to each other in the intimacy of the truck cab as she cried on his shoulder. He listened as she sobbed out the tale of what had happened. Most of it was unintelligible, but he didn't stop her. She needed to get it out.

He was jolted from his thoughts when she mentioned Danny's name. He concentrated on what she said.

"If he'd been there...it would've been...been all right."

"What?" Jeff said.

"If Danny had been there, it wouldn't have happened."

"Are you serious?" Jeff said, unable to keep the surprise and rising anger from his voice. Tori raised her head from his chest to look at him.

"Of course, I am. He would've protected me."

"Jesus, Tori. He was behind the whole thing."

She stared at him for a moment before answering him in a smooth, soft voice.

"I know he was behind the plan to trade me for Chantal, but he'd never allow anyone to harm me. I expected to see him, but he wasn't there."

"Tori, if we hadn't been there, God knows what would've happened to you. Those guys had every intention of killing you."

"I agree with you. I'm sure they did, but I have no idea why. I'm certain Danny isn't responsible for what those men did, and he would've been furious with them if they'd hurt me."

Jeff's heart plummeted. He'd been sure this would've been the final wakeup call for Tori. Instead, if anything, she was even more loyal to Danny Wilcox. He had no clue how to convince her otherwise.

Chapter 43

Despite having the heater at its maximum setting, they shivered all the way to the city as cold air and snow streamed through the broken window.

"I think I may have hurt someone. There was a man hanging onto your truck. I'm sorry, but he broke the window."

"That's okay. Don't worry about it," Jeff said, not wanting to pursue this conversation.

"He tried to strangle me. I had to get him to stop, so I drove close to a telephone pole, hoping to get him to jump off."

Jeff heard the tremor in her voice and imagined her fear at the time.

"You did the right thing."

"Did you find him?"

"Yep, we did."

"Was he seriously hurt?" she said.

"I didn't hang around very long. I had to get to you as soon as possible. I didn't know if you were hurt or not."

"I see."

There was a pause, and Jeff sensed she wanted to ask him another question.

"Jeff?"

"Hmm."

"I'm sorry about your truck. I'll find some way to pay you back, I promise."

"What are you talking about?"

"Your beautiful truck. Apart from the window, I think I may have smashed the side a little."

Jeff hadn't given a second thought to the damage. He knew the truck was badly scraped and dented, but it didn't bother him. Tori had saved her life with her quick thinking, and the insurance company would cover the damage.

"Don't worry about it."

"You're just being nice."

"I *am* being nice, but you still don't have to worry about it."

They were on the highway, and Jeff drove as slowly as possible to avoid being frozen to death. He'd pulled a blanket out of the back seat, and Tori was bundled up snugly, but the cold air invaded any protection they'd found.

"Jeff?"

"Hmm?" he murmured absently, absorbed in negotiating the truck through the snowstorm as he was blindsided by intermittent blasts of snow to the side of his head.

"How did you find me? At that house, I mean. I can't understand how you followed me through the woods without them noticing you."

Jeff glanced at her, his expression sheepish.

"Well, um," he said, "do you remember that hamburger I made you eat?" He paused and waited for her nod of assent. "There was a very tiny tracking device embedded in the meat."

"What? You made me eat a tracking device? I've got an electronic thing in my stomach? Are you crazy?"

"It's very tiny, almost microscopic. You won't even notice it's there. In a day or so, it'll be gone."

She glared at him.

"Why do you have to be so sneaky about everything? Is it part of your nature to do things behind someone's back all the time? Why couldn't you have just asked me to swallow the damn thing instead of hiding it in my food?"

He returned her look.

"Because you're so pigheaded when it comes to Wilcox, you would've refused to swallow it."

Tori opened her mouth to deliver a comeback but shut it hastily. Jeff imagined the thoughts going through her head. The device had saved her life. He watched as she swallowed the retort along with a large piece of humble pie and forced a submissive smile to her lips.

"You're right, Jeff. You're absolutely right."

Chapter 44

The atmosphere was tense in the room where Captains Bouchard and Meunier worked with a half-dozen other men. Tori prepared for bad news about Chantal as the guilt gnawed at her insides. She felt she was responsible for whatever happened to the police officer.

The room had fallen into silence as she was led to a chair beside a long, battered, wooden table. She looked expectantly at Captain Bouchard until she couldn't take the suspense any longer.

"Is she okay? Is Chantal going to be all right?"

"She's in surgery at the moment. Her left arm is severely broken, and she has internal bleeding along with a severe concussion, but the doctors feel she'll make a full recovery."

Tori exhaled a breath. At least Chantal would survive her physical wounds, but she shivered to think of the emotional scars that would remain. The fact she was an experienced police officer may have hardened her to many aspects of violence, but surely it was different when the violence was directed toward yourself. Tori's own recent ordeals had left her with a quivering sense of horror.

Glancing around the room, she realized the men spoke in French, as if she wasn't present, or she wasn't worthy enough to participate in the discussion. She caught Jeff's eye and, with a raised eyebrow, communicated her disapproval. His response was a shrug of resignation. Anger welled up when it dawned on her that they purposely shut her out, and Jeff was in complete agreement with the scheme.

"Excuse me, but I'm having trouble following the conversation," she said, not bothering to conceal her sarcasm.

Captain Bouchard shifted his narrowed stare toward her.

"I'm sorry if we're being rude, but there's a valid reason for not including you in our meeting at this point."

Tori bristled.

"Then why did you bring me in here? Why not just lock me up in a room as you're accustomed to doing?"

Before he could answer, the door opened, and a young woman came in carrying a file, which she placed in front of Captain Meunier. Everyone stilled and stared expectantly at the folder. Meunier glanced at Tori and Jeff in turn before he flipped it open. Tori gasped when she saw what was on the table in front of her.

The face of the latest man who'd tried to kill her was exposed in a photo on top of a pile of documents half an inch thick. It took a moment before she got over the shock of seeing that terrifying face and found her voice.

"Where...how did you know...who is he?" she said.

"He's a well-known gang member, Claude Fortin," Bouchard said.

Tori hoped Jeff would fill her in with more details, but when she saw his expression of dismay, a sense of terrible foreboding came over her.

"Is he...dead?" The last word was hardly audible, but it didn't have to be spoken aloud. Everyone in the room read Tori's thoughts by the look on her face.

Jeff's arms circled her at the precise moment that her shoulders caved inward and her hands covered her face. She trembled violently, as she had done when he found her in the truck.

"Oh my God, that's three. I've killed three men," she said, her voice muffled by his sweater.

"You didn't kill them, Tori," Jeff said, "Not intentionally, and you had nothing whatsoever to do with Yvon Picard's death."

He blatantly ignored the sceptical glance Tori aimed at him.

"The other two deaths were a clear-cut case of self-defence. They tried to kill you, and you were justified in your actions."

Tori looked at Captain Bouchard and a few of the other faces in the room as if expecting them to deny Jeff's opinion and his decision to become judge and jury in her case. The expressions were either blank or sympathetic, and another wash of emotion swept over her.

She looked at Jeff with eyes wet from tears.

"I know that. Deep down, I know it, but it's still a shock. I can't believe that up until a few weeks ago, I was an ordinary, boring, law-abiding citizen. And now I'm responsible for the deaths of three people, and I'm involved in some crazy scheme concocted by the police to run down Danny."

"Well, it's nice of you to heap such praise on all of us, but we have to share a lot of the credit with our wonderful criminals without whom this whole operation wouldn't be necessary," Jeff said.

Captain Bouchard stepped into the fray.

"It's time for the Quebec City contingent to return to their own turf," he said, nodding toward his officers. "After her surgery, and when she's well enough to be transported, Chantal will be sent to a hospital in Quebec. All we can do now is regroup and work on another strategy."

CHAPTER 45

Tori and Jeff made the trip to Quebec in an unmarked police car that had been loaned to them by the Trois-Rivières unit of the Sûreté du Québec. Jeff's truck was left behind to be held as evidence in the death of Claude Fortin. Repairs would follow.

They spent the night at Jeff's house in Valcartier. Out of sheer exhaustion, Tori slept deeply and peacefully. When she woke in the morning, she was rested.

She had to give credit for her good night's sleep to Jeff. Although they slept in separate rooms, she felt unconditionally safe in his orbit. He may be a lot of things, but Tori knew he'd never let any harm come to her if it was humanly possible to prevent it.

Later, at police headquarters, they were greeted with varying degrees of warmth by Sébastien and Captain Bouchard. The former appeared happy to see Tori, while the latter treated her with remote politeness. She pondered why he'd summoned her here and what his intentions were.

Her mind wandered in uncomfortable directions as she sat on a bench in the corridor while Bouchard held a private meeting with his officers. Chantal was foremost in her thoughts, and she prayed the woman would recover from her injuries. The idea that Danny may have had a hand in those injuries worried her. Could he have stooped so low that he'd attack a police officer and a woman? It couldn't be possible. The Danny she knew had bad qualities – Tori was well aware of them – but he'd never resort to violence against women. That, she couldn't believe. In contrast, the people he associated with had no scruples, and she would lay the blame at their door.

The session in the room beside her lasted twenty minutes but, judging by the sound of the raised voices and the grim expression on Jeff's face when he stepped into the corridor, it'd been tumultuous. He stood over Tori and glared at her.

"You can come in now," he said tersely.

"What's wrong? Why are you looking at me like that?"

"Just come into the room. Bouchard will tell you."

The people sitting at the table were bedraggled, and Tori knew, without a doubt, it didn't bode well for her.

"Sit down, please." Captain Bouchard rose and gestured to a chair as he took up his characteristic pacing.

Although she preferred to stand, Tori realized she'd follow the conversation more easily if she was firmly seated. She noticed Jeff pull a chair over and place it at a right angle to hers, close enough she could reach over to touch him if she wanted. He sat with his elbows on his knees, and his hands clasped together, and she saw the anguished expression on his face. Her heart clenched in dreadful anticipation.

"Miss Anderson..."

The captain's formality made Tori's shoulders stiffen, expecting bad news.

"Four times now, we've intervened to pull you out of the clutches of criminals. I am including the instance where Jean-François, or Benoit as you knew him then, refused to hand you over to the two men who showed up at his cabin. We've placed you under round-the-clock protection, at a great expense to the province of Québec. We've done everything we could to accommodate you and to ensure your security. In return, you've given us nothing."

Bouchard held up his hand when Tori opened her mouth to protest.

"Please, let me finish. You'll have your chance to speak."

As he said those last words, Tori saw him glance at Jeff, but she refrained, with difficulty, from looking in the same direction. Instead, she kept her attention pinned on Bouchard, her mind working feverishly, attempting to guess in which direction he was headed.

"We believe you may be able to provide us with a great deal of information about Danny Wilcox. We know you have some kind of personal connection to him and have been able to make contact with him in the past. We had desperately wished for your cooperation in our efforts to arrest Wilcox, but you've stubbornly refused to give us that cooperation."

His jaw tightened, and she felt Jeff stiffen beside her.

"As a matter of fact," Bouchard continued, "You've done everything possible to hamper our investigation. So, I regret that I've no choice but to arrest you for obstruction of justice."

Tori's mouth went dry. It wasn't possible.

"That's not true. I never did anything to impede you. I never stood in your way. I just refused to help you. It's not the same thing," she said, desperately. "It's not my fault you couldn't capture him. You followed me everywhere."

She turned when a large, warm hand closed over hers, and she looked into Jeff's troubled eyes. He shook his head but, in her anxiety, she didn't comprehend his gesture. A thousand images flashed through her head; Danny, her mother, herself sitting in a jail cell in a foreign country, her home in Florida.

Tori saw this decision by Captain Bouchard as the one to change her life and send her on a tailspin to doom. She'd planned to go back home and pick up where she'd left off, living with the anguish of leaving Danny behind, but at least able to retrieve most of what she had before. If the captain carried through with his threat, she may never be able to do so.

She swallowed heavily.

"I want a lawyer."

"You can have one," Bouchard said. "But, I'm still placing you under arrest. When you've been booked and assigned a cell, you may speak with your lawyer."

The words were harsh, and they cut a path through Tori's gut. Her most serious offense so far in her life had been a single speeding ticket. She'd never imagined she would be paraded through the procedures she'd only ever seen on television. Fingerprinting and mug shots had never been on her bucket list and her eyes filled with tears.

Jeff's hand tightened on hers. She'd momentarily forgotten it was there. She gave him a blurry look and wondered at the anger she'd seen on his face earlier. Had it been directed at her? Because of her unwillingness to cooperate? Or was he angry with his boss?

Apart from the worry in Jeff's eyes, she saw a flicker of accusation. She was aware he blamed her for the predicament she was in, even as he wished she didn't have to be in it.

She straightened her back and tugged her hand from Jeff's. Well, so be it. What she'd done had been done for love. At least, she could remind herself of that, and hopefully, it'd bring her comfort. She'd need it.

•   •   •

Tori gazed at the stark cell that was her temporary home and reflected on what had happened in the past few hours. She'd been booked and escorted to a cell. A court-appointed lawyer was assigned to her, but two hours passed before she was summoned to a private room to speak to him.

Jacques Simard was a short man, in his mid-fifties, with a rotund build and the beginnings of a receding hairline. His English was quite good, and she wondered skeptically if they'd sacrificed quality in their hunt for a lawyer who could converse with her in her mother tongue. Her doubts were put to rest when she had the time to speak with him for a few minutes. He expressed concern for her welfare as he laid her case out concisely.

"I've been informed of the situation by the police, and, with what you've told me, I don't believe they have a strong case against you. What you say is true. You didn't help them, but you didn't try to hamper their case or alter evidence. However, you'll still have to be arraigned in front of a judge, and possibly tried in a court of law."

He hesitated for a moment.

"Ordinarily, it would be my job to get you out of here on bail, but since you're a foreign citizen, the police feel the flight risk is too great. Also, after hearing about all the experiences you've suffered, and being informed they no longer intend to keep you under police protection, I think it'd be better for you to stay here, no matter how disagreeable the circumstances."

Tori's arms crossed over her stomach, and her shoulders caved.

"Of course, they've offered you the option of being released and nullifying the arrest record if you help them in their search for Danny Wilcox."

Tori's shoulders straightened, and her mouth settled into a hard line.

"I'll stay here, thank you very much."

She should've known they'd send a lawyer who'd work in their best interests, she thought. If she had the money to hire a lawyer of her own choosing, this wouldn't happen. He'd fight to have her released.

Instead, the police had maneuvered her into a winning situation – for them. They no longer had to expend the manpower to protect her, yet they had her in captivity and within their sight at all times. Well, she'd let them have their way for now. They had no case against her, and she'd find a way to fight them, she thought rebelliously. She wouldn't give in.

Chapter 46

Jeff adjusted his suit and tightened his tie as he gazed at his reflection in the washroom mirror at police headquarters. The only time he dressed like this was when he had to appear in court, he thought grimly.

That was where he'd be today. He had the odious task of testifying at Tori's arraignment, and whatever he had to report to the judge, it wouldn't weigh in her favor.

Jeff recalled the meeting in Captain Bouchard's office when they'd told her they were placing her under arrest. He'd witnessed the expression on Tori's face, and it brought a pain like a knife stab to his heart. Once again, she'd made the decision to stand by Danny.

She'd go to jail for him, and even as that knowledge hurt, he was awed that anyone could be so loyal, so willing to give and give, even when they received nothing but misery in return. The irony of that idea struck him. He had travelled down the same path, and if he didn't stop soon he'd be destroyed by it.

His colleagues involved in the case had assumed Tori's arrest and confinement would convince her to change her mind and decide to cooperate, but it seemed to have had the opposite effect. It didn't surprise Jeff. When he went to visit her at the jail, hoping to change her mind, she was rigidly cold toward him and refused to respond to a word he said. Jeff wanted to offer Tori comfort and support, but that was a fantasy. She neither wanted nor needed his help.

Now, he was in the nefarious position of helping Bouchard carry through with his threat. He had to play the part of the villain, and he'd soon drive another wedge between them. It was hopeless and had been hopeless from the beginning.

Jeff sighed and shook his head. It'd be better for all of them if they could get it over with. Maybe Tori's lawyer would convince the judge to be lenient and release her, and they could put it in the past. Tori would go back to Florida, and he'd get on with his life, chalking up the whole experience as a major life lesson.

He met Sébastien in the corridor, and they walked to the parking lot together. They'd meet Captain Bouchard at the courthouse, where Tori would be escorted with an armed guard to the arraignment chambers.

Inside the large, modern building that housed the courthouse of Québec, Jeff and Sébastien were joined by their superior officer. They'd each have their piece to say at Tori's arraignment. They'd talk about her meeting with a man who was wanted by the police throughout the province of Quebec. They'd talk about when she escaped from Chantal's apartment and provoked a full-scale search. They'd have to reveal the fact that she stubbornly refused to cooperate with the authorities despite the deaths, injuries, and close calls that had occurred since her appearance in the province.

They wouldn't lie, and they wouldn't exaggerate any of their claims, but they wouldn't need to. The testimony would stand on its own, and it would be damning enough without any need for embellishment. They didn't derive any joy from this knowledge. It was part of their jobs to accept it.

Sébastien was the first to spot her, and the others, seeing his reaction, turned to see Tori being led along the corridor in handcuffs, a burly guard at her side with his hand on her elbow.

A shiver ran down Jeff's spine at the sight of her. Tori was dressed in a tailored pale-blue shirt and navy pin-striped pants, matched with a pair of low-heeled sensible shoes. Jeff knew the clothes were taken from Chantal's closet. He was the one who'd picked them up. He didn't know if Tori was aware who they belonged to, or if she even cared.

Her head was held high with her hair demurely tied back, and she carried herself with as much dignity as possible for a person wearing handcuffs. Tori must have seen the group of people she'd once considered friends. She avoided making eye contact with any of them. Instead, she focused on a wall far down the corridor.

The explosion of a gunshot rang through the building, echoing off the cement walls and huge glass windows. It was followed by screams and the thud of bodies hitting the floor or scrambling out of harm's way.

Jeff and his companions flattened themselves against the walls, their weapons drawn and their eyes exploring the area. Sébastien and Bouchard searched for the source of the shot, but Jeff looked for Tori among the bodies that fervently fought to escape the building, no doubt believing there was a mass murderer on the loose.

Despite the pandemonium, a panic-filled voice, shouting in French, reached his ears.

"Over here. She's been shot."

His heart leapt into his throat before dropping into his stomach when he saw the guard bent over the still form of Tori lying on the floor, a pool of blood beneath her.

Jeff didn't remember making his way to Tori, or the amount of people he shoved out of his way to get to her side, but he was aware of putting his hand to her throat to feel for a pulse. His touch was answered by a fluttering of her lashes and a creasing of her forehead. She lay face-down on the floor. The bullet had entered her from behind, just beneath her collarbone. The blood seeped from her body at an astonishing rate.

As he removed his suit jacket, he spun around to face the stunned guard.

"Call an ambulance! Get help right away!"

"It happened so fast. There was nothing I could do."

Jeff growled at him once more.

"Never mind talking. Just get an ambulance."

Out of the corner of his eye, he saw the man pull his radio from his belt, requesting assistance. Jeff struggled to staunch the flow of blood with his jacket, as he spoke urgently in Tori's ear.

"It's going to be okay, baby. Help is on the way."

"It hurts."

Her voice was just above a whisper, but it vibrated with the pain contained in those two words.

"I know it hurts, but we'll take care of you. You're going to be all right. Do you understand, Tori?"

She nodded feebly, and he knew he'd do anything to take the pain away from her. If he could draw it into his own body, he would.

Jeff scanned the area, searching for someone to tell him the medics were almost there, and the police had caught whoever had shot her. He knew who was responsible, and he wished he could be granted five minutes alone with him before he was handed over to the strong hands of the law.

Jeff glanced up to see Sébastien kneeling next to him. Meeting his gaze, Sébastien briefly put his hand on his shoulder before leaving to help manage the havoc being wreaked around them.

Panic pulsed through the building, drawing people from various chambers to see what caused the commotion. Security personnel scurried to control the crowds and keep them from generating further injuries, while allowing the police and emergency workers to do their jobs. The exits were barred, preventing anyone from leaving until they caught the person responsible. Although it served the purpose of keeping the criminal inside the building, it also created an atmosphere of hysteria among the remaining innocent bystanders who desperately wanted to get out.

Jeff kept his full attention on Tori, speaking soothingly to her, pressing firmly on the wound as someone else – a stranger – lifted her head to place a rolled-up jacket beneath it.

"Come on, Tori. You can do it," he said when she shivered from reaction, and keeping her eyes open seemed to be an effort. "You're too damn tough to give in to this. Stay with me. Help will be here soon."

Under his breath, Jeff cursed the length of time it took for an ambulance to get to the courthouse. Hôtel-Dieu Hospital was less than a kilometer away.

Six minutes passed from the moment of the call and the arrival of the ambulance. The medics bundled Tori onto the stretcher and were out the door a few minutes after that. Jeff was right behind them as they headed for the vehicle. When one of the medics instructed him to sit in front with the driver instead of riding in the back with Tori, he was silenced by Jeff's glower.

Luckily, the Hôtel-Dieu of Quebec, North America's oldest hospital, was so close it was visible from the courthouse and, minutes later, the vehicle entered the ambulance bay. Inside, Jeff was stopped by a nurse who was short in stature but tall in determination.

"You can't go into the emergency ward. I don't care who you are," she said, as Jeff flashed his badge at her. "You'll stay in the waiting room while we examine her. As soon as possible, someone will come get you."

As soon as possible wasn't soon enough for Jeff. He took a few minutes to contact Captain Bouchard and began the interminable wait as he paced the floor of the waiting room.

Although he'd seen plenty of violence and gunshot wounds, Jeff didn't have any medical training. He used his imagination to fill in the blanks and assess Tori's injuries. However, when using your imagination with someone you care deeply about, the injuries tended to become worse with each minute that passed. Jeff was convinced Tori hadn't survived the attack.

"She'll be taken up to surgery in a few minutes," the nurse said, when he was called to the emergency desk.

"Can I see her?" Jeff's question came out in a rush. He was weak with relief to know she was alive.

The nurse gave him a stern look, but any protest died on her lips. Jeff hurried into one of the examining rooms with the order to stay for just a few minutes ringing in his ears.

Tori's eyelids were almost translucent, emphasized by the dark circles underneath. Her skin was as pale as the white sheets on which she lay.

Jeff had no idea if Tori was conscious or not, but he picked up a limp hand and leaned over to place a soft kiss on her brow. When he drew back, her tired and pain-filled eyes were focused on him.

"It's going to be okay, Tori. They're going to take good care of you."

"They have to take out the bullet," she said, her voice scarcely above a whisper. "But it didn't hit any major organs or arteries. The doctor said the damage should be minimal."

Jeff nodded, unable to hide the wave of relief.

"Good. That's great. You'll be better in no time." He clutched her hand, wishing he could hang onto her.

"Jeff?"

"Yeah?"

"Did they get him?"

Jeff knew to whom she referred. He'd prepared himself for the question and had hoped against hope she'd wait until after the surgery to ask it. But, he should've known Tori would always have the subject uppermost in her mind.

"They caught the shooter, but it wasn't Wilcox."

His heart cracked a bit when he saw the small smile come to her lips and the gleam of triumph sparkle in her eyes.

"I knew it wasn't him," she said.

Jeff couldn't respond. There were a thousand things he wanted to say, but he couldn't bring himself to utter the words. They'd do nothing but hurt her. She'd been hurt enough, and there'd be more to come before all was said and done.

Jeff didn't tell her the man was being interrogated, and everyone was convinced he was one of Wilcox's men. He didn't tell her they were working hard to wring a confession from him and were willing to offer him leniency in exchange for Wilcox. There'd be an opportunity for that conversation later.

A gruff clearing of the throat sounded behind him, and Jeff spun to face the nurse in the doorway.

"It's time. You'll have to leave. There's a waiting room on the second floor if you wish to stay. Otherwise, you can give us your coordinates, and we'll contact you when we have news."

"I'll wait upstairs."

Jeff turned back to Tori with an encouraging smile and lifted her hand to his lips to give her fingers a parting kiss. As he walked past the nurse, she laid her hand on his arm.

"Don't worry. She's in good hands. Dr. Jobin is one of the best we have."

Chapter 47

The walls were beige, a sickly pale beige, and they were nicked in several places, presumably by stretchers, walkers, or wheelchairs. The windowsills were high and deep. All she could see was sky; an endlessly blue, winter sky. Even though the sun was bright, it was likely bitingly cold.

Tori didn't have any sensation of cold or hot at this moment. She felt disembodied. It worried her. Had something gone wrong? Maybe a major nerve had been damaged, and she was paralyzed from the neck down. Every once in a while, you heard about a major medical snafu that changed a person's life forever. It wouldn't be impossible.

Tori concentrated on moving her legs, and they shifted a fraction of an inch. She did the same with her left arm with the same result. She wasn't paralyzed after all, just sluggish. When she tried to move her right arm, she couldn't do more than wiggle her fingers. With great effort, she turned her head to look at her arm and saw it was securely strapped to her body. She let her head fall back. Worrying about it was too much work. She'd think about it later.

When Tori opened her eyes again, the sunlight had faded to dusk, and she knew in a few minutes it'd be dark. She was less groggy now, better able to pivot her head and view her surroundings. There was another bed in the room, but it was empty. That was good. She didn't feel like having to keep company with a stranger. She preferred the quiet.

The quiet was broken by the entrance of a male nurse. He greeted her in French with a loud, jocular voice. He seemed to feel it was his duty to boost her spirits. What he didn't realize was that she couldn't understand him. Nevertheless, she was comforted by his good cheer.

It didn't take long for the nurse to realize Tori didn't speak French, but he was unfazed. He stumbled and stammered in very poor English, speaking mostly nonsense, while he checked her vital signs and the fluid in the intravenous bags before leaving her on her own.

Tori stared out the window at the night sky. She thought about the fact that twenty-four hours ago she'd sat in a jail cell with nothing more to look forward to than her outing of the following morning. She'd anticipated a short session with the judge and had expected to be released until her trial, if there would ever be a trial.

Tori remembered walking along that long corridor and seeing Jeff with his back to her while in conversation with his colleagues. She saw Sébastien spot her and she knew Jeff would turn to look at her soon. She deliberately moved her gaze from the group.

The rest seemed to happen in slow motion. A loud bang erupted and something powerful hit her in the back and propelled her to the floor. At first, she assumed the guard had hit her with his fist. As she tried to lift herself, the pain seared through her body. It wasn't until she heard his shout that she was aware of the sound of screams and scrambling feet. The warm stickiness of blood soaked into her shirt, and the reality of what happened dawned on her.

At first, Tori was stunned and furious. Hearing Jeff by her side, those emotions morphed into fear. His voice was filled with terror. For what reason, she didn't understand.

But terror surrounded her. It echoed and bounced off the walls. People screamed and ran for their lives, and the knowledge did nothing to calm her.

Tori was afraid she was dangerously exposed and would be shot again. She was afraid she'd bleed to death on the floor. She was afraid this would be the end for her, and her mother would receive the news that her only daughter had died a dishonorable death while trudging through the courthouse in handcuffs.

Then Tori felt another fear, a different kind of fear, more like trepidation, when a thought sinuously crept into her mind. Did Danny shoot her? *No.* She couldn't and wouldn't accept that. It was impossible. She'd listened to the police for too long, and their garbage had taken root in her brain. This was a kind of fluke thing that had happened. She'd been in the wrong place at the wrong time. Which appeared to be the way things had been ever since she'd arrived in 'la belle ville de Québec'.

Tori was startled out of her deliberations by the creak of the door opening. She twisted her head to see Jeff come into the room. He shuffled in sideways as he spoke to someone outside the door. She caught a glimpse of a dark blue uniform, and a frown formed on her forehead. When Jeff swiveled to face her, his frown rivaled hers.

"Hey, how do you feel?" He ran his gaze over her prostrate form.

"Why is there a cop outside my room?" she said.

Jeff blinked at Tori in surprise. He mustn't have expected her tone of voice, nor the question.

"Jeff, why is there a cop outside my room?" she repeated.

"He's here as a precaution."

"Are you afraid I'm going to hop out of bed and escape?"

"Of course not. We're not trying to keep you in. We're trying to keep other people out."

Her anger deflated, replaced by worry.

"Keep people out? Like who? Do you think someone's going to try to kill me again?"

CHAPTER 48

Panic vibrated in Tori's voice.

Jeff hastened to calm her fears. He grasped her hand and squeezed hard enough to make her focus on him.

"It's standard procedure. We're not taking any chances."

"I thought you said the shooter was in custody. Why would there be danger now?"

Jeff sighed and momentarily bowed his head, bolstering his patience. He'd spent the last several hours at police headquarters interrogating the man who'd caused her such pain, and him such terror.

The accused was a skinny little thug who looked like he'd spent his life living on the streets. He'd been an impossible nut to crack. Despite their threats and offers, he refused to incriminate Wilcox, claiming he'd acted on his own and it had been a random shooting. It was further proof of the power and terror that Wilcox wielded.

It had been a long and frustrating day for everyone involved, and several times Jeff had itched to circle his hands around the guy's skinny throat and throttle him for all he was worth. The memory made him clench his hands and forced him to take a steadying breath before he spoke. He met Tori's gaze and answered her question.

"We have him in custody, but we don't believe he worked alone."

Her eyes narrowed.

"Who do you think he worked with?"

Jeff didn't answer. He merely stared at her with his eyebrows raised.

"No. I know what you're thinking, and it's not true."

Again, Jeff remained silent.

"Who is this guy? Did he say he knows Danny? Did he claim Danny had sent him?" Tori said.

"His name's Alain Marquis. He's a guttersnipe with a prison record as long as your arm, although this is the first time he's going down for attempted murder."

"So there. He has a grudge against the judicial system, and I just happened to get in his way," she said.

Jeff sighed. "I almost wish it were the case, but we happen to know this guy's been on Danny's payroll in the past."

"That doesn't mean Danny paid him to do this."

"You're right," he responded, resignedly. "It doesn't."

Jeff saw Tori didn't have the strength to argue with him anymore. Her eyelids were heavy, and everything appeared to be an effort for her. Jeff put his hand on her forehead and brushed back her hair. Her eyelids fluttered.

"Hey, why don't you rest for a little while? I'm going to sit in this chair and put my feet up for a bit."

Jeff made himself as comfortable as possible in the hard vinyl chair and watched as Tori's eyelids slammed shut, and she fell sound asleep. He leaned back in the chair and began his vigil, avoiding thoughts of the way Tori's loyalty to Wilcox managed to tie his insides in knots.

CHAPTER 49

If she wasn't already depressed by her situation, Tori would've been by the fact that the only visitors she had were members of law enforcement. At the moment, her bed was flanked by Sébastien and Captain Bouchard. They'd enquired about her health and showered her with the appropriate amount of sympathy, but did nothing to allay her suspicions.

Tori didn't have any illusions about this being a social visit. Even the small bouquet of colorful chrysanthemums, although appreciated, didn't make her lower her guard. These two men were nothing if not committed to their jobs, and she imagined all of their waking hours, and even most of their sleeping ones, were dedicated to the cases on which they worked. And, she was aware their most important case now was the one involving Danny.

They made small talk to which Tori responded appropriately until an awkward silence fell over the group. Sébastien fidgeted beside her. She knew the two men were here with a specific purpose in mind, and she had no intention of making it easy for them.

She laid her head back on the pillow and pretended fatigue. Let them feel guilty for harassing a recent gunshot victim, she thought. When Bouchard self-consciously cleared his throat, she knew he was about to take the leap.

"Miss Victoria, we know this is difficult for you, but I'm afraid we don't have a lot of time to waste. I wouldn't have bothered you with this until you had recovered, but I feel the situation has become desperate and it would be better for everyone involved if we resolved it now."

"In other words, you don't want to pay a guard to stand outside my door much longer," she said.

"If it was my choice, and it was necessary, I would pay someone to follow you for the rest of your life," he said. "Unfortunately, I have superiors to which I have to report. But the issue is not about the guards. It's about finding Wilcox, as you well know."

He paused for effect.

"I know you're skeptical, but we firmly believe Marquis worked under Wilcox's direct orders. We don't post guards outside every victim's door, I can assure you. We are certain Wilcox wants you dead, and he'll go to any length to achieve that end."

"You're wrong."

She didn't make an effort to hide the venom in her voice.

"Then prove it. Help us apprehend him, and he'll face a fair trial. If he's as innocent as you assert he is, he'll go free, and we'll no longer have to bother with him."

She scoffed disbelievingly.

"You have a vendetta against Danny. You'll do anything to see him behind bars for the rest of his life."

"Maybe that's what you see, but I'm a fair man. It's my job to bring the suspects before the court. The rest is left up to the justice system."

She didn't respond. She tightened her lips and focused on the wall in front of her, willing these men to leave the room and her life.

"I'm asking you for your cooperation. I don't have an unlimited amount of time to play with. It's now or never."

She looked him in the eyes.

"Are you going to throw me back in jail?"

Bouchard stared back at her with such solemnity her breath caught in her throat. She thought she knew what the answer would be, but when he spoke, his words took her by surprise.

"No. I don't see the use of burdening the justice system with another person when it'll serve no purpose."

He shared a look of resignation with Sébastien, and Tori understood they'd decided to move on to Plan B. The captain continued.

"When you're fully recovered, you'll be free to leave the country and go back to your home. In the interim, while you're within our borders, we'll see that you remain safe."

Those words should have evoked joy and relief, but something about the atmosphere in the room nagged at her. She wouldn't be satisfied until she found out what Plan B was, and how it would affect her and Danny.

The older man inclined his head toward the space by the window. Sébastien crossed the room, and the two of them huddled in the corner. They'd switched to speaking French, and they discussed a subject Tori couldn't understand.

Nevertheless, she strained her ears and eyes to pick up some words or gestures that would give her a clue. During her short stay in the city, she'd learned a few basic words of French, but everyone spoke so rapidly the whole conversation was a blur to her inexperienced ears. Tori saw by their expressions that the subject matter was serious and urgent.

They hadn't bothered to lower their voices below a normal pitch, convinced Tori couldn't grasp what they said. But, she made out the name "Jeff" as it entered into their conversation. Another word also stood out.

Tori noticed that the Quebecois had a tendency to incorporate English words into their slang vocabulary by pronouncing them with a French accent and, in this instance, she made out the word 'undercover'. It didn't take long to connect the two words and come to her own conclusions.

"No!"

Hearing her expletive, both men swiveled in her direction with identical looks of surprise.

"*Pardon?*" Bouchard said.

"I know what you're thinking, and you can't do it." She glared at the captain and saw him glance at Sébastien.

"It's too dangerous," she said vehemently.

"What are you talking about, Tori?" said Sébastien.

"You know what I'm talking about. You're going to send Jeff in there undercover."

Tori's scowl dared them to deny it.

Captain Bouchard spoke softly and precisely.

"Victoria, we'll make our own decisions about how to carry on this investigation. I'm afraid you're not able to tell us what we can or cannot do."

She continued as if she hadn't heard him.

"They know what he looks like now. They'll be ready for him. It's too dangerous for him to go in there with those people."

"You're contradicting yourself," the captain said. "You've been telling us Wilcox is innocent. Now you're saying he's dangerous."

"I'm not saying that Danny himself is dangerous. I just don't have faith in the people he hangs out with," she said.

The senior police officer shrugged dismissively.

"At any rate, we'll do as we see fit," he said.

"Can't you send someone else?" she insisted, glancing pointedly at Sébastien.

"No offense to any of my other detectives, but I think Sébastien will agree Jeff is the best undercover cop I have. Even you have to admit he does an excellent job at immersing himself in a role."

Tori winced.

"They'll expect him now," she said. "They won't trust any newcomer into their group after what happened last time. He wouldn't last an hour among them."

Tori couldn't believe Bouchard could be so dense. It was obvious to her that sending Jeff into the den of criminals was all but signing his death warrant. The more she thought about it, the more horrified she was. She couldn't allow it to happen. No matter what Jeff may have done to hurt her, she didn't want to see any harm come to him.

"I won't let you," she said emphatically.

Captain Bouchard let out a short, humorless laugh.

"I'm sorry, Victoria, but I'm forced to remind you that you've washed your hands of this case, and as a result, you've no input as to what happens. As you say in English, you are out of it. Once you're sufficiently recovered, you'll leave. You can learn about the outcome in the newspapers or on the Internet, whichever you prefer."

With that, he turned his back to her and resumed his conversation with Sébastien. Tori's thoughts swirled in her head, and she was plagued by images of Jeff being tortured and killed. She vividly recalled what Chantal had looked like lying on the icy ground, her face battered, and her bones broken. God knew what they'd do to Jeff. Tori was in the terrible predicament of having to choose between the worthiness of two lives, Jeff's and Danny's.

Pictures flashed through her mind of the two men who, to her knowledge, had never come face-to-face, but who were bitter enemies. Each of them, in their own way, had a place in her heart, and she had to sacrifice one of them in order to save the other.

Tori was certain that Jeff would be in mortal danger if he infiltrated Danny's camp. His blood would be on her hands if she allowed it to happen.

One way to prevent it was to cooperate with the police and help them capture and arrest Danny. The idea brought a stab of pain to her heart. She'd be responsible for taking away his freedom even if it was for a short period of time. He'd never forgive her, and she wouldn't blame him.

How could she do it? Tori had gone through so much and fought so hard to tear Danny from this terrible life he'd chosen for himself, and she couldn't believe she contemplated siding with the police to have him arrested.

But then again, how could she not? Tori couldn't let Jeff risk his life. She vividly remembered the sensation of a bullet ripping through her body, and she closed her eyes in horror when she imagined several more tearing through Jeff's flesh.

"Will he get a fair trial? You won't just shoot him?" she said. Her words were whispered, but loud enough to gain the attention of the two men in the corner of the room.

Through a fog of tears, she saw them move toward her bed.

"Miss Anderson," Captain Bouchard said. "It's my responsibility to bring suspects before a court of law. It's never my intention to harm anyone. And I've always considered the Quebec justice system to be a fair one. You need not fear for that."

Tori nodded in response. She knew if she tried to speak she'd burst into tears. Her heart broke, and the weight of her betrayal was heavy on her chest. The men remained silent, clearly waiting for her to compose herself, probably not daring to hope she'd chosen to collaborate with them.

Tori refused to look at them, staring at the wall beyond their shoulders until she found the resolve to continue.

"I'll help you," she said.

Captain Bouchard didn't congratulate or thank her, getting down to business right away.

"We need information, Tori. We need to have any knowledge you can share with us that will give us a clue as to where he could be hiding. We need to know where he is at this moment. Did he give you any indication of where he was going?"

She shook her head.

"No. Believe it or not, he didn't fill me in on any details of his plans for the near future. He mentioned he had a new partner, someone very powerful from South America. He said there'd be a big job coming in soon that'd bring him a lot of money, and he'd go to South America, at least for a while."

Sébastien and Captain Bouchard exchanged glances before the senior officer spoke.

"We'd heard there was a large shipment of drugs on its way to Canada thanks to Wilcox, and that's why we feel a sense of urgency. We need to intercept that shipment before it makes it into the network. And, we don't want to be forced to search for Wilcox in a foreign country where it'll be almost impossible to get him extradited. That's why we need your help."

Tori shook her head, her emotions numb.

"You've been expecting more from me than I'm able to give. You won't find him in any of the places where I've been, even if I could tell you where they were. You seem to know more about his hideaways than I do. As for Danny, he knew it could come to this, and he's found somewhere else to hide by now, somewhere new where no one can get to him."

Bouchard nodded, apparently agreeing with her logic.

"So, what do you suggest, Tori?"

"We'll have to do it another way. The way that has a chance to work," she answered glumly.

CHAPTER 50

Jeff was more than a little irritated. His boss had ordered him to meet with another team of detectives to review one of their cases. He couldn't understand why he had to do such a thing. Their supervisor was more than capable of handling the case, and Jeff had never been asked to oversee another team's work before. Besides, Bouchard knew Jeff wanted to go to the hospital to see Tori that morning, and now he was delayed.

Shoving open the door to her hospital room, he was surprised to see both Bouchard and Sébastien standing by her bedside. His surprise was replaced by alarm as he imagined possible reasons for them being there.

"What's going on? Has something happened?" He looked around the room searching for evidence of violence. "Are you all right, Tori?"

"I'm fine."

She moved her attention to the other two police officers. His eyes narrowed when he saw both of his colleagues looking anywhere but at him.

"What's going on?" he said warily.

Captain Bouchard cleared his throat before speaking.

"We had a discussion with Tori."

His boss hesitated and threw a glance at Sébastien before continuing.

"She's decided to assist us."

Under normal circumstances, such news would've been welcomed by Jeff. But, for some reason, he had a feeling he wouldn't be happy about the manner in which she'd offered to assist them. Seeing Sébastien brace his arms across his chest, he was convinced.

"Oh really," he said. "That's good news. And how will she be helping us?"

Jeff pierced Tori with a glare, daring her to tell him what crazy plan she'd hatched with his cohorts. He was both pleased and dismayed to see her squirm and turn to Bouchard for support.

Tori was saved the unpleasantness of having to respond when Captain Bouchard unveiled their plan to Jeff.

"After studying a few possibilities, we've determined the one most liable to succeed is to...uh... sort of re-create what happened two days ago."

Jeff's eyes widened in disbelief when he understood the significance of what he'd heard. They couldn't mean it, he thought.

"Bait? You're going to use her as bait?"

"No, I think 'bait' is too strong a word," his boss said defensively.

"What else would you call dangling her in front of a man with a gun? A man who's determined to kill her. Don't you realize she's lucky to be alive? A few inches lower and we'd be standing around her grave, not a hospital bed."

Jeff threw his hands up in exasperation.

"I can't believe you'd even suggest such a thing to her," he said, running his hands through his hair.

Bouchard cleared his throat once more.

"Actually..."

Tori interrupted him.

"It was my idea."

Jeff whirled to stare at her incredulously.

"You? Tori, you don't understand the danger..."

"I understand it completely. I also know it's the only way."

"No, it isn't. You can tell us about the places where you met him, how you know him, the people you saw him associating with, your conversations with him, his habits, his preferences. There are other ways of tracking him."

Jeff was desperate to get through to her.

"Like I explained to your boss and Sébastien, none of that information will help you. Danny is long gone from any of those places and has found a new cave in which to hide. I was never able to find him on my own. I had to use Yvon." She grimaced at the thought of the dead man. "We have to draw him out."

"What makes you so sure you can draw him out? He sent a lackey last time. He'll just send another one. One with better aim," he added, his voice teeming with bitterness.

"I know Danny. If he's behind this, as you believe he is, then he'll be tired of leaving it in the hands of incompetents."

Tori's voice had treacherously broken on the last few words. Obviously, she'd admitted to herself there was a possibility Wilcox was determined to take her life. Despite all they'd apparently been through together, and the bond they'd shared, she knew he might eliminate her before she could do anything to come between him and his new way of life. Jeff watched as she got a grip on her emotions and continued in a controlled voice.

"I'm convinced if he's given the opportunity he'll want to take care of me himself," Tori answered, her voice low and tight.

"What if you're wrong?" Jeff said, knowing how much it hurt her to admit defeat. "What if he sends someone else this time?"

"Then we'll come up with another plan."

"What if you don't survive the first plan?"

"That's not going to happen," she said.

Realizing she was serious about this, and hardheaded enough to go through with it, he felt a surge of anger, and it was directed toward all of them. His astounded look swung from one to the other.

"I can't believe you're all crazy enough to cook up something like this."

Sébastien spoke up.

"We'll take every precaution, Jeff," he said.

"Every precaution? We all understood every precaution was taken at the courthouse, and look what happened. Someone managed to make it inside with a gun. Don't tell me this is foolproof."

"Of course, we're not so naïve as to think everything is foolproof," Bouchard intervened, "but we'll do everything we can to keep Tori safe. She'll wear full body armor…"

"Why don't you have someone stand in for her, a female police officer? We can fool Wilcox into believing it's Tori."

"No," Tori said. "I'm doing this myself. Besides, Danny won't be fooled. You should know that by now."

"Exactly. He can't be fooled. What makes you presume he'll fall for this trap?"

"We'll do everything we can to ensure he falls for it," said Captain Bouchard. "You may not be aware of this, Tori, but we're sure we have an informant in the department. There's someone within our ranks feeding Wilcox information. That's how he could take you from the safe house, and how he was aware you'd be at the courthouse the other day. We'll use that to our advantage, and we'll ensure he knows where you'll be when we're ready for him."

A shiver ran down Jeff's spine at these words. There were so many things that could go wrong.

"What if this informant tells him it's a trap?" Tori asked, having the same concerns as Jeff.

"No one outside of this room will know what we're planning, and I assure you, Miss Anderson, I would trust either Jean-François or Sébastien with my life."

Tori nodded, apparently accepting his words unquestioningly, but Jeff wasn't willing to let it drop.

"I still don't see how you can be so sure Wilcox will make an appearance and take matters into his own hands," he said.

"I know he will. I know him," Tori said. "I know he's desperate now, and if we let word out that I'm going to be working against him, he'll make a move."

"I won't allow it. It's too dangerous," Jeff said.

"Jean-François, it isn't your decision. It's mine," said Captain Bouchard.

"I'm involved in this case. I should have some input," he said, his voice rising.

"I agree, and I always take everyone's input under advisement, but I know you're no longer working objectively, and I have to take that into consideration."

Jeff and his superior spent several moments glaring at each other, the former's look angry and the latter's resolute. Jeff had half a mind to threaten to withdraw from the case, but after Bouchard's words, he was afraid he might take him up on it. That was a chance he wasn't willing to take.

No matter how much it bothered Jeff, he had to remain closely involved if he wanted to have a hand in protecting Tori. So, instead of ranting and raving, he crossed his arms over his chest and seethed inwardly. The decision had been taken out of his hands.

Jeff worked with his colleagues to decide how to set up the sting operation. One plan had been to stage it as it had happened in the courthouse, except with Tori clad in bulletproof material from head to toe, but the idea was discarded. It was too dangerous for the many innocent bystanders who'd be present in the ever-crowded building, and the police would have a difficult time setting up a discreet S.W.A.T. team inside.

Numerous suggestions were bandied about, and Jeff knew his attitude didn't go unnoticed. He was still angry that none of them could see the danger involved, and he wanted nothing more than to race to the hospital, pluck Tori out of bed, and drag her, kicking and screaming if necessary, to somewhere safe. Somewhere out of the clutches of Wilcox and the well-meaning hands of his colleagues. All he could see forthcoming was disaster.

They decided the mission would be better handled outside the courthouse where they could have control over bystanders without it being too obvious. This plan would also allow Wilcox easy access to Tori, yet the police could cover her unobtrusively from all angles. Captain Bouchard would allow the information about her appearance in court to be leaked, and they would set it up to appear as innocent as possible, without having to sacrifice security.

Tori would remain in the hospital for another two days, under close guard, after which she'd be given a few more days to convalesce in a more comfortable environment.

"I've been in touch with Chantal," Captain Bouchard told Tori during one of his visits to the hospital. "She wanted me to pass on an invitation to stay at her apartment. You can recuperate together."

Unsure what Tori's reaction would be, Jeff was surprised and pleased when she accepted the invitation. His own offer of room and board had been refused by the captain before it could reach Tori's ears, but at least Jeff had the consolation of knowing she'd be with his partner, and both of them would be well-guarded.

Chapter 51

Two days later, Tori was discharged from the hospital and moved to Chantal's apartment. The two women were now, more or less, working on the same side, although Tori had grave misgivings about what she'd agreed to do.

She'd stood by Danny for so long, she could hardly fathom the idea of betraying him. But, he'd finally succeeded in breaking her spirit, and because of his actions and her fear for Jeff, her loyalties had swayed. Tori's sole consolation was that Danny would be treated fairly under the law. If indeed he had done all the terrible things they accused him of, he deserved to face the punishment doled out to him.

Tori had always known Danny was involved in the drug trade. It wasn't something she condoned or was proud of, but she'd believed he could be reformed. Perhaps, with a good lawyer and some leniency on the part of the judge, the charges could be disproven, or he could be asked to leave the country to never come back.

Tori hoped Danny was innocent of attempted murder. She strove to convince herself that he wasn't guilty of that particular crime, but she had a nagging feeling of doubt. No matter how difficult it was to admit, there'd been too many attacks against her since she'd arrived in Quebec. He had to have been aware of them, and if so, been able to prevent them. Instead, they'd continued and became more vicious with each attempt.

Tori knew she couldn't let her natural optimism slip away, drowned by the memories of the horrors she'd experienced. Instead, she focused on the positive. After all, maybe nothing would happen at the courthouse. Maybe no one would try to kill her. Maybe there'd be no threat. Maybe.

Tori was nervous about coming face-to-face with Chantal. The last time they'd spoken Tori had been angry and resentful. Since then, Chantal had been beaten, abused, and used as a bargaining tool, leaving Tori overwhelmed with guilt. She was afraid Chantal would be bitter toward her, despite the offer of housing that apparently had been freely offered.

Entering the apartment and seeing the expression on Chantal's face – a face that still showed signs of mistreatment – Tori's fears were eased.

"I'm so happy to see you," Chantal said. Her hug, although gentle, was warm and unforced. A small portion of the burden was lifted from Tori's shoulders. Her eyes filled with tears as she returned the hug.

The women were left alone in the apartment, but police officers were posted on all sides of the building to make sure no threats were made against them. The authorities had a willing and valuable collaborator, and they wouldn't allow any harm to come to her.

Tori needed to set things straight with Chantal. She urged her to sit on the couch facing her.

"Chantal, I'm so sorry for what happened to you. You have no idea how…"

"Stop. You've nothing to be sorry for. You didn't do anything."

Tori bowed her head.

"Exactly. I didn't do anything, and that was part of the problem," she said, Jeff's words of admonishment coming back to her.

"I understand what it's like to feel loyalty toward someone, even if it's misplaced. It can destroy you."

Chantal's tone of voice sparked a question in Tori's mind.

"Are you talking about Jeff?" she said, her breath clenched in her chest. The words were out, but she didn't know if she wanted to hear the answer.

The other woman met her look with surprise.

"Jeff? No, he's always been a good friend and partner. I couldn't have asked for a better one."

Tori tried her best to hide her sigh of relief. She realized she'd worried too much about Jeff and Chantal having a romantic relationship.

"There was someone else who hurt you?"

"Yes," Chantal said with a snort of derision. "Hurt is a small word compared to what he did to me."

Her expression told it all, and for the first time, Tori saw past the tough, energetic, generous woman, and knew she'd found someone who understood her. She didn't press her for more details.

Tori never saw Jeff during her stay with Chantal, although he phoned to chat with his colleague, and he always inquired about Tori's health. She didn't know if he was honestly worried, or if he was simply polite, but she knew he was still angry about the decision that had been made by her and his associates.

Tori knew Jeff thought they all wore blinders and couldn't see the risks involved, but she believed this was the only alternative, and she wasn't afraid. She trusted Captain Bouchard when he said he'd do his utmost to protect her.

Tori also realized the captain had done an excellent job manipulating her into agreeing to this scheme. In hindsight, she was convinced the conversation between Bouchard and Sébastien in her hospital room had been a set-up. They'd intentionally used Jeff's name and the word 'undercover' to frighten her and get her to capitulate.

Strangely, it didn't bother Tori. It would've eventually come to this point. Knowing Jeff, he'd want to infiltrate the gang to get results, and that was something she couldn't allow. What surprised her was the fact the captain knew her feelings for Jeff were strong enough that she'd go to such lengths to protect him.

The morning of the day of the sting, Tori was struck by a case of nerves. It wasn't fear for her life that made her palms sweat. She was afraid of letting everyone down. She'd never claimed to be an actress and felt certain her reactions and emotions were easy to read on her face.

"I'm worried I won't be able to do this," she said to Chantal. "Anyone watching will know I'm faking it."

"Not at all. It'll be normal for you to look around nervously. After all, it wasn't very long ago that you were shot in that building. It'd be natural for you to be worried and nervous."

Tori chewed on her bottom lip. They were at police headquarters, going over the last-minute details. Chantal had insisted on being there for moral support. The rest of the team talked and pored over drawings of the courthouse yard.

"I suppose you're right."

"Remember to keep staring straight ahead," Captain Bouchard said, having overheard their conversation. "Don't look for the sharpshooters."

The mention of sharpshooters sent Tori's mind on another tangent.

"What do you mean? You said you wouldn't harm him. You *are* going to arrest him, not shoot him, aren't you?" she asked.

"That is definitely our intention," Captain Bouchard said. "But we have to take precautions. What if he's not alone? What if there are many of them, and there's a possibility of having a full-scale slaughter on our hands? That isn't what we expect, but we have to be prepared for everything. As Jeff pointed out, we weren't prepared for what happened in the courthouse last time, so now we're not taking any chances. You have to understand that."

"But you promise to be careful, don't you? I don't want anything to happen to him."

"I promise we'll do our best."

Tori peered at Jeff and saw the anger on his face, along with a flash of hatred that she presumed was directed toward Danny.

Despite his obvious feelings about the police operation, Jeff remained calm while helping Chantal encase Tori from head to toe in body armor. She wore a suit of the black material and when they were done, she resembled a scuba diver. On top of the armor, she wore an orange jumpsuit reserved for prisoners. A story had been leaked that she was incarcerated until she appeared before the court and been considered for bail.

On her head was a matching orange cap that had been lined with a thin layer of lead and felt uncomfortably heavy. The collar of her jumpsuit had also been lined with lead and had been lifted to protect her neck. There was hardly an inch of Tori that wasn't covered in bulletproof material.

Jeff wasn't satisfied. He insisted the area be searched by K-9 dogs to sniff out any explosive devices. The van that would be used to transport Tori was inspected and guarded to prevent any tampering.

Bouchard allowed Jeff free rein. He knew it served the dual purpose of providing extra protection for Tori and of giving the cop something to occupy his mind. He'd been bad-tempered all week, getting on everyone's nerves, especially Tori's, scowling at her at every opportunity.

"I'll be Tori's escort at the courthouse," Jeff said to his boss during the planning process.

"That's not a good idea. We'll have someone else do it."

"I'm available, and I'm the best one to be there," he said, his brows furrowed.

Bouchard sighed.

"I don't agree. You're too emotionally involved. You have to remain detached."

"I'm going to walk beside her, that's all. It's not that difficult a job."

"And, if there's shooting? What will you do?"

"I'll protect her with my life," Jeff said, his voice deep with emotion.

Bouchard's expression was unhappy.

"Yes, that's one of the things I'm afraid of."

In the end, Jeff got his way, but not without a long lecture about what Jeff's responsibilities were, a lecture grudgingly received.

Tori was torn between relief that Jeff would be by her side, and fear he'd also become a target.

"He'll have to wear body armor too," she said, addressing her words to Bouchard.

"I'll wear a vest," Jeff said.

"No. You'll have to be dressed like me, with full armor."

"I don't need full armor. I'm not the target."

"You could be," she said. "Or, you could be hurt accidentally. If you don't wear full armor, neither will I."

"He will wear full protection," Bouchard said, earning him a resentful glare from Jeff.

"This stuff is too damn tight. I can barely move in it," he said, as they sat side by side in the back of the van, on the way to the courthouse.

"It's just as tight for me," Tori said.

"Yeah, but for you, it's necessary. For me, it isn't."

"That's not true. You could be hit by a stray bullet."

"The chance of that happening is slim. You just want to get even with me."

"Do you think I spend all my time coming up with ways to get even with you? You give yourself too much credit."

She admitted to herself that he was right. She got a certain amount of satisfaction from seeing him squirm in the hot, tight, bulletproof material.

Jeff sighed.

"Tori, I don't want to fight with you. I know I've been out of sorts lately, and I may have taken it out on you, but today we have to work as a team."

"I have no problem with that," she said stiffly.

A few moments of silence passed. Despite Tori's determination to ignore Jeff, she couldn't push aside the doubts creeping into her mind, and she was even less able to prevent them from being spoken aloud.

"What if it didn't work? The leak, I mean. What if Captain Bouchard didn't manage to get the information out to the right people?"

"It'll work. He knows what he's doing. Four people know it's a set-up, and that's the Captain, Sébastien, you, and me."

"What about Chantal?"

"No. Technically, she's still on sick leave, and we didn't want to worry her with any more details than necessary. Not that we don't trust her, but there's no need for her to know."

Tori nodded distractedly. Her nervousness surfaced as the time approached, and she was assailed by doubts.

Jeff opened his mouth to say more but was interrupted by the driver announcing they had arrived at the back entrance of the courthouse. The location had purposely been chosen because it was out of the public eye but held a multitude of hiding places for the police to set up their men.

When the van pulled to a stop, Tori took a deep shuddering breath. Jeff squeezed her hand. He reached over, adjusted the cap on her head, and fiddled with her collar.

"I'm going to be okay," Tori said, unsure who she wanted to reassure, Jeff or herself.

Their gazes met, and Jeff grasped Tori by the chin, leaned close, and kissed her long and hard. The driver discreetly kept his head face-forward and his eyes from the rear-view mirror. Thankfully, the windows were tinted, but it wouldn't have mattered. Tori knew Jeff would've kissed her anyway, and she was glad he had.

Breaking contact, Jeff looked into her eyes. Tori sensed he wanted to say something, but this wasn't the time or the place. Hopefully, there'd be plenty of both at a future date. For now, they had to get this ordeal over with, and she needed his moral support more than anything else right now.

They jerked away from each other in surprise when the side door of the van was slid open, and a uniformed policeman stood waiting to escort them into the building.

Tori wondered if he was also suited up in body armor beneath his uniform. She realized everyone was well-informed about the danger involved, given what had happened the last time, but they weren't privy to all the details of the planned sting. She took a deep breath, and closed her eyes for a brief second, before sliding from her seat.

Tori stepped onto the pavement, heard Jeff's footsteps behind her, and resisted the urge to look at the surrounding buildings. The memory of being hit by a bullet momentarily slowed her pace. She reminded herself of the precautions they'd taken, and she walked with more sureness. She felt Jeff's hand on her elbow even through the layers of material, and she experienced another surge of something close to confidence.

Staring ahead of her, Tori calculated the distance to be about fifty steps from the van to the entrance of the building. She was acutely aware of the fact that if nothing happened within those fifty steps, they'd have to come up with another plan, and she had no idea what it'd be.

As she walked, Tori counted the footsteps, striving to keep her mind off what she was really doing; setting a trap for a man she'd sworn she'd never betray.

When she reached the halfway mark – twenty-five paces – it happened. It was the same sound, and yet it was not the same. It didn't have the enhancement of an echo this time, but was released into the air to mingle with the horns and engines and bustle of a city.

Tori recognized it. She recognized the impact of the projectile hitting her square in the back and pitching her to the ground. Without the constriction of handcuffs, she broke her fall with her hands, but the breath was knocked from her lungs. She lay gasping while her brain focused on what was happening around her.

There was a cacophony of gunshots, and panic rose in her chest. Had someone else been shot? Was Jeff okay? She attempted to force herself into a sitting position. Her lungs and back ached, and her previous wound felt like it was torn open.

"Stay down!" she heard, as a hand shoved her back to the ground.

Tori recognized Jeff's voice. She peered over her shoulder to see him squatted over her with his gun pointed in the direction of a building across the street.

Shifting her attention, she saw several police officers in the same position pointing in the same direction. She followed their gazes to see four S.W.A.T. team members on the roof huddled around something in front of them.

"No," she whispered. She pulled herself up again. Jeff gripped her arm, restraining her.

"We're going inside, Tori."

"No, I have to see. Who is it?"

"It's too dangerous out here. Come on. We have to go inside."

Jeff's tone of voice made Tori's heart pound faster. She detected pity and concern in it, and that wasn't what she wanted to hear. She jerked her arm out of his grasp and ran toward the building. Jeff grabbed her from behind and pulled her against him.

"Tori, don't go up there," he warned.

"Let me go. Don't you understand? I have to see."

Chapter 52

Jeff reluctantly released Tori and followed her as she raced up the stairs. By the time she fought her way through the crowd of police officers, he was behind her and witnessed with his own eyes what she saw through hers.

Lying before them was a tall, blond-haired man whose blue eyes stared sightlessly upward as if pleading to be allowed a space in heaven instead of in his more probable destination. In the middle of his chest was a gaping wound. It had taken one shot, and the person behind the trigger had known his business.

Jeff stood behind her as Tori fell to her knees beside the body. When one of the other officers reached out to hold her back, he put out a hand to stop him. Tori needed to have this moment, however difficult it was to witness.

And, it was difficult. When she grabbed Danny's arm and lowered her head to his shoulder, great sobs racking her body, Jeff felt as if his heart would break.

Her constant cries of 'No!' and 'I'm sorry' were heard by the silent crowd. It was obvious Tori would spend the rest of her life mourning this man who'd aimed a bullet at her back minutes earlier. Who could compete with that kind of love?

Gradually, most of the other officers left, knowing Danny Wilcox was no longer a danger to anyone, and the woman's suffering didn't need an audience. The surrounding area was cleared. Wilcox's one other accomplice had been captured.

Jeff remained on the rooftop with Tori. Even to the end, he'd stay by her side, he thought, amazed at his own stupidity.

She lifted her reddened eyes to his and said in an accusing, grief-stricken voice, "You promised. You promised he wouldn't be shot."

Jeff couldn't respond. She was right. They'd promised. Why that promise hadn't been kept would be revealed in the ensuing investigation, but Jeff knew no matter what answer he gave her now, it wouldn't be enough to relieve her agony.

Out of the corner of his eye, Jeff saw the forensic crew arrive and knew he'd soon have to remove Tori from the scene. They'd go about their thorough, clinical job, and, in her present state, it would appear inhuman to Tori. It was over now. There was a lot to be done and a lot they couldn't do to bring closure to what had happened.

CHAPTER 53

Tori sat in the brightly-lit conference room with a long, twelve-foot table in front of her, but she didn't acknowledge her surroundings. Her eyes were red-rimmed, puffy, and swollen, but, for the moment at least, the tears had stopped flowing.

She stared at the beautiful painting of the Château Frontenac hanging on the wall opposite her, but the image she saw through her eyes was that of Danny lying lifelessly on the concrete.

His face, even in death, was handsome. He looked so angelic you'd think him incapable of any wrongdoing. She felt a stab of pain in her chest as she thought of his death; her sense of loss and the knowledge of what was to come combining to send her spirits plummeting even further.

Jeff sat tolerantly beside her, but Tori wasn't capable of speech. She couldn't face him. He was the reason she'd agreed to this plan. She'd wanted to ensure his safety. But, she'd been promised Danny would be left unharmed.

It'd be easy to blame Jeff for the outcome, but she couldn't. She was the one to carry the blame. She'd made the choice between Danny and Jeff and, because of what she'd done, Danny lay in a morgue and Jeff was alive. She'd spend the rest of her life reconciling those two realities.

Dimly, Tori heard the door open behind her and the soft shuffle of feet entering the room. A hand set a cup of coffee on the table in front of her, and in her peripheral vision, she saw Jeff reach up to accept one of his own.

Across the table from Tori, Captain Bouchard and Chantal took their seats. Upon hearing the news, her friend had insisted on being present to offer support even though she was officially off-duty.

There was an uncomfortable silence, no one wanting to take the first step. None of the police officers could bring themselves to feel any grief for the dead drug lord, yet they felt sympathy for the woman whose grief was all too obvious. They also knew whatever words they had to state would sound empty and trite to her ears. Instead, quiet prevailed for several minutes until Tori broke the silence.

"Why did you kill him?" she asked, lifting her head and staring into Bouchard's eyes. "You promised."

He faltered before speaking.

"Believe me, it wasn't our intention for it to happen. We were convinced, if he succeeded in trying to shoot you, he'd make an attempt to escape immediately afterward. We were prepared to trap him. Unfortunately, he had other plans. After the first shot, the one that hit you, he was spotted by a sniper. But instead of leaving, he turned his gun toward Jeff. There were other officers in the area. They were unprotected. We couldn't take a chance and let them lose their lives. My sniper was under instruction to take whatever measures were necessary if he tried to continue his shooting spree."

Tori absorbed this information. Danny had wanted to eliminate all of his problems. Both she and Jeff would be dead, along with God knows how many others, if the sniper hadn't done his job.

"I'm sorry, Victoria," Bouchard said. "I know I told you it was my responsibility to bring him before the justice system, but it's also my responsibility to protect the lives of my officers and the citizens of Quebec."

"What will I say to her?" she said, tears rolling down her cheeks.

The three other occupants of the room glanced at each other. Jeff leaned closer and took hold of Tori's hands, holding them between his.

"What do you mean, Tori? Who are you talking about?"

"My mother. This will kill her."

She cried harder, as the reality of what was ahead swept over her once more.

Jeff wouldn't let it go.

"Your mother? What does she have to do with this?"

Tori looked at him with despair, his image a fuzzy blur through her curtain of tears.

"She has everything to do with this. How can I tell her? How can I tell her I was responsible for killing her son?"

•   •   •

Her last words were almost inaudible as she sobbed, but they were clear enough to plunge the room into a stunned silence as everyone seemingly recognized their meaning. The only sound was Tori's weeping.

Jeff never took his gaze from her face as he reconciled what she'd said with everything that had happened over the last weeks. Clearing his throat, he found his voice.

"Your brother? Danny was your brother?"

Tori's expression revealed the depth of her misery.

"Yes, and I killed him."

Jeff shifted gears, putting the information into a storage compartment to be taken out and studied at another time. He grabbed her hands and squeezed them hard enough to focus her attention on him.

"Listen to me. You didn't kill him, Tori. He was responsible for his own fate. He chose the life he wanted to live. No one forced him into it, not even you. You have to stop blaming yourself. You also have to remember that he tried to kill you, several times."

As the words were out of his mouth, the true horror of the situation hit Jeff. It had been hard to accept the fact Wilcox had tried to kill an unwanted lover, but it was mind-boggling to know it was his sister he'd wanted to murder. It was no wonder Tori had judged him incapable of harming her.

Tori looked beseechingly at the people in the room.

"You didn't know him. He was such a sweet kid. We were so close, and we had so much fun together. He loved me, I know he did. He was always so protective."

She paused to blow her nose.

"But he changed after my father died. He started taking drugs, and he became involved with some bad gangs. Then...then he left. We had no word from him until a friend of mine told me she'd seen his picture in the news one day while she was vacationing in Quebec. My mother's very sick, and she always spoke of seeing Danny again. I knew I had to get to him, and now..."

Tori couldn't continue. She dissolved into tears as the three law enforcement officers watched helplessly.

CHAPTER 54

At the time of Danny's death, Tori was convinced things couldn't get much worse, but she was wrong.

The other man who'd been captured on the day of the shooting had been questioned. Not fearing any reprisals from the now-dead Danny, the felon was more than willing to give up information in exchange for leniency. The police were rewarded with an abundance of knowledge regarding Danny's mini-empire. They were given locations, dates, times, and names.

Within hours, a series of raids were executed at specifically-revealed locations, and at least twenty arrests were made, along with the discovery of thousands of kilos of drugs. By the next day, without Danny's leadership and influence, the finger-pointing and the butt-covering were in full swing. In reality, Danny's organization hadn't been held together by loyalty, but rather by fear. And, since the source of that fear was no longer among the living, everybody's skin was fair game.

The most disturbing information for Captain Bouchard and Jeff was the name of the leak in the police department, Sébastien Marois.

During the early stages of his stint in the narcotics division, Sébastien had been lured into Danny's clutches with a simple bribe to look the other way. What began as a one-shot deal had snowballed into something that had grown out of control.

Sébastien had been blackmailed into agreeing to provide information about the ongoing investigation into Wilcox's illegal career, thereby allowing the criminal to remain one step ahead of the police.

After witnessing Tori's shooting inside the courthouse, Sébastien made a personal decision. He'd help the police carry out the sting operation by informing Wilcox of the time and location, and by convincing him the job would be better taken care of if handled by Danny himself.

Sébastien had decided his life would be easier if Wilcox was dead, and he'd banked on the criminal being killed that day. However, he made the mistake of naively believing Wilcox when he was told only the drug lord was aware of Sébastien's involvement in his criminal activities. Now, his associate had pointed the finger at Sébastien, and the cop faced criminal charges. His life was in ruins, and his fellow police officers were stunned by the unexpected news.

Meanwhile, Tori stayed with Chantal in her apartment, not because she needed protection, but because she needed a comforting presence, and she couldn't accept it from Jeff, who had wanted her to return to Valcartier with him.

In Tori's mind, she viewed the lives of Danny and Jeff as being interconnected. One life had been sacrificed for the other, and she'd been the reluctant and unqualified judge and juror. She realized Jeff wanted to comfort and protect her, but she couldn't bring herself to accept his well-meant offers.

Despite everyone's best efforts to keep her in the dark about the case against Danny, Tori broke through their protective shield. Danny's death and the subsequent raids were summarized and covered by the television news channels. She went to see Captain Bouchard and insisted on having more details.

Throughout the session, Jeff stood stone-faced against the wall behind Bouchard's desk, his arms crossed over his chest. Even though Tori had made it clear to him she didn't want his sympathy or compassion, he'd insisted on being present.

As she listened to the list of crimes committed by her brother, Tori's emotions morphed from skepticism, to disbelief, to horror, and at last, to a deadened acceptance. The worst part for Tori was the revelation that Danny had given direct orders to his men to kill his sister. His paranoia was so severe, he didn't hesitate or show the slightest remorse about eliminating the sibling he'd loved and protected for so many years.

When Captain Bouchard set down the documents and lifted his head, Tori felt nauseous and weak, but she refused to give in to those sensations. She spent several minutes staring at the floor, gathering her wits.

"Tori, is there anything I can do for you?" the captain said.

Tori acknowledged the question with a weak shake of her head.

"Would you like me to arrange transportation for you to Chantal's apartment?"

"Yes, please."

"I'll take you back," Jeff said.

"That isn't necessary. I'm sure you have plenty of other things to do," Tori said listlessly.

"Not at all. I'm going in that direction anyway."

Tori was certain it was a lie, but she didn't have either the strength or the inclination to argue. She shrugged her shoulders and stood. She approached Captain Bouchard, who'd come to his feet.

"Thank you for all your help, Captain. I know I didn't make your job easy, and yet you always went out of your way to be fair with me."

The words were softly-spoken but they rang with sincerity, and the older man accepted them like a gentleman.

"You made it very easy to be fair, Miss Anderson. Despite the situation, you were a delightful visitor to our city, and I wish the circumstances hadn't been so dreadful. I hope with time you'll overcome your ordeal."

Her return to the apartment was conducted in silence. When they arrived, and Tori opened the door of the car, Jeff stopped her with a hand on her forearm.

"What are your plans now?" he said.

"My plans?"

She was surprised. Tori had assumed her plans were self-evident.

"I'm going to go home as soon as possible," she said.

"Do you have to leave right away? I mean, I thought it'd be good if you stayed here for a few days longer. We could spend some time together, under normal circumstances."

Tori didn't think her life would ever be normal again, not after Danny's death and all she'd heard today. So many emotions churned inside of her. Grief, regret, and anger fought for her attention, but it was overshadowed by a feeling of despair, knowing she'd been too stupid and naïve not to have seen the truth when it had stared her in the face. Tori shook her head disconsolately.

"I'm sorry, Jeff. I'm going back to Florida and the sooner the better. I need to see my mother and pick up the pieces of my life."

Tori suspected Jeff had expected her answer, no matter how painful or difficult it was. She had a rough road ahead of her, and she'd have to travel it alone before she'd have the confidence to take another path.

It took a few days for Tori to make the arrangements, during which time she was so busy it was easy to avoid Jeff. When everything was taken care of, she was on a plane to Florida.

Chantal had insisted on lending her the money for the flight, even though Tori was prepared to take a bus. Her friend reminded her she'd been away from her mother much longer than planned and needed to hurry home before her parent's condition worsened.

Apart from concerns about her mother and how much she should tell her, Tori had to deal with the problem of Danny's remains. Initially, she'd considered arranging his burial in Quebec, his chosen home, but her heart wouldn't allow such a choice. Deep down, she felt he belonged with the family upon which he'd turned his back. She made the decision to have him cremated, and he accompanied her on the plane.

The irony of the situation didn't escape Tori. She'd been granted her wish to bring Danny home with her. Her throat tightened at the thought, but she fought back the tears. She wouldn't cry for him anymore.

Saying goodbye to Jeff, knowing she'd never see him again, had been painful. She'd reluctantly accepted his offer of a ride to the airport, certain it was a mistake to drag out their eventual parting, but unable to refuse a few more minutes of his company.

"Tori," he'd said during the drive to the airport, "Why did you never tell me Danny was your brother? I don't get that part."

She stared out the window for several seconds before answering.

"A couple of reasons, I guess. I didn't want to give away any information about him to anyone, particularly the cops. It would help them to capture him, wouldn't it?"

She glanced at Jeff and saw his shrug.

"I'd have to say the biggest part of it was shame. I wasn't proud of his career, even when I assumed it was limited to drug-dealing. The one favor he did for my mother and I was to change his name from Anderson to Wilcox.

There was that much, at least."

Their farewell was stilted and uncomfortable. The last few days had been difficult for both of them. Tori was torn apart with guilt and self-recrimination, while Jeff held himself away from her.

When Tori turned from Jeff at the airport, she ambled almost blindly to the departure gate, her chest aching from the desire to look back one last time. Seated on the plane, she peered out the window, blinking back her tears. She decided to put her experiences in Quebec, both the good and the bad behind her and resolved to concentrate on the ordeal ahead of her.

Tori had called her mother's neighbor to have an idea of what she'd face when she arrived. She was dismayed to discover her mother had been hospitalized the previous day. Tori took a taxi straight from the airport to the hospital and was at her mother's bedside within an hour and a half of her arrival.

The sight of her parent's relieved smile sent a shaft of guilt through Tori. She knew her long absence had worried her mother, and she prayed she hadn't contributed to the declining condition of her health.

The doctors explained to Tori that her mother's heart condition had deteriorated to the point where there was nothing they could do to help her. They left Tori with few expectations of ever seeing her mother return home.

Despite her weakness and ill health, Clarissa was eager for news of Tori's trip to Canada.

"Did you find Danny? Is he all right? Is he coming home?"

"How did you know I was looking for Danny? I never told you that," Tori said, unable to hide her surprise.

"Oh honey, I knew you were up to something, taking off like that in the middle of winter. I called Sherry and she told me about you learning Danny was in Quebec. You could've said something, you know."

"I didn't want you to worry, and I didn't want you to get your hopes up. I had no idea if I'd find him or not."

"So, did you? Find him, I mean. Is he well?"

Tori forced a happy expression onto her face and chuckled.

"Slow down, Mom. I'll tell you all about it."

And she lied. She lied like she'd never lied before in her life.

"I found Danny, and he's doing great. He picked up a lot of French, and of course, his English is perfect, so he has a job as a tour guide in Quebec City."

Tori went on to tell her mother about the beautiful city, using memories of her time with 'Mario'. Clarissa's eyes took on a faraway look and she knew her mother imagined the sights Tori described to her of the old city, the quaint restaurants, the horse-drawn carriages, and the snow.

She omitted all the harrowing details; her accident, the attempts on her life, her imprisonment, her betrayal of Danny, and his subsequent death. Tori forced herself not to glance toward her luggage that sat in the corner of the room and in which her brother's ashes were packed.

She must've given something away, because her mother's expression became suspicious.

"What's wrong, honey? What aren't you telling me? You seem sad about something."

Tori told another story, one that was true, but didn't uncover the whole truth.

"I met someone while I was there, and it was hard to say goodbye."

"So, that's it. What's his name? Tell me about him."

Tori told her mother about Jeff, leaving out the fact that he'd originally been Ben and then Mario, and she changed his profession from an undercover cop to a computer analyst.

Her mother tried to console Tori by saying she was sure there was a need for computer analysts in Florida, and maybe he could be convinced to move there. Tori smiled, neither agreeing nor disagreeing with her mother's plan. A cloak of sadness draped over her. None of those plans concerning Tori, Jeff or Danny would ever come to fruition.

Tori went on to tell her mother about her skiing and snowmobiling adventures, enjoying the sight of her mother laughing with real joy. At the end of the day, Tori experienced a bittersweet happiness, knowing she'd lifted her mother's spirits, but also realizing their time together was short and not to be wasted.

Tori didn't feel guilty about the lies she'd told. It was better for her mother's health, both physical and emotional, if she didn't know the truth, and nothing would be gained by darkening the last few days she had on this earth.

Later that day, Tori arrived at her apartment, weak with exhaustion. The travel early in the day and the stress of maintaining a cheerful disguise when her mental state was anything but cheerful had taken its toll. The effort it took to make up more lies to support her initial lie was a strain almost beyond bearing.

When her mother had asked why Danny hadn't returned home, Tori had replied, "You know Danny, Mom. He let the paperwork slip for his working visa, and now he's not able to come and go freely across the border. He should be able to get everything together soon."

Now, back in her own home, Tori unpacked the urn containing Danny's ashes and placed it with care on a small table in her apartment. She'd make arrangements for his burial later on, when she wasn't so worried about her mother.

CHAPTER 55

Tori spent every day with her mother, and every day she was more apprehensive. Clarissa's condition went from bad to worse, until she was on a respirator, her breathing controlled by a machine. Talking was almost impossible for her, but she did her best. Tori, in turn, worked to interpret the grunts and hand signals. Giving up, she simply sat and held her mother's hand, hoping to bring her some comfort.

A week after Tori's return to Florida, her mother slipped peacefully to her death, her daughter by her side. Tori's emotions were so battered she felt like a punching bag that had been given its final blow before it fell to the ground in tatters.

Tori dragged herself home to her empty apartment, opened the door, and burst into tears when her gaze fell upon the urn in the corner. For hours, she sat on the floor with her back up against the couch, holding the urn, and alternately crying and staring blankly at the opposite wall.

She had lost everyone; her brother, Jeff, and her mother. She was alone in the world, and she couldn't have felt more wretched. Her determination to fight had left her. Both Danny and her mother were beyond needing her help, and Jeff was out of her reach.

Tori resumed her job, thankful her boss had been patient and understanding. Weeks passed in a vacuum while Tori worked, ate, and slept like an automaton, not taking any pleasure in anything.

After her mother's funeral, and when her life returned to normal – as normal as she expected it to be –she realized how much she'd come to care for Jeff and how much she missed him.

Knowing what she now knew, she saw her behavior the way Jeff and all the others must've seen it. She'd worn rose-colored glasses when it came to Danny. But Jeff had seen things clearly from the beginning. She would've done the same if she'd been in his shoes. The ensuing intimacy had been happenstance. The fact remained that she'd been wrong, and she'd paid dearly for it.

Tori had inherited her mother's house. She spent her weekends sorting through Clarissa's possessions and moving her own into what would be her new home.

Winter had given way to spring, and the weather was hot and muggy. Often Tori found herself thinking about Quebec and speculating what it would be like in the springtime. Would it still be cool? What were their summers like?

She imagined Jeff in a spring-like setting, having shed his heavy coat and winter boots. With a pang, she pictured him contentedly relaxing at his cabin with Riley, possibly fishing, maybe with someone else in his life.

One day, when she arrived from work, Tori was surprised to discover a box wrapped in plain brown paper on her doorstep. She approached it cautiously, noticing it had only her name written across the top of it. No address, no return address, and no postage stamps. She stared at it for several minutes, unsure what to do. Was there something dangerous inside? Had some of Danny's friends found her and sought some sort of revenge against her?

Tori shook her head at the idea. She didn't think Danny's death was mourned by anyone other than herself.

Tori picked up the box and sat on the wicker love seat on her porch. She shook it but didn't hear any rattling. It wasn't heavy, and it seemed innocent enough. She unwrapped the paper until she had a large, plain box sitting on her lap.

Tori lifted a corner of the lid and peeked inside. Her brows drew together in interest when she saw the contents. She flipped off the lid, letting it clatter to the wooden floor. She lifted out a light brown, suede, winter boot. It was knee length and lined with fur.

Dazedly, she slid off her sandal and slipped her bare foot into the boot, noting its perfect fit and the cozy sensation of the fur against her skin. Tori admired the look of her foot and speculated about the unexpected gift. There were very few people who'd give her such a present. She was afraid to hope.

Her reflections were interrupted by a deep voice coming from the line of trees beside the house.

"It seems to fit pretty well."

Tori looked up to see Jeff at the end of her porch, advancing toward her. For a moment, she stared in disbelief. As he drew closer, Tori saw he'd changed. He appeared thinner, more strained. She shook off her daze.

"It fits perfectly," she whispered.

"Just like you and me," he said, not smiling, but watching her expectantly, warily.

"Do you think so?"

"Oh, yeah," he said.

"It seems to me we had difficulty getting along before."

"That's because we were living through some pretty difficult times, especially you. And I know things haven't improved since you came home. I'm sorry about your mother, Tori," he said, as he settled on the love seat beside her.

"How did you know?"

"I'm a detective, remember," he said, with a smile. "We have our ways of discovering things."

They both looked at the boot covering Tori's right foot.

"Thank you for the boots, Jeff."

"You're welcome."

"I don't have much opportunity to wear boots like this here."

"I know, but I was kind of hoping you'd wear them in Quebec."

"Do you still have snow there?"

Jeff chuckled.

"No, the snow has been gone for a few weeks. As a matter of fact, we should be snow-free until at least October now."

"So, you mean, if I were to go there again on vacation, sometime in the winter, I could use the boots?" Tori said, avoiding his scrutiny.

"I guess," he responded hesitantly. "Or, if you decided to come to Quebec to live, you'd get to use them every day, if you wanted."

She turned her head to look him in the eye.

"Why would I go there to live? What could I do there?"

"There are lots of things you could do. You might have to learn to speak a little French, though. And, you'd have to get used to snow and cold, and cars that won't start every once in a while. But you'd never have to worry about hurricanes or tropical storms."

He hesitated.

"And you'd have to get used to being a cop's wife...if that was something you were interested in doing, that is."

"Are you proposing to me, Jeff?" Tori said.

He nodded, looking unsure.

"I am. When I said we fit, I meant it. Ever since you left, I've felt like a piece of me was missing. I wanted to give you time to get over everything that'd happened, and I was hoping, maybe by now, you'd have forgiven me for my role in the whole affair. I love you, Tori. I didn't feel the timing was ever right to tell you that...until now."

He studied her expectantly, one knee bouncing.

"That's a big move...Quebec, I mean," she said, skirting around his comments.

"It is."

There was another short silence.

"Tori, can you put the past behind you?"

She hesitated for a moment before answering him, gathering her thoughts.

"After all that's happened, I've realized how short life can be. I saw how Danny wasted his life," she said with a grimace. "I was wrong about him. And, because I was wrong about him, I was wrong about you and your involvement in the case. It made me stop and think about what was left in my life that I wanted to keep."

"And? What was left?" Jeff said.

Tori looked into his eyes.

"You were," she said with a smile. Jeff's face relaxed in relief, and his arms circled her as they tumbled back onto the love seat together, boot and all.

ABOUT THE AUTHOR

A.J. McCarthy is the author of two published novels, *Sins of the Fathers* and *Cold Betrayal*. She's a member of Sisters in Crime and International Thriller Writers. When she's not writing, she can be found reading or planning her next travel adventure.

Thank you so much for reading one of our **Mystery-Thriller** novels.
If you enjoyed our book, please check out our recommended title for your
next great read!

Sins of the Fathers by A.J. McCarthy

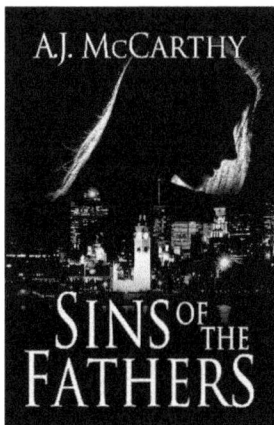

"McCarthy has certainly established herself as a writing force to be

reckoned with." *–Authors Reading*

BLACK ROSE
writing™

CPSIA information can be obtained
at www.ICGtesting.com
Printed in the USA
LVHW041201041218
599215LV00001B/2/P

9 781684 331963